"MEMORIZE THESE NUMBERS. . . ."

At the end of the training cycle, the team was met by a stranger. The man stood in front of a blackboard with several toll-free numbers written on it.

"Memorize these numbers," he said. "Don't ever forget them. There will be someone at each of those numbers twenty-four hours a day, seven days a week."

He paused. "Ladies and gentlemen," he went on, "it has taken millions of dollars and several years to turn this conception into reality. You are the crème de la crème. Your training—not that any of you really needed it—is over. You are a team unlike any other in the world. You all know that much, if not all, of what you will be doing is not only very dangerous, but also illegal and unconstitutional. You agreed to that when you signed on."

"Only way out of this team," Paul said, "is in a body bag. Is that what you're saying?"

The man smiled at the gathering. "I believe that sums it up rather well." He took a sip of water and looked into each face for a few seconds. "Are there any questions?"

"When do we start?" Mike asked.

"Immediately."

BOOK YOUR PLACE ON OUR WEBSITE AND MAKE THE READING CONNECTION!

We've created a customized website just for our very special readers, where you can get the inside scoop on everything that's going on with Zebra, Pinnacle and Kensington books.

When you come online, you'll have the exciting opportunity to:

- View covers of upcoming books
- Read sample chapters
- Learn about our future publishing schedule (listed by publication month *and author*)
- Find out when your favorite authors will be visiting a city near you
- Search for and order backlist books from our online catalog
- Check out author bios and background information
- Send e-mail to your favorite authors
- Meet the Kensington staff online
- Join us in weekly chats with authors, readers and other guests
- Get writing guidelines
- AND MUCH MORE!

**Visit our website at
http://www.pinnaclebooks.com**

CODE NAME: PAYBACK

William W. Johnstone

Pinnacle Books
Kensington Publishing Corp.
http://www.pinnaclebooks.com

PINNACLE BOOKS are published by

Kensington Publishing Corp.
850 Third Avenue
New York, NY 10022

First Pinnacle Printing: March, 2000
10 9 8 7 6 5 4 3 2 1

Printed in the United States of America

The more I see of the representatives of the people, the more I admire my dogs.

De Lamartine

One

The last thing John Barrone carefully placed in the cardboard box was the eight-by-ten-inch framed picture of his long dead wife, Michelle. He wanted to be certain the glass would not be broken. He placed the lid on the box, and with that final touch, twenty-two years of service with the CIA was ended—almost twenty years of it in the field. He walked out of his office, closing the door behind him, and took the elevator down. He exited the building and did not look back. Several blocks away, he stopped and checked his car, looking for electronic hound dogs. He could find none. He made certain he was not being followed by making a confusing series of left and right hand turns until he finally reached the Beltway. He followed that for a few miles, then cut off and headed south.

John had met several times with several different men, never with the same man twice. He had listened to what each had to say and he knew, almost immediately, that his personal history had been painstakingly gathered and carefully studied. Once he agreed to the proposal offered him, the last man he met with confirmed that John, along with men and women from various government and civilian agencies, had been studied thoroughly for months.

"How many people?" John had asked.

"There will be ten of you."

And that was all he was told at that time.

John spent his first night on the road in Roanoke. The next day he connected with Interstate 40 and followed that all the way to Little Rock, breaking that up into a two-day trip, making certain he was not followed. In Little Rock he followed instructions and left his personal car at a local garage for 'servicing." He drove away from there on Interstate 30, behind the wheel of a different vehicle. He spent the night in a motel in Dallas, and the next morning he connected with Interstate 20 and headed for West Texas. It was early fall and the nights were becoming quite pleasant, but it was still hot as the fringes of Hell at midday. He spent a night in Odessa and pulled out early. Just a few miles after I-20 merged with I-10, John cut south on a state road and began his drive into some of the most desolate country he had seen in a long time.

He had lunch in Alpine and continued south for sixty miles before turning off to the east on an unpaved road. A few miles farther, he once more turned south and headed into a range of mountains. He drove until he came to a closed and locked gate. He got out of the car and waited. A few minutes later an old Jeep came down the road, kicking up dust behind it. An old man who looked to have a lot of Indian blood in him got out and walked up to the gate and stared at John for a long moment.

"Name?"

"John Barrone."

"Wait a minute."

The old man unlocked the gate and waved John on through. John pulled in and stopped. The old man closed and locked the gate, then walked up to John's car and said, "Just keep on drivin' 'til you can't drive no more."

"And then what?" John asked.

The old man looked at him, amusement in his eyes. "Then you'll be where you wanted to go."

He walked back to his Jeep, sat down, pulled his cowboy hat down over his eyes, and to all appearances went to sleep, seemingly oblivious to the blazing sun beating down.

John turned the car's air-conditioning up to high and drove on. After several miles he reached a complex of buildings, with cars and pickup trucks parked off to one side. He got out and stood for a moment. He could hear the faint hum of a big generator coming from the rear of what he guessed was the main house. The front door opened and a man waved.

"Mr. Barrone," the man called. "Come in, please. Leave the keys in your car. I'll have a man get your luggage."

In the welcome coolness of the house, John was ushered into a large den, joining two men and a woman.

"I'll let you introduce yourselves," the man said. "There will be others coming in later on this afternoon." He smiled. "But I believe you and Don know each other."

"We've seen each other a few times," John replied, walking over and extending his hand to Don Yee. "Computers, isn't it?"

"Mr. Barrone," Don said, standing up and taking the hand. "Yes, sir. I left Langley a couple of months ago." He pointed to another man. "The ugly one is Mike Rojas, and the lovely lady is Jennifer Barnes."

John shook hands with Mike. Powerfully built man. John guessed him to be one eighty or so. Maybe thirty years old.

"IRS, sir," Mike said. "Internal Security Division. At least, I was," he amended.

"Call me Jenny," the very cute lady said, standing up and shaking hands.

About five-four, John guessed. Blond hair, blue eyes.

"Formerly of the FBI," Jenny said.

"Field agent?" John asked.

"Yes, sir. Explosives."

"Interesting," John said.

"How about something to drink, Mr. Barrone?" the unnamed host asked. "The cook just made some ice tea."

"That would be fine."

"Sweet or unsweetened?"

"Unsweetened, please."

"I guarantee you it's good," Don said. "But unsweetened?" He shuddered.

John smiled and sat down.

"The New England Barrones?" Mike asked.

"Yes," John replied. "Don't tell me my family's in tax trouble."

"No," the former IRS man replied. "But their returns are gone over very carefully."

John laughed and took the glass of ice tea handed him by a lady. *Another Indian,* John thought, looking up at the woman, who neither smiled nor spoke. She disappeared silently into another room. "I'm sure they are."

"I hate the goddamn IRS," Jenny said. "And the goddamn mealy-mouthed politicians who won't lift a finger to straighten out the tax mess. Those assholes!"

John frowned. He was not accustomed to females who slung profanity and vulgarity around with every breath.

Don Yee laughed at the expression on John's face. "Don't hold back, Jenny. Let us know how you really feel."

Jenny gave Don the rigid digit.

Interesting group of people, John thought, taking a sip of his ice tea. It was very good—just a hint of lemon, not over-powering.

Before anyone could launch a topic of conversation, the host reentered the large den and said, "Another member of the team has arrived. They should be arriving now every half hour or so." He walked out of the den and into the foyer.

Jenny leaned forward and whispered, "Mr. Barrone, what is that guy's name?"

John shrugged. "I don't know. He didn't tell any of you?"

She shook her head. "No. Everything so far is so hush-hush."

John smiled. "Just like the Company. Makes me feel right at home."

The newcomer was ushered in and introduced as Chris Farmer. He was young, maybe thirty at most, John thought.

Former Secret Service. Trained as a sniper. Chris was a big man, 220 pounds, six feet, four inches tall.

The luggage was brought in from the various vehicles and the team members were shown to their quarters—some in small cottages outside, others in spacious rooms in the main house. The team spent the next half-hour or so unpacking and resting. When they again met in the den, two more team members had arrived—Al Durstman and Linda Marsh. Al was former FBI, and Linda had spent ten years with the Los Angeles Police Department. Both were in their early to mid-thirties.

"Three to go," their host said. "Everybody should be here in time for a drink or two before dinner." Their mysterious host smiled and walked out of the room.

So far, no one had touched on why they were gathering in this desolate spot. Linda Marsh broke the ice on that subject. She lifted her freshly poured cup of coffee in a salute.

"Here's to the success of the team, people."

"I'll drink to that," Don Yee said, lifting his glass of ice tea.

"It seems we all have different specialties," Mike Rojas said. "This is shaping up to be a team that can tackle just about anything that comes up."

"I worked with you on a job," Al Durstman said to John. "I thought you looked familiar."

"Now, you know the Company is forbidden by law from working in the good ole U S of A," John said with a smile.

"Right." Al returned the smile. "Of course."

"What was the outcome of that operation?" John asked.

"It never came to trial," the former FBI man replied. "The charges were eventually dropped."

"Naturally," John said with a frown. "The primary reason we're all here."

Mike spoke up. "One of the reasons. But I still can't figure out why I was approached. What do our . . . ah, employers think one small team can do to change the IRS's way of collecting taxes?"

"They don't," the host said, walking into the room. "We

feel the people will eventually rise up in revolt and settle that issue."

"Armed revolt?" Jenny asked.

"Perhaps," the host said, and he continued walking toward the foyer.

John figured another member of the team had arrived.

"Count me in," said Jenny.

Mike looked at her. "Dangerous talk. It isn't the employees of the IRS who are to blame. It's the politicians who make the laws."

Jenny's gaze was filled with ice and fire. "Any time bad laws are enforced, it's very much the fault of those doing the enforcing. I don't see how you can argue that."

The host paused for a moment and chuckled. "The next few weeks are going to be very interesting."

"I certainly believe that," John agreed. "What happens if it's decided that we can't work together as a team?"

"That won't happen," the host said. "It's already been determined that you're all very compatible. If not, I assure you, you wouldn't be here. Excuse me, more team members have arrived."

Paul Brewer and Lana Henry were introduced. Paul was a forty-year-old black man who had spent fifteen years in government service, the last five with the Border Patrol. Lana was a very attractive woman in her mid-thirties who had spent ten years with the Bureau of Alcohol, Tobacco, and Firearms, better known as BATF.

"I know that name," John said after greeting Paul. "Have we met before?"

Paul smiled. "No, sir. I played football in college, and then in the Canadian League for a few years."

"Ah!" John said. "I lived in Montreal for a while. That's where I heard the name."

Mike Rojas then said, "Are you sure you're black, man? You don't look black to me."

Paul was at first startled, then burst out laughing when he

realized that Mike was putting him on. "My parents were Jamaican. With a little Spanish in them, as well."

"We might be cousins, man! Lend me twenty bucks?"

"Get out of here!" Paul said, grinning.

Mike's wicked sense of humor would come in handy in the months ahead, when things got tight in the field, as would Don Yee's.

John shifted his gaze to Linda Marsh. She had not cracked so much as a tiny smile during the exchange, while everyone else, including John, had laughed. She was a beautiful woman with a knockout figure, but her eyes were cold. John wondered about that.

During a lull in the conversation, their host said, "I believe number ten is here. If so, that completes the team."

Bob Garrett was in his middle forties. He had spent the past fifteen years working for the National Security Agency and five years before that working for the CIA. John knew him slightly. Bob could blend in and not be noticed in a crowd of two. He was shown his room and his luggage was brought in.

"The bar is now officially open, ladies and gentlemen." The host pushed a button on the wall and sliding doors opened silently, revealing a bar that would put many public bars to shame. "Help yourselves. Dinner will be served at seven. Until then, get better acquainted and relax. I'll see you at dinner." He walked out of the room.

"Is that the man we'll be working for?" Lana asked.

"No," Bob Garrett answered. "As soon as I was approached I began doing some monitoring on my own at Meade. I hit a stone wall at almost every direction I turned. I doubt we'll ever know who's financing this team, but I can tell you it's a group of billionaires and multimillionaires. . . . I found out that much before a solid freeze went in and I could get nothing. And I mean it was a hard freeze."

"Americans?" Mike asked.

"For the most part, yes. But I'd guess, from the number of overseas calls made, that there are several men and women involved from England, France, Germany, and Italy . . . maybe two or three in the Scandinavian part of the world."

"Who could freeze out the NSA?" Don asked. "That doesn't seem possible."

"Oh, it's possible," Bob replied. "Both technologically and politically. Take your pick."

"I'd opt for politically," John said.

"You got it, John."

"Any idea who that person might be?" Al asked.

"Not a clue."

John walked over to the bar and fixed a vodka martini on the rocks, with olive. Don Yee joined him, fixing a gin martini, straight up. Jenny rummaged around in the cooler and chose a beer. When all the team members had the beverage of their choice, they returned to their seats.

Paul looked at his watch. "An hour before dinner. Wonder what we're having?"

"You can bet it'll be good," Mike said, looking around him. "This complex must have cost a fortune to build."

"I wonder who owns it," said Lana.

"It would probably take a team of CPAs and lawyers to discover that," Al Durstman opined.

"Anybody getting cold feet?" Chris Farmer asked.

"Not me," Linda stated firmly. "I didn't have to think twice before agreeing to join this team."

Jenny looked at Paul Brewer. "Why did you join, Paul?"

Paul smiled. "Are you asking because I'm black?"

"Frankly, honestly, yes."

Paul nodded his head. "Good. We'll clear the air about race right now. . . ."

"We were all grilled very hard about prejudice, Paul," Bob Garrett said. "Obviously we all came through clean."

"Oh, I didn't mean to challenge anyone on the team," Paul was quick to state. "Not at all. I think we've all been checked out very thoroughly on that. What I meant was: just because

I'm black doesn't mean I approve of every issue that's raised by minorities."

"Just to really clear the air," John said, "name some issues you disagree with, and some you don't." He looked at Mike Rojas. "And the same goes for you, Mike."

"How about me, Mr. Barrone?" Don Yee asked.

John smiled. "Your ancestors came to this country from China about two hundred years ago, Don. I read your file once."

"Damn!" Don said with a grin. "I was really gonna have some fun, too."

"Yeah, I bet you were," John said. "I saw that coming."

"I got no kick with anybody," Mike said. "Hell, one of my ancestors died fighting *with* the defenders at the Alamo. He was one of the few in the Alamo who was actually born in Texas."

Paul said, "Well . . . I do believe that many blacks are stopped by the police simply because of their color. And that is something that must be corrected."

Linda started to speak and Paul held up a hand. "I think I know what you're about to say, Linda: A disproportionate number of crimes in this country are committed by blacks. Right?"

"That's right, Paul," she acknowledged.

"Sad, but true," he said. "However, certainly not all blacks are criminals, are they?"

"No," she replied. "Of course not. The majority aren't."

"With that said, then . . . how do we correct the aforementioned problem?"

John quickly stepped in before the discussion took a turn down a street he preferred not to travel at that time. "That isn't up to us. That isn't why this team was formed."

"But some minorities are certainly going to die at our hands," Jenny said. "Perhaps a great many of them. I say get the air clear now."

"I agree, Mr. Barrone," Paul said.

John spread both hands in a gesture of surrender. "OK. You folks have at it."

In his office, the host was listening to every word. The den was bugged with very sophisticated listening devices. *Good, good!* he thought. *This is exactly what we wanted: Get all the petty disagreements out of the way now. Then they won't surface at some inopportune time and put a mission in jeopardy.* The host leaned back in his chair and sipped his drink. *This should be interesting.*

Paul took a sip of his drink. When he spoke his voice was calm but his eyes were cold and hard. "Let me say this one time, and then I'll speak no more about it. There are good and bad people of all colors. Respect is something that must be earned. It isn't handed out like bubble gum. I hate rap music. I hate hip-hop music. I enjoy classical music and opera. My favorite pop singers are Lou Rawls and Mel Tormé. I despise drug pushers, of any color. I despise violent gang members, of any color. My kid brother got hooked by a slick-talking punk and died a couple of years later after shooting himself with a hot shot. He was eighteen years old. The law never did anything with the punk who hooked him and supplied him with dope. My father was driving home from work one night and got caught in the middle of a gang war. He was killed by a burst of automatic weapons fire. The gangs sent an anonymous letter to the newspaper saying they were so sorry it happened. The shooters were never caught; no one was ever punished. My kid sister was mugged by a doped-up asshole. She was in a coma for weeks before she mercifully died. She left behind two small children and a very angry and bewildered husband . . . and about a half million dollars in hospital bills her insurance didn't pay. I have a very simple solution for solving the drug problem in America: kill all the drug dealers, the growers, the drug lords, the pushers, a sizeable number of defense lawyers, and all the violent gang members. And I don't give a damn what color any of them are. Does that clear the air, people?"

"Sure does for me," said Chris Farmer. "Not that I had any doubts."

"All right," John said, standing up and heading toward the bar to fix another drink. "That issue is finished and put to bed. Anything else?"

"Who's in charge of this team?" Linda asked.

"I am," John said. "Anybody got any complaints about that?"

No one did.

Short and sweet, the host thought. He drained his glass and stood up. Time to see about dinner.

Dinner was nothing elaborate, but it was delicious. Huge charcoal and mesquite grilled T-bone steaks, baked potatoes with butter or sour cream or both, and salads that were meals in themselves.

The dinner dishes were swiftly and silently cleared away and then dessert was served: hot apple pie with rich homemade ice cream. After that ashtrays were put on the table and coffee was served.

No one questioned how the host knew how everyone liked their steaks, or who smoked and who didn't. They had each been interviewed several times, each time by a different person, and the interviews had been intensive.

"Have we passed so far?" John asked innocently.

"What do you mean?" the host asked.

"The den is bugged. I found one of the pickups. Very nice one, too."

The host smiled, but it was a tad forced. "Those were put in place by experts, John."

"You're sitting at a table with ten experts," John countered.

The host lifted his coffee cup in a salute. "Touché, my friend. Point taken."

"So what now?"

The host shrugged. "You all relax tonight. Tomorrow another man will take my place, and your relaxing days will be over for several months."

"Then we get to work?" Al asked.

"Yes."

"Can you tell us what our first assignment will be?" Lana asked.

"No, I can't. I don't know. That's not my area of responsibility."

"Just what is?" Don asked.

"I'm a psychiatrist, among other things. Oh, don't misunderstand: I'll be here after tomorrow, for a time, studying you all."

"What if one of us fails your study?" Linda asked.

"You can't fail. Or, let me amend that: failing would be extremely difficult. You're all part of a team. A team unlike any other in the world. You all know that much, if not all, of what you will be doing is not only very dangerous, but also illegal and unconstitutional. You agreed to that when you signed on."

"Only way out of this team," Paul said, "is in a body bag. Is that what you're saying?"

The host pushed back his chair and stood up. Then he smiled at the gathering. "I believe that sums it up rather well."

Two

For the next sixteen weeks the team practiced their various skills. During the morning, John Barrone, Al Durstman, and Bob Garrett soaked up reports on criminal activities worldwide; in the afternoon they honed their shooting skills with various weapons. Don Yee spent hours in a computer room. Jenny Barnes blew things up with different types of explosives. Mike Rojas and Paul Brewer familiarized themselves with the faces and habits of known terrorists, and practiced with firearms. Linda Marsh and Lana Henry sharpened their martial arts skills and worked on the shooting range. Chris Farmer had his choice of various sniper weapons and honed his skills to a razor-sharp edge. Then each member was cross-trained—as much as time would allow—in another's specialty. The entire team did an hour of physical training every morning, starting at 0600, and another hour in the middle of the afternoon.

The physical training was the easiest part, for all were in good physical shape to start with. By the end of the sixteen-week program, they were in even better physical shape. They ate nourishing food, got up at the same time, and went to bed at the same time. And due to the South Texas weather, they had all sweated buckets.

At the end of the training cycle the four instructors disappeared, and the team was met by a stranger for breakfast one Saturday morning. The man was dressed in casual clothing, but the team members got the impression that he would be much more at home in an expensive business suit. Behind the man was a blackboard with several toll-free telephone numbers written on it.

"Where is Mr. Host?" Don asked, using the nickname the team had hung on the mysterious psychiatrist.

"He's gone. The only ones left are the caretaker and his wife; they live here year-round. My name is Wagner. I will be one of your contacts for as long as the team is operational." He pointed to the blackboard. "Memorize those numbers. Don't ever forget them. There will be someone at each of those numbers twenty-four hours a day, seven days a week. This will probably be the last time any of you will ever see me in person. And I hope it will not be necessary to explain the why of that.

"Ladies and gentlemen, it has taken millions of dollars and several years getting everything in place to turn this conception into reality. The backgrounds and philosophies of several hundred people have been carefully looked into, in various ways. Then the first, ah, rather innocuous interviews began. Without going into a lot of detail about the final selection process, let me just say you ten are the crème de la crème. Your training—not that any of you really needed it—is over. Now it's time to go to work." Wagner took a sip of water and looked into each face for a few seconds. "Before I proceed, are there any questions?"

"Do we have a free hand in dealing with criminals?" Paul asked.

Without hesitation, Wagner said, "Yes. You people are, to use a rather distasteful historical expression, the final solution."

"How do we get the supplies we need?" Lana asked.

"Call one of the numbers you memorized. Anything you need will be available to you within twenty-four hours—in many instances much quicker than that. The men and women who make up the strands of this organization—ah, web, so to speak—are highly motivated, one hundred percent loyal, richly rewarded monetarily speaking, and do not have the vaguest idea who any of you are . . . and never will."

"None of this could be accomplished without assistance from some highly placed government officials," Bob said. "When the current administration changes, what happens then?"

"Nothing that will affect any of you. You'll have to trust me on that. A lot of time, effort, and money have been spent insuring there will be no hitches in your ability to function."

"When do we go to work?" Mike asked.

"Immediately."

"We don't know if this group of terrorists is even in the United States," Linda said, after reading the reports Mr. Wagner had left for each of them.

"They aren't," John replied. "But they have left the final training camp, heading for the port of Los Angeles." He then passed out ID cards to each member of the team. The cards were issued by the National Security Agency—NSA—and Mr. Wagner had assured them the cards were not fake and would stand up to any kind of check the authorities might want to run. In addition to the cards, each team member was given a national concealed weapons permit.

"I've never seen one like this," Bob Garrett said.

"There aren't many of them," John told him. "It covers everything up to nuclear weapons. Somebody—probably more than one person—is very highly placed in government."

"We driving to Los Angeles?" Al asked.

"Flying. A private jet is picking us up at 0700 tomorrow morning at the airstrip just east of here."

"Must be nice," Don muttered. He shook his head. "That private strip, right in the middle of nowhere, capable of handling jets, must have cost a fortune."

"How much money you figure is behind us, John?" Paul asked.

"Millions, at least." He then passed out credit cards to each member. "None of those cards have a limit."

"My ex-wife would have loved these," Al said with a smile.

"Yeah, so would mine," Paul agreed. "Wherever she is."

"You lost contact with her?" Lana asked.

"About a month after we divorced. And that suits me just fine."

"Must have been a wonderful marriage," Linda said.

"Delightful," Paul said. "I caught her screwing a friend of mine about eighteen months after we said, 'I do.' "

"Ouch." Don grimaced.

"What did you do to him?" Mike asked.

Paul shook his head. "Nothing. It was as much her fault as his. Takes two. I didn't lay a hand on either of them. Just turned around and walked out of the house."

"Any children?" Jenny asked.

"No. Thank goodness."

"Let's go over this material once more," John said. "We've got to memorize these names and descriptions."

Jenny held up the file on the international team of terrorists. "This sure is a mixed bag of assholes. Some of these people have Anglo names."

John had grown used to Jenny's language. "About half of them are Americans. The rest are German, French, and Middle Eastern."

"Americans," Linda said. "And according to the files, they're all well-educated. University of California, CCNY, Harvard. What the hell's wrong with these people?"

"Start with the professors who taught them," Mike said. "Bunch of ultra left-wingers."

John said nothing, letting the team talk it out.

"Some of them are, yes," Al said. "But that trend began years ago. Those types are so firmly entrenched with tenure you couldn't blow them out with dynamite."

"I wouldn't use dynamite to rid the world of those socialistic bastards and bitches," Jenny said with a straight face. "C-4 or Semtex would be much better."

Don shifted his gaze to the woman. "Why do I get the feeling you're only half kidding?"

"I'm not kidding at all," Jenny replied.

"Did you have a bad time with one of your professors?" Chris asked.

"I just called him a communistic prick," Jenny said. "Which he was . . . is."

"You did that publicly?" Paul asked.

"Standing up in class."

"How'd you do in that class?" Don asked.

Jenny smiled. "I squeaked through . . . barely."

"Did you contest the grade?" John asked.

She shook her head. "No. I think the grade was legitimate. After I realized the bastard was an avowed leftist, I attended just enough to get a passing grade." She shrugged. "It was an elective." She grinned. "Let's don't talk anymore about my grades. It's embarrassing."

"I've reviewed your grades, Jenny," John said. "You breezed through every chemistry course you took with high marks. Nothing embarrassing about that."

The team knew that John Barrone had studied all their very extensive files and knew just about everything there was to know about them—likes, dislikes, habits.

"You're right, John," Jenny replied. The team had stopped, at John's insistence, calling him Mr. Barrone. They would be working too closely together for formality. "But that was fun. I was learning the chemical composition of every explosive known to humankind. And making them and testing them. I even improved on a couple."

"I couldn't help but take notice," John said drily. "When you destroyed half of a mountain the other week."

The old Indian caretaker walked into the room. "You're wanted on the phone, Mr. Barrone."

"I didn't hear it ring," John said, standing up.

"It didn't ring in here. But I switched it over from where I was." Without another word, he turned away and walked out of the room.

"That's the strangest man I ever met in my life," Linda remarked.

"He's a Comanche," Mike said. "Almost full-blood."

"How do you know that?"

"I asked him."

John was on the phone only for a few seconds. He hung up and looked at the group. "Pack up your things and do it quickly. The plane will be here in half an hour. The terrorist team has landed three days ahead of schedule."

The team rose to their feet as one, Al asking, "Do we know yet what their objective is?"

"New York City."

"To do what?" Don asked.

"As far as we know, kill several million people."

Three

"These people we're after, according to the dossiers, are suspected terrorists," Linda said to John as the private jet blasted its way west. "Right?"

"That's correct. But suspected is the key word."

"And they have valid passports. Right?"

"That's also correct. It's all there in the files. You read it."

"And they are now being detained in Los Angeles by immigration officials?"

"Correct."

"John—"

"Immigration can't do a thing with them. They haven't done anything wrong, and none of them have a criminal record."

"But this group they represent, the PLF, the Peoples' Liberation Front, is a known terrorist group, responsible for the deaths of dozens of people. Forgive me, John, I'm babbling, trying to make some sense of all this."

"I understand, Linda. This type of situation is something the CIA has been facing for years. We know a person or group is guilty of the most heinous of crimes, or is planning to do something awful, but can't prove it. Therefore, no action can legally be taken. What you're saying is: why not just take out these people right now, right?"

"That's it."

"Because the authorities aren't positive that this group is actually going to do anything illegal. There is some agreement that these people who have just entered the country are here to lay down a false trail, to blow a smoke screen to cover the real team of terrorists."

"And your opinion is?"

"At this time, I personally believe they're the real team. That might change. But they don't appear to be on any timetable. They look and behave like genuine tourists, just wandering and seeing the country."

"So all we're going to be doing for . . . however long, is bird-dogging?"

"That's it."

"And if we decide conclusively that the group is planning a terrorist act?"

"We take them out."

"Unconditionally?"

"One hundred percent, and to hell with any political ramifications."

The pilot's voice over the intercom stopped conversation. "Telephone, Mr. Barrone."

John was back in a few minutes. He picked up the intercom mic and said, "Give me your attention, please. The FBI has intercepted a small cache of supplies that was presumably meant for the terrorists once they reach New York City. The cache included grenades, automatic weapons, rocket launchers, and several boxes containing vials of hydrogen cyanide. No delivery system for the cyanide was found. I imagine the bulk of the supplies are coming in by various routes. That's it."

"Hydrogen cyanide," Lana said to her seatmate, Jenny. "Good God!"

"Real nice people we're dealing with," Jenny replied. "Maybe by the time these crackpots are released we'll have confirmation that they're the genuine article. Then we can do our thing and go see a good movie."

"You're a cold one, Jenny," Lana replied after a few seconds of digesting what her seatmate had said.

"I'm a realist, Lana. We live in an evil world, and our system of justice is just not working. Checks and balances are all screwed up."

"I won't argue with you there."

"As far as I'm concerned, both our ex-departments have been busy kicking down the wrong doors."

"You support the militia movement? If that's what you're referring to."

"I don't see anything wrong with most of them. I know that some groups are nothing but a bunch of whackos, but the majority are good decent Americans who are tired of what they perceive as this country's constant downhill slide toward socialism. They're not criminals."

Lana smiled at her. "I think we're all going to get along great, Jenny. The entire team seems to be of one mind."

"You can bet that was carefully planned, too. I wonder whose idea this was. The team, I mean."

Lana shook her head. "That's something I doubt we'll ever know. What I can't figure out is how we're going to stay out of jail."

"Simple: we do our thing and walk away, keep our mouths shut, and don't look back."

"There's got to be more to it than that."

Jenny tapped the side of her head with a fingertip. "Right here is where the secret lies."

"If we were all that bright, you think we'd be mixed up in something like this?"

Jenny laughed. "Maybe it's because we have the courage to do what others just dream about."

Lana smiled at her. "I'll buy the courage part. But I'm glad you didn't say anything about common sense."

Across the aisle and several rows up, John wondered what in the world the two women had found so amusing.

Rooms were booked for the team in several motels, all in close proximity, and all very close to the motel where the INS had booked rooms for the suspected terrorists. The suspected terrorists had been told either to stay put or go to jail. The choice was theirs. Of course the rooms were bugged, and of course the INS and the FBI knew the members of the PLF suspected that, and therefore would say nothing of importance while in their rooms.

"What do we do while we're here?" Paul asked. Several members of the team had gathered in a parking lot close to the motels.

"Nothing," John told him. "When the PLF members decide to pull out we'll know fifteen seconds after the Bureau does."

"So the organization has someone placed very high in the Bureau," Al said.

"Your guess is as good as mine," John said. "But I would assume so. All I know is we'll be informed when the PLF makes a move."

"I'm hungry," Don said.

"I saw a Chinese restaurant just up the street," Mike said with a smile, knowing what Yee's response would be.

"I hate Chinese food," Don replied. "Stuff makes me wanna barf."

"That remark will not please honorable ancestors," Mike told him.

Don flipped him the bird. "Honorable ancestors are in the spirit world. They don't have to eat that crap. I'm going back to the motel and grab a hamburger. How about you, Paul?"

"Lead the way."

John walked back to his room and checked the phone for messages. He didn't expect to find any, and there were none. All the team had pagers and extremely secure cell phones. The cars that were waiting for them upon landing were equipped with the latest in encoded two-way radios. An assortment of weapons were in each trunk.

He sat down in the chair and wondered, as he almost always did, why motel chairs were so damned uncomfortable. He opened his attaché case and took out the latest intel on the

PLF. Whoever put this report together was convinced that the group of members who had just docked in Los Angeles were the real threat.

"So am I," John muttered.

He looked at the picture of one of the young ladies of the group. She reminded John of his daughter, sort of, in a vague way—the hair, he concluded.

And that kicked in memories of his wife.

Michelle had been dead for years, more years than John liked to think about. She had been killed by a mugger when John Jr. and Ellen were small. They had only very misty memories of their mother. The mugger was caught and sentenced to twenty-five years in prison. He served eight years and was released on parole. He had been a model prisoner, the courts said. He was so sorry he had killed the woman, the mugger said, but now he had found Jesus. Besides, the prison was overcrowded and they needed the cell.

A week after the punk was released from prison he attacked another woman in a parking lot, raping her, robbing her, and then beating her head in with the butt of a pistol he had bought off the street. The woman survived the attack, more or less. She suffered major brain damage, remained in a coma for weeks, then was institutionalized for the rest of her life.

John phoned the head of the parole board. "Looks like he forgot Jesus, doesn't it?"

John found the punk a month later (with the help of friends of his from Langley) and shot the mugger/rapist/murderer in the head, leaving the body in a ditch.

John rose from the chair and, using the motel coffeemaker, fixed a pot. He settled back in the uncomfortable chair and tried to concentrate on the report, but his thoughts kept returning to Michelle. He finally laid the report aside and stared at the wall.

John was questioned by the police after the punk's death, but he had an ironclad alibi in the form of his friends, and the police couldn't break it. They strongly suspected, but couldn't prove, that John had killed the human vermin, and they finally dropped the matter.

After the state police had left, a sheriff's deputy had lingered for a moment, smiled at John, and said, "One lousy no-good punk who got exactly what he deserved, Mr. Barrone. One rotten piece of shit the courts wouldn't flush down the crapper. Watch yourself. Some of the state boys will be looking at you for a time. See you, Mr. Barrone."

John was sent overseas on assignment a few weeks after that and stayed overseas, off and on, for several years. The kids were in boarding school and John missed them. The years rolled by swiftly, and John looked up one day and his kids were both in college and he had a lot of gray in his hair.

John, John Jr., and Ellen had grown apart. When they met now there was some strain evident between them. He wanted to tell them that he had done the best he knew how, considering his job. But those would have been wasted words and John knew it, so he said nothing.

Ellen had grown into a beautiful young woman, and John Jr. a tall and handsome young man. John Jr. worked for an advertising agency in New York City, and Ellen was an attorney in the same city. Neither had married.

John did not have to work after retirement. He had money, from his family and from sound investments, but fifty was far too young to retire. If this job had not come along, he would have worked at something else. But this way, John figured, he was striking back at a justice system that, in his opinion (and in the opinion of millions of other Americans), was unworkable, ponderous, unfair, and in many cases, just plain lousy.

John put his brain to rest for a time by field-stripping his pistol, a Colt Double Eagle in .45 ACP. He had carried one for years and liked the autoloader. John figured that if a .45 wouldn't stop a man, the next best thing to do was throw it at the guy and take off, for you sure as hell didn't need the extra weight while running.

He had just finished reassembling the .45 when a knock came at the door.

"Yes?" John called, slipping the magazine into the butt of the autoloader.

"Bob Garrett."

John opened the door and waved the man inside. "Something up, Bob?"

"No," the ex-NSA man replied. He lifted a sack. "Not a thing. I thought you might like some company and a drink. I've got the vodka, a small bottle of vermouth, and a little jar of olives."

"I'll get the ice," John said. "And you were sure right on both counts."

As evening gently pushed day aside in Southern California, John and Bob lifted their glasses in a silent salute.

"Were you thinking about your family when I knocked, John?" Bob asked.

"Are you a mystic?"

"No. But I was doing the same thing a few minutes ago, sitting in my room."

"Yes, I was doing just that. The two minutes each week I allot to feel sorry for myself, I suppose. If 'feeling sorry' is the right phrase."

"Things that might have been, as the saying goes, can sure play hell with a person. How long's it been since you've seen your kids?"

"Almost six months. And the meeting was a bit strained. My son cut it short."

"I've got two boys, as you're aware. They were five and seven when my wife and I split. Over the years she's turned both of them into raging liberals. They despise the work I do . . . or did, I should say."

"My kids feel the same way. I gave up trying to explain the necessity of our work a long time ago."

The ringing of John's cell phone stopped conversation. He listened for a moment, then broke the connection.

"The PLF members are all in their rooms," he said. "Released by the INS, and others, with no charges."

"So they're free to move." It was a statement, not a question.

"Anytime they choose to go, anywhere they choose to travel. No restrictions."

"Why do I get the feeling some group of national civil rights attorneys got involved in this?"

John chuckled and took a sip of his drink. "You'd sure be correct."

"How are the PLF members moving east?"

"They've rented several vehicles."

"Aren't they being a bit obvious?"

"Yes. Bob, I think they're definitely going to play a major part in this crazy scheme, but whether or not they're the primary players is very much up for grabs in my mind."

"A backup role, perhaps?"

"Possibly. What I may do is split the team, send half on to New York to get set up."

"Good idea."

"If I decide to do that, you'll be in charge of New York."

"All right."

"You'll take Al, Linda, and Paul."

"Want me to advise them of that now?"

"Finish your drink. The PLF boys and girls are under heavy surveillance. We'll know as soon as they make a move."

Bob drained his martini glass and stood up. "I'd better do it now, John. Before I decide the first one tasted so good I want another."

"I do know that feeling. OK, I'll tell my half of the team what's going on. You people get packed and get ready to take off. If for some reason we can't maintain radio contact, we'll use the computers."

"Good deal."

"I'd better call in right now and advise Control of what's taking place."

"Good luck," Bob said. He held out his hand and John shook it.

"Bob. And good luck to the people of New York City if all our combined groups can't stop this bunch of nuts."

"Does anybody know yet how these screwballs plan to disperse the cyanide? It isn't something you can just toss up into the air and hope for the best."

"I haven't got a clue. Or even if that's the chemical of choice."

"You think that might have been planted to throw everybody off?"

"That thought has entered my mind."

"But our intel confirms the target is New York City?"

"That much is solid."

Bob moved toward the door. "I'll see you in New York . . . or before."

"Let's hope it's before. I really don't like the idea of being in Manhattan if we fail to stop this bunch."

"John . . . my kids are in New York City."

"I know, Bob. So are mine."

Four

John had a hunch the PLF would not pull out that night, and his hunch proved to be correct. None of the eight members of the alleged terrorist group so much as left the motel area until eight o'clock the next morning. Shortly after breakfast they packed up and pulled out, John and his team a few minutes behind them. Bob and his team had left hours before. The voice on the receiving end of the toll-free number had noted the change in plans without emotion or question and hung up.

"We've got them tracked by hound dog," Chris said. "We'll know where they are at all times."

"They might drop those rental cars off in Las Vegas," John told his group before they pulled out. "These people aren't amateurs. They're highly trained professionals."

"But you don't believe this bunch is the primary group?" Mike questioned.

"I have some doubts," John replied. "Time will tell. Let's roll, people."

John, Mike, and Jenny rode in one car. Chris, Don, and Lana were in the lead car. Don was handling the electronic equipment, keeping track of the suspects from the signal that was bouncing back to them from satellite. Don was handling the inboard computer for more than one reason. He was a recognized expert with computers, but he was also a lousy driver—probably the worst driver ever to receive a California license. After seeing him slam-bang around the training area and put dents in the fenders of every vehicle he drove, absolutely no team member wanted to ride with him.

"I think I'm not well-coordinated," Don had explained after his fifth fender bender back in Texas. "I've been told that."

"I think you're a menace to public safety," Paul countered.

"I do have my pilot's license," Don proudly informed them all.

"God help us," John muttered.

"How can you fly a plane and not drive a car?" Jenny asked him.

"There's more room in the sky," Linda said.

"I'm not very good when it comes to landing," Don admitted.

"Let's hope none of us ever has to experience that," Bob replied.

It was mid-morning before John and his team managed to wind their way through the LA traffic and hit Interstate 15 heading for Barstow.

"Catch up with the PLF convoy and pass them," John radioed to Chris. "They're maintaining a speed just below the legal limit. Stay about a quarter of a mile ahead of them, just in case they have a change in plans and find those hound dogs and stick them on a truck heading for Vancouver. I'll lay back about a mile."

"Ten-four, John."

But the PLF group, traveling in three vehicles, headed straight for Barstow. There they ate lunch, gassed up, and bought jugs of water in case they broke down during the trek across the desert. John and his team ate lunch and bought water for the trip. Chris, Don, and Lana ate on the east side of Barstow, while John, Jenny, and Mike had a sandwich on the west side, keeping an eye on the PLF from across the street.

Back in the car, there was a message on the computer. The PLF group had made reservations at a hotel on the strip. John's team would stay at a hotel across the street. Reservations had been made for them.

"Now, it gets dicey," John said. "None of us is going to get a lot of sleep tonight. We'll check out both hotels and then I'll assign shifts."

Both hotels were new, and they were huge. John silently cursed when he saw the size of them.

"Let's check in and then get across the street and take a look."

"Why weren't we booked in the same hotel?" Mike griped.

"Full up. There's some sort of convention taking place across the street. This is the best our people could do. The town is jam-packed."

Jenny studied John's face for a few seconds. "They know they're being followed, don't they, John?"

"Oh, they suspect it, I'm certain of that. As I've said before, these people aren't amateurs. I'm wondering how many other government teams are following them, and from how many countries. Most importantly, are *we* being bird-dogged by a team from the PLF?"

"I haven't detected any signs of us being followed," Mike said.

"Neither have I," John admitted. "But I've got a creepy feeling on the back of my neck."

"You think agents from other countries are working this operation?" Chris asked.

"British intelligence is certainly working it. The PLF is responsible for a dozen bombings in that country. France has people over here, and probably the Mossad has agents on this op. The PLF hates Israel."

"Germany?" Lana asked.

"Could be. There are some German nationals involved in the PLF."

"But no one knows about us, right?" Don asked.

"Supposedly," John replied. "But as you all know, or should know, the intelligence community is small, made up of very intelligent and highly curious people. I would hazard a guess that they know of the existence of the team, but not our identities."

"But they will," Chris said.

"Oh, yes. They will."

"Now you've got me looking over my shoulder," Jenny said.

"Good habit to get into," John told her and the team. "Let's get to work."

This PLF contingent was made up of men and women in their mid to late twenties. They were dedicated to the cause, even though that cause—if any were asked to fully explain the whys and hows of its worldwide implementation—would be rather fuzzy and ill-defined. They were dedicated to destroying what they believed was the oppressive capitalistic system—a form of government highly repugnant to the PLF, one that many people around the world gleefully embraced.

In this group André was the leader. His second in command was Brigitte, followed by Akal-Keerat, Winifried (called Wini), Alain-Gerard, Jan, Max, and Hurran. The last names on their passports were all false. Brigitte and Max were Americans by birth; André and Alain were French. Winifried had been born in England, and her parents still lived there. Akal and Hurran were believed to be of Middle Eastern origin. Jan was thought to be Belgian.

Standing in the noisy casino, André told his people, "We have several teams of agents following us. The FBI, MI6, the Mossad, and the French."

"We expected that," Wini said.

"But there is yet another group trailing us that no one can positively identify."

"The CIA," Akal said, looking as though he wanted to spit. "I despise those pigs."

André shook his head and smiled at a security guard who

was walking by the group. The guard gave the group a long look and did not return the smile.

"Let's go for a walk," André suggested.

Outside, strolling down the strip, André said, "The unknown group is not the CIA. That has been determined. No one seems to know who they are."

"Our deep-planted people cannot find out the identity of this group?" Jan asked.

"No. They have tried. None of their usual sources know anything. It's all very strange."

"What can they do?" Max asked. "We're not carrying weapons. We're not carrying anything contraband. We've been cleared by the INS, the FBI, and the State Department. We're tourists, that's all."

"They might be an assassination team," Alain suggested.

"Nonsense!" Wini scoffed. "An American assassination team? Americans don't do that sort of thing. The government here is too cowardly. That is why America is going to be such an easy target."

"I didn't say they were American," André said. He shrugged his shoulders. "But they very well may be. No one knows who they are. But our people will find out. It's just a matter of time. And we have lots of time. We're on no inflexible timetable."

"So what do we do?" Jan asked André.

"We do nothing. Not unless we receive orders countermanding our original orders. We let our backup handle it."

"They get all the fun," Wini said.

"I'm hungry," Akal said.

The others laughed at that. Brigitte patted her terrorist-in-arms on the back. "We'll find you something to eat. But we might have some difficulty finding dates and goat's milk in this den of opulence and debauchery, Akal."

"Vegetables will do nicely," Akal said.

"You come with me, Brigitte," André said. "You, too, Wini. The rest of you go with Akal and get something to eat. And all of you be very careful in what you say and do. The night has eyes and ears."

When the others had strolled away, vanishing in the crowds that milled about—all of them looking for yet another place to try to win a fortune at the drop of a token into a machine or the turn of a card—André said, "I have a very bad feeling about this unknown group. I think they are American, and I think they are new and dangerous. Very dangerous."

"You have nothing to base that assumption on, André," Brigitte reminded him.

"I struck my first lone blow against the establishment when I was ten years old, Brigitte. The policeman carries the scars of that rock to this day. That was eighteen years ago. I have lived by my wits ever since. I have learned to trust my instincts."

Brigitte said nothing in reply, but her eyes spoke volumes.

Wini said, "So what are you suggesting, André? That we confront these people? How? We don't even know who they are. How do we find them?"

"Our goal is to bring terror to the people of New York City," Brigitte said. "We can't risk putting hands on weapons until we reach the city."

"And if we are stopped before we get there?" André asked. "What do we fight with, sticks and stones?"

"Good point," Wini said. "I never did agree with this weaponless trek across this fat and bloated country."

Before one or the other could launch into a tirade about the evils of capitalistic America, André said, "There is a source here in this city. I shall make a call and soon we will be armed. Then let the new group of American agents stop us. We will soak the land with their blood."

"Bravo." Wini uttered the word softly. "I feel naked without a weapon."

"Let's go downtown," André said. "We'll mingle with the crowds and I'll make the call."

"I must admit I feel better already," Brigitte said. "As always, you're right, André."

"Thank you."

"André is always right," Wini said.

"Thank you both," André said again. He hailed a cab and the three headed for Fremont Street. Mike Rojas and Lana Henry, in another taxi, were only a few seconds behind them.

In the backseat, Lana used her cell phone to call John and tell him what was happening.

"They're probably going to make a call or a personal contact," John replied. "None of them have used a public phone since they arrived. And they wouldn't be stupid enough to use a room phone. Stay with them."

"How about the other group?"

"They've stayed together, and are in a restaurant eating."

"There are two of us. If these three split up?"

"Stay with André. He's the head honcho."

"Ten-four."

"It's gonna be a very long night," Mike said.

"You can always put in for overtime," Lana told him with a smile.

Five

The three members of the PLF gave Mike and Lana the slip in the crowds on Fremont. John had expected they would do that, so the news came as no surprise.

"Don't worry about it, Mike," John told him when he phoned in. "We've got the others under surveillance and he's not going to leave them behind. André made contact with someone. They might be planning to switch cars in the morning; they might change routes. We'll know in the morning. Walk around for a while, gamble some, and look like tourists. If you don't pick them up in an hour, come on back. No point in staying downtown spinning your wheels."

"Will do, John."

"I want the front and back of that hotel covered," John said. "At all times. We'll work two-hour shifts. Chris, you and Don take the first shift, then Jenny and me. Mike and Lana will follow us. Then we'll start all over. That way we'll all be able to grab a little sleep."

"We're gone," Chris said.

John looked at his watch. It was ten o'clock. "Jenny, we'll relieve them at midnight. You sleepy?"

"Not a bit."

"All right. Let's walk across the street and get a sandwich and some coffee."

While waiting for their club sandwiches, Jenny asked, "Why

didn't you ever marry again, John? If the question isn't too personal."

"Not at all. I don't know, Jenny. I suppose the right woman just never came along."

"You must have loved your wife very much."

"I did. I still do."

"After all the years?"

John smiled at her. "Yes. Not with the intensity that I once had, of course. But I still think about her."

"She was a lucky woman to have found you."

"Thank you. And why are you still single, Jenny?"

Her blue eyes twinkled with undisguised mischief. "Because no man could put up with me."

"That's a cop-out."

"Sure, it is!" she said with a quiet laugh. "I might get married someday. Probably will. But for now, I'm not looking. I've found what I want to do . . . finally."

"The team?"

"All the way."

"According to your file, which was extensive, you've had no personal encounters with criminals, and neither has any close friend or member of your family. Yet you were picked out of several hundred applicants. That puzzles me."

Jenny sugared and slowly stirred her coffee. "This country has become a huge immoral and directionless ship with no rudder and no captain, John."

"Interesting response to my question. You think this little team of ours can replace the rudder and serve as captain?"

"No. But I believe if we do our jobs right, we can help plot a course."

Before John could reply, his small cell phone softly chimed. He listened for a moment, then pocketed the miniphone. "Our missing PLF members have returned. They were driven back here by an as-yet-unidentified woman. She left the van she drove over in and took a cab back to wherever. Don got the plate number and is running it now."

"Vehicle switch?"

"Looks like it. There are several others outside who have also taken a great interest in André and his group."

"Agents?"

"Don seems to think so. We'll take a look as soon as we've eaten."

"You're sure not in a big hurry."

"André and his group aren't going anywhere just yet, and neither are the newcomers watching them."

"Whoever they may be."

"We'll soon know," John said as their food was placed in front of them.

"How?"

"Oh . . . I'll ask them."

"We are covered like a blanket," Brigitte said in the elevator. "I spotted three easily."

"I saw Henry Thompkins from MI6," Wini said. "That bastard has been hounding me for years."

"Jacques LaBlanc made it a point to show himself to me," André replied. "That damned pig!"

"Brigitte?" Wini asked.

"I saw several people, but I recognized none of them."

"Jacques is DGSE?" Wini asked.*

"Of course."

"Forgive me. The name is not one I'm familiar with."

"I am sorry. Jacques came over from DST. It was he who tortured me during my time in their hands."**

"The scars on your feet?" Brigitte asked.

"Yes. He was dismissed from the DST immediately after the torture was found out. Then last year he went to work for

*French Direction Général de Sécurité Éxterieur
**French Direction de la Surveillance du Territoire

the DGSE. I suppose all was forgiven within the two departments. I hate the bastard."

"I wonder who the others are," said Brigitte, as the trio walked up the hall to their rooms.

"I suspect we'll know when they make their move," André replied. "But won't they be in for a shock when we step out armed?"

"I will feel better when we actually have our hands on those weapons," Wini said.

"In the morning," André assured her.

"Hans Bruner," John told Jenny as they walked through the parking area of the hotel. "German BND—Bundesnachrichtendienst."

"Did you just clear your throat and spit, or is that a proper name?" Jenny asked.

Despite the situation, John had to laugh. He knew that Jenny was well aware of the German Federal Intelligence Service, the German equivalent of the CIA and MI6. "I've known him for years. He's a good man. I don't know the woman with him."

"My God, how many countries are interested in the PLF?"

"Obviously, quite a few. It's just too bad they're not all working together. But as you well know, that's practically an impossible objective."

"And that's where we come in?"

"Precisely. But in this situation we're going to be falling all over each other, and that could prove dangerous."

"Is the Pickle Factory in on this?"*

"I haven't seen any I know. Not yet. Have you seen any Cabbage Patch Kids?"**

*The Central Intelligence Agency
**The Federal Bureau of Investigation

"Not a one that I recognize, but they're certainly lurking around somewhere."

"The field is getting crowded, too damn crowded. I don't like it."

"Is there anything we can do about it?"

"Not a thing. Let's find our people and do a slow walk past."

John and Jenny spotted Chris standing alone at the edge of the parking lot. He waved them over.

"No point in pretending we're not here. I've already been made."

"By whom?" John asked.

"Perkins, from the Los Angeles office."

"The Secret Service is in on this, too?"

"I guess so. He's here with a couple of other people."

"Hello, John." The voice came from behind him.

John turned and stared. He was not surprised at what he saw. "Kemper. What the hell are you doing here?"

"I might ask you the same thing."

"Strictly a private matter. I have my own business, now."

John and Jenny exchanged glances.

John reached into his jacket pocket and handed his old company associate a business card.

Kemper held it up for better light and read aloud, "John Barrone and Associates. Security Services. That isn't very original, John. Is this phone number legit?"

"Staffed twenty-four hours a day."

"Yeah. I'm sure it is. No address?"

"The number is toll-free, Kemp."

"I can see that, ole buddy. Impressive card. Raised letters. Looks like gold, too, but I'm sure it isn't. May I keep this?"

"That's what they're for."

"Fascinating meeting you here, John. In a parking lot in the middle of the night."

"We're on a job."

"Yeah. I bet you are." He shrugged his shoulders. "Well, you may be, at that. See you."

"Later, Kemp."

The CIA man strolled away.

"Cards?" Jenny asked. "What cards?"

"They were waiting for me in my hotel room," John said. "I called the number. It's real. There are cards for all of you."

"In gold lettering?" Jenny said with a grin. "With our very own names? Wow!"

"Absolutely," John replied, unable to hide his smile at Jenny's words. Her humor was infectious. "The business cards are something I discussed with Mr. Wagner back at the training site."

Don Yee stepped out of the darkness. "Are we having a convention, folks?"

"We certainly could, Don," John told him. "The parking lot is full of spooks."

"Sure is. We're falling all over each other."

"You and Chris go get something to eat and some sleep. Jenny and I will take over."

"OK," Chris said. "Y'all have fun in this fishbowl."

"Yeah," Don said. "Let us know when they start passing out the funny hats and party favors."

The two walked off.

"Seven government agencies, representing at least four countries," Jenny said. "This is approaching absurdity."

"We might even see the Japanese Naicho show up before it's over," John replied.

"Why them?"

"Because of the Supreme Truth cult."

"Ah! The poisonous gas and biological group. But they aren't a part of the PLF, are they?"

"No connection whatsoever, but paranoia is highly infectious. And that group is growing in membership once again. They're also heavily involved in computer-related equipment. There will probably be a few in the intelligence community who will see some sort of tie-in."

"Do you?"

"No, not at all. So far as we've been able to determine the PLF acts alone, but it's larger than we originally thought. They obviously have contacts here in Las Vegas, and that means they probably have contacts in other major US cities. Especially in New York City."

"And probably in cities along the way."

"Yes."

"That means they'll be switching vehicles several times."

"In all probability."

"Damn!"

"And they're smarter than we are in at least one respect."

"What do you mean?"

"There are a dozen agents milling around this hotel in the middle of the night."

"So?"

"The PLF people are in bed, asleep."

Six

By dawn of the next morning, the team was able to confirm at least twenty-one agents from various US and foreign agencies gathered in Las Vegas. John had reported in and was told, "Play it any way you think best. It's your show."

"We'll lay back," John told his team. "We have the equipment and we're able to monitor the frequencies of all the US agencies involved. Phone calls are iffy, but our people can tag some of them. I think that's the best we can do at this time."

"What are the odds of the press finding out about the objectives of the PLF?" Lana asked.

"I don't know," John admitted. "But I sincerely hope they don't. If the press went public with the PLF's plan, it would create panic in New York City the likes of which you have never seen."

"New York would be a ghost town," Don said.

"With hundreds of dead bodies of people trampled by others attempting to flee," Mike added. "The tunnels and bridges would be blocked by dozens of wrecks. It would be chaos."

John cut his eyes for just a second as André strolled nonchalantly into the hotel dining room and was shown to a table. "The head honcho of the PLF just walked in. Time for us to walk out and get ready to move. A couple at a time."

Packed up and checked out of their hotel, the team waited for the PLF.

"It's going to be a damn parade," Jenny said. "All we need to make this complete is Peter Sellers."

Mike shook his head in disgust. "By now these people have to know they're being tailed."

"They knew that before they pulled out of LA," John replied without removing the long lenses from his eyes. "I'm sure by now they've spotted some of the agents bird-dogging them." He adjusted his binoculars. "There they are. Getting into a van, a sedan, and an SUV."

"Are we checking out the person or persons here in Vegas who supplied them with these new vehicles?" Jenny asked.

"No," John told her. "That isn't our job. The Bureau is taking care of that."

"You hope," Mike said.

John lowered the binoculars and looked at the man. "If they're not, somebody screwed up big time."

"You know they're not going to move against these people without some hard proof. Not with all the civil liberty lawyers looking at them. These people have been cleared by the federal government to move around the country."

"Then when they get close to New York we'll detain them . . . maybe."

"Maybe?"

"If Bob's people have found where the cyanide is stored and neutralized the team already in place, we'll make our move. If not . . ." He frowned. "We'll wait."

"And tackle them in the city?" Jenny asked.

"We have no choice. We've got to locate the cyanide, or whatever poison these nuts plan to turn loose in the city."

"You still have doubts about the cyanide ampules that were found?" Mike asked.

"Yes. I don't know how they could deliver the gas in sufficient quantity to achieve their objective . . . which is to kill thousands and thousands of people. Cyanide is tricky. I did some exploring on the Internet with my laptop last night. To be really effective, cyanide takes extremely high concentrations

CODE NAME: PAYBACK 53

in the air. A certain amount of cyanide—more than I thought—can be endured for as long as an hour without effect."

"Is there an antidote?" Jenny asked.

"To some degree, yes. Something called PAPP. There is also another method used—something about speeding up the body's own ability to excrete cyanide. But I'm no doctor or scientist. You can read it on the Net yourself if you like." John straightened up in the seat. "There they go." He lifted his mic and said, "They're pulling out now, Chris. You have them?"

"Yes, sir. On it. Along with five or six other vehicles. This really *is* going to be a parade."

"I know. It's ludicrous. Just stay with them."

"Yes, sir."

John waited until all those involved had pulled out of the various parking lots, then motioned for Mike to follow. "We'll just tag along, bring up the rear for a while. We sure can't lose them."

"If this didn't have such serious overtones," Jenny said from the backseat, "it would be funny."

"Yeah, all we need is a marching band," Mike said.

"You're both right," John replied. He picked up his cell phone and punched out the toll-free number of the team's HQ. It was answered immediately. "You people are aware of all the agencies involved in this chase, are you not?"

"Yes. The field certainly appears to be getting a bit crowded."

"Suggestions?"

"None at this time. Continue shadowing suspects."

"That's it?"

"The Canadian SIS is now in on the chase. You can expect more countries to become active."

"Oh, that's just wonderful. One correction: this isn't a chase, it's a damn comedy. Can you give me a clue as to just who else might be joining this crowded field?"

"Not at this time. Control out."

John clicked off the phone. "Incredible. Obviously, Control

did not anticipate all these agencies becoming involved. I was just informed that more agents from overseas are probably coming in."

"More?" Jenny said. "From where, Monte Carlo?"

John turned his head to hide his smile, but not before Mike saw it and grinned. "Canada's Security Intelligence Service is here."

"I didn't spot them," Mike said. "Of course, I don't know anyone from the SIS."

"Who else might be joining us?" Jenny asked.

"Control didn't tell me. I think they might be a tad irritated about the chase becoming something out of a Three Stooges movie."

"Interesting comparison, John. I would have said the Keystone Cops."

"We're all going to stop laughing when this mess takes a violent turn."

"That's coming, I think," Mike said. "Too many people pushing this group of whackos."

"Nine agencies, including ours, and more coming in. Jeez!" Jenny shook her head.

"Probably thirty people or more," John said. "As a secret op this is joke."

"John, do you think our powers-that-be knew all along that this op would draw worldwide attention?" Jenny questioned.

"I really don't think so. They probably knew the Bureau would certainly be in on it, but not all this bunch."

With Mike handling the wheel, the team rode in silence for ten minutes, maintaining a couple of miles' distance behind Don, Chris, and Lana.

Mike broke the silence. "I wonder if our would-be killers are going to take the northern route."

"I doubt it," John said. "They'll probably cut south up ahead and pick up I-40 at Kingman."

"Why do you think that?"

"Arizona, New Mexico, and Texas offer lots more places for an ambush, and lots more places to hide bodies."

"I never thought of it that way. Then you believe things are about to get nasty?"

"I sure do. I'd make a substantial bet the PLF will stop only for gas and fast food today, and keep on driving well into the night. They might even exit I-40 and take Highway 93 down toward Phoenix. If they do, they'll stage an ambush somewhere along this hundred-mile stretch down toward Wickenburg. Anybody want to take the bet?"

"You have information you're not sharing, John?" Jenny asked.

"Not a bit. It's just a hunch. We don't know what kind of weapons came with those new vehicles they picked up last night. We don't even know for sure this is the primary group of terrorists. They may well be a suicide squad sent out to sacrifice their lives in order to create a diversion. Jenny, warn our people up ahead to be ready for something to pop if the suspects take Highway 93 south."

"Do I warn the other people?"

"No. How can we? We're not supposed to know they're here, and we're not supposed to know anything about this group of alleged terrorists."

"This is getting stranger and stranger."

John twisted in the seat and looked at her. "Welcome to the world of international espionage, Jenny. Each knows the other is working in the host country but can't say a word about it. That's just the way it is."

The three-vehicle PLF group picked up I-40 at Kingman, and the multicar convoy stretched out. Twenty-five minutes later, the PLF cut south on Highway 93.

"Fall back a few hundred yards," John radioed Chris. "They're going to pull something."

"One of the agents' cars just passed the PLF group and took the lead," Chris replied. "I'm dropping back."

"Which car?"

"The French, I think, but I'm not sure."

"I can understand that. I don't know who's driving what." John hooked the mic. "I wish I knew what was going on." He then uncharacteristically said, "Shit!"

Jenny giggled. "You are human, after all, John. Congratulations."

Mike was struggling to hide his smile.

"We have a big tanker truck and two out-of-state vehicles behind the PLF people," Chris radioed. "Everything is slowing down.

John picked up a state map and studied it for a moment. He radioed, "Stay well back, Chris. I've got a bad feeling about this."

"Ten-four, John."

"This would be a hell of a spot to pull something," Jenny said after glancing at a map for a few seconds. "No towns for miles."

"Everybody is slowing down," Chris radioed. "I don't know what's happening. I'm at the beginning of a long curve and can't see."

"Pull over and stop," John instructed him. "Wait for us."

"Stopping."

Out of sight of the team, the three vehicles of the PLF slowed and then stopped a short distance from a bridge over a dry creek bed. Akal stepped out of the van, a Russian-made RPG in his hands. He knelt down, checked behind him to make certain none of his people would be hit by the back-blast, then leveled the rocket launcher at the tanker truck and took aim. He fired just as the tanker reached the middle of the bridge.

The tanker was suddenly enveloped in a ball of flames as the gasoline it was carrying exploded with a powerful whooshing blast of fire and heat concussion. The car carrying the agents from the French DGSE quickly stopped, wheeled around, and headed back just in time to be hosed down with automatic weapons fire from Brigitte and Hurran. The car slewed off to one side and went off the road and into a ditch, the front windshield shattered and spider-webbed, both front tires flattened, and steam rising from the bullet-shattered radiator. No bullets struck the three French agents, but they were badly shaken and bruised from being tossed around when the car impacted with the ditch bank and came to a very abrupt stop.

The PLF terrorists jumped back in their vehicles and were gone down the empty highway. The entire act of violent fiery death had taken less than fifteen seconds.

The lead car of out-of-state visitors suddenly slammed on its brakes, and the car behind it plowed into it and locked up bumper to bumper, both vehicles sliding into the wall of flames. The passengers of the lead vehicle never had a chance. They were trapped in their car and incinerated within seconds. Those in the second car bailed out and ran for their lives.

The road was blocked and would remain so for several hours.

The terrorists disappeared down the highway, laughing as they rolled along.

Seven

The driver of the tanker truck never had a chance, either. He was probably killed instantly when the rocket exploded in the front of his rig. At least, John hoped he had been. That death would have been a lot more merciful than burning.

Those in the lead four-wheeler were all dead, burned to blackened char. The smell was terrible.

John observed the various agents milling around, all frantically talking on cell phones—all except for Kemper and his people. He walked over to John.

"I guess you took this route because you were sightseeing, hey, John?"

"That's right, Kemp. We're just poking along, taking our time heading east."

"You wouldn't be heading to New York City now, would you?"

"How in the world did you guess? That's truly astonishing."

"Who are you working for?"

"Myself, as I told you. Gave you my card."

"Yeah. I called the number. Big deal. I think your Security Services is all bullshit."

"Think whatever you like."

"It's bullshit. You're freelancing, and you're in over your head on this op. You don't know what's going on. My suggestion to you is to back off before you get tangled up in something you can't handle."

"I haven't found anything yet I couldn't handle, Kemp. But you tell me: what op are you talking about?"

"You're an asshole, John!"

"I assume someone here has notified the state patrol about this accident?"

"My people did."

"What caused the tanker to explode?"

"Oh, horseshit, stop the game playing. You're bird-dogging the same people we are . . . all of us," he added with no small amount of disgust.

John smiled at him just as the breeze shifted, bringing with it a whiff of burned human flesh. John lost his smile and grimaced. "Yes, there does seem to be quite a crowd."

Kemp stared at him.

"Going to be very interesting when all the IDs are shown to the police. That might create a very awkward incident, don't you think?"

"And you'll be right in the middle of it, John. Don't forget that."

"Not me. I'm not a government agent. I'm retired. I don't have to sidestep a lot of embarrassing questions. Besides, I was a mile back. I didn't see a thing."

Traffic was beginning to back up on both sides of the blocked bridge. People were getting out of their cars and walking as close as they could to the still-burning vehicles.

Still farther in the distance, the faint sounds of sirens could be heard.

"See you," John said, turning away.

"Wait a minute! Where the hell are you going?"

John shrugged his shoulders. "I can leave. I didn't see a thing." He smiled at the CIA man. "Besides, I'm not blocked in like you are."

"You can't leave!"

"Watch me. See you around, Kemp. Have fun with the state patrol."

Jenny fell in step with him halfway back to the car. "I contacted control like you said. They punched up their maps on the big board and found us a road around all this crap—not much of a road but it's passable. I've got it on the screen."

"Good. The others will be tied up here for an hour or so. We'll get the jump on them. Let's get out of here, and do it quickly."

The fast-moving state police cars didn't slow down when they saw John and his people heading back in the opposite direction. They blasted on south, emergency lights on and sirens screaming a warning. A few miles further on, Mike cut off to the east on an unpaved dirt road.

"A couple of miles more and we'll hit an intersection," Jenny told him. "Go straight on through."

"Got it."

"Jenny, you gave Control the tag numbers of the PLF's vehicles, right?"

"Sure did."

"Wagner told me the organization has eyes and ears all over the United States. That tells me that at least some cops are also a part of this operation. How many, I don't know. Hell, it might even be a bunch of older retired people. Whatever. But I'm going to bet our naughty boys and girls are heading for Phoenix and a motel. They'll surely switch cars there. They're going to have to do that. Maybe we'll get lucky and some of the eyes and ears will spot them and call in."

"And if they don't?"

"Do you know how to pray?"

"Sure. But I haven't in a long time."

"If we lose this bunch, I would suggest you pick up the habit again. Quickly."

The members of André's contingent were ecstatic. They had struck their first blow against the United States. That their victims had been a truck driver and a tourist family from Iowa made no difference. They were racist, money-hungry, materialistic, capitalistic Americans, and that was all that mattered. They all needed to die.

André had used his cell phone to call in to a cell of the PLF in Phoenix, but there had been no answer. He tried repeatedly with no success.

"They have left to join us in New York City," André said. "I was afraid of that."

"So we are on our own?" Hurran asked.

"Until we reach Dallas, yes."

"We must get rid of these vehicles," Akal said.

"We will. In Phoenix."

"But our people have left!"

"Phoenix is a large city with plenty of vehicles." André smiled. "Lots of rich Americans living in fine homes with fences around them and lots of privacy."

"And they won't be missed for several days," Akal said.

"Hopefully."

"Then we can drive straight through to Dallas, and we'll be halfway to our objective."

"Yes."

An hour later the terrorists were approaching the outskirts of Phoenix.

John and his team had traveled in a half-circle, over some really bad roads, and picked up Highway 93 at Wickenburg. They figured they were about ninety minutes behind the terrorists . . . if, as John pointed out, the PLF members had actually gone to Phoenix.

"Our chances of finding them are about a million to one," Mike pointed out.

The team was sitting in a truck stop just outside the city, having sandwiches and coffee and wondering what to do next.

The federal authorities had issued a nationwide alert—not for public dissemination—just moments before John and his team pulled into the truck stop: if the vehicles are spotted, report your location immediately, follow, but do not attempt to detain.

"At least the cops are finally in on it," Don said, signaling the waitress for more coffee.

"If they'd been brought in sooner, we might have had a chance," John replied. "But the vehicles the terrorists picked up in Vegas have been tucked away in some obscure place, or will be very soon. Bet on it."

"Then we start all over," Lana said.

"Just about," John agreed. "But these nuts had their first taste of American blood back on the bridge and I'm sure they enjoyed it immensely. If they don't have a cell here in Phoenix, they'll kill to get vehicles. And they'll kill again and again on their way to New York." John sighed, and was silent for a few seconds. "And of course, there is the college connection we have to worry about."

"The report wasn't very clear about that," Chris said.

"Because information on the connection is so ill-defined," John replied. "The organization knows there are college cells in Tucson and in Dallas who support the PLF. But how much support is not clear."

"The report didn't state if those college cells would support killing," Jenny said.

"Because whoever put it together didn't know. At least at the time. Personally, I believe some, perhaps all, of the young cells would support violence. The PLF has had the time to recruit lots of young minds overseas . . . before they came to this country to attend college—or as much as I hate to say it, even high school."

"High school!" Lana said. "John, the report didn't say anything about high school kids."

"I don't believe it can be dismissed out of hand. There are hundreds, perhaps thousands, of young people from all over the world attending high schools and colleges here in America. Who knows how many? I sure don't."

"State would," Mike suggested.

"Sure," John agreed. "But the big clock is ticking, working hard against us. There just isn't time or personnel to check them all out. Hell, that would take months. And God knows how many people are in this country on work permits who might support the PLF."

"Control, or whoever is running this group of ours, sure gave us one hell of a first assignment," Jenny said.

"One we had damn sure better complete," Mike added.

"Yeah," Don said with a smile. "That's why we're getting the big bucks, folks."

No one added anything to that, for each team member was paid exceedingly well.

"John, do we start looking around Phoenix?" Chris asked.

"The needle in the haystack syndrome," John replied. "We'll be wasting our time. But . . ." He spread his hands. "We've got some daylight left. We can check the motels along the interstate. Although I suspect we'll just be spinning our wheels."

"Beats sitting around here," Lana said.

"Before we go," Jenny said, "I have a question: Does the president know about this situation?"

The team looked at John. "I suppose he does," John said. "Something of this magnitude, I don't see how he could be left out of it."

"Evacuating New York City . . ." Chris let that statement fade away into silence.

"Virtually impossible," John said. "Many people just wouldn't leave. Besides, we're talking about millions. Where would they go? Even if it were feasible, the terrorists would just strike another city."

"And most of the nation's business is conducted out of New York City," Don added. "Banks, Wall Street, the stock market. It would play hell with the economy."

John laid out a map of Phoenix and studied it for a moment. "I have to make a guess, so I'm going to guess the PLF will take I-10 out of here toward Tucson, then on to El Paso until they link up with I-20 to Dallas. We'll prowl the motels on the south side of the city. It's all we can do. Let's hope some of our unknown eyes and ears out there spot something and call in."

"Oh, shit!" Jenny said, as the team stepped out of the truck stop.

"What is it?" John asked.

"The FBI," she replied, nodding her head toward the left. "Standing right over there. The grim-looking one is Inspector Ballard."

"You know him?"

"Unfortunately. He is a right-by-the-book, cut-no-slack, I-claim-to-be-a-born-again-Christian type. On top of all that, he's a humorless asshole."

John sighed. "You have such a way with words, Jenny. I gather you have had a run-in with him?"

"Oh, I think you could safely say that."

"They're sure giving us the evil eye," Lana said.

"The woman is Libby Carson. She's a bitch. She's WMDOU and HAZMAT."

"What the hell did you say?" Don asked. "Or should I just ignore it and chalk it up to very vulgar, unfeminine bodily noises?"

Jenny smiled. "Weapons of Mass Destruction Operations Unit and Fire and Hazardous Material Unit."

"I guess being called a spook isn't that bad, after all," Don muttered. "She's a womdoo and a hasmat," he said, and shook his head. "Wonderful."

"Here they come," Jenny warned.

"Miss Barnes," Inspector Ballard said, marching up. "How nice to see you once again. I thought I spotted you back at the scene of the accident. I wondered about that."

"Wonder on, Ballard," Jenny told him.

The inspector's eyes narrowed for just a second. "Your tongue has not lost its sharpness, Miss Barnes. Nor its impudence."

"I'm out of the Bureau. I can call you a dickhead if I so choose. And I so choose."

John stepped forward and extended a hand. "I'm John Barrone, Inspector Ballard."

Ballard looked at the hand as if wondering if it was germ-free. He took it reluctantly. "Formerly of the CIA. I know something about you, Mr. Barrone."

"Oh?"

"Yes. I spotted you earlier today, as well. Interesting that you and Miss Potty Mouth are traveling together."

Don could not contain his laughter. "Potty Mouth?" he questioned.

"You find vulgar language appealing?" Libby Carson asked.

The third FBI agent looked heavenward and quietly sighed.

"It really doesn't bother me, Miss Womdoo Hasmat."

"What?" she asked sharply.

"Now, wait a minute!" John said, a noticeable edge to his words. "Let's all back off the name-calling." He turned his attention to Inspector Ballard. "You have something on your mind, Inspector. Say it."

"You left the accident scene rather quickly today, didn't you, Barrone?"

"Put a Mr. in front of it, *Ballard!*"

The inspector blinked and tried a smile. It came across as forced and totally insincere. "Excuse me, Mr. Barrone. I didn't realize you were so sensitive."

"I'm not. But I do enjoy good manners. As to the incident earlier today, I didn't see the accident. I was at least a half a mile or more back. There was nothing I could add to any investigation. When I arrived, the dead were dead, and those in the second car did not appear to be hurt. I left. You have any more questions?"

"I have lots of questions, but they can wait until I run into you one more time . . . if you get my drift."

"I'm afraid I don't. My associates and I are working. I have my own investigative service. Security Services. Let me give you a card."

Ballard looked at the card for a moment, then tucked it away in the breast pocket of his suit coat. He leveled a cold gaze at John. "Nice talking with you, Mr. Barrone."

"The pleasure was all yours."

The third agent, younger than Inspector Ballard or Miss Womdoo Hasmat, smiled at that, his eyes twinkling with good humor.

Ballard wheeled about and stalked off, the other two agents trooping along behind him, but not before the third agent gave them all a friendly thumbs-up.

"That Ballard is a real jerk," John said. He looked at Jenny. "And he doesn't like you, Jenny."

"Believe me, the feeling is mutual."

John chuckled at that. "I never would have guessed. OK, people. Let's get to work."

Eight

André looked at the bodies of the man and woman, sprawled in bloody death on the den floor of their suburban home. "All their money did not protect them," he said scornfully.

"And they did not die well," Hurran said, wiping the blood from his knife blade with a washcloth he'd taken from one of the four bathrooms of the sprawling home. "Typical Americans. Whining and begging for their lives. Pigs!" He threw the bloody washcloth on the floor beside the body of the small dog that had been the beloved family pet for years. Alain had stomped the animal to death to still its incessant barking.

"I hate dogs," Alain said. "Filthy beasts."

"We now have a Cadillac, a pickup truck, and an SUV," André said. "Transfer our equipment and then clean up. We will leave here glowing with cleanliness."

"Three vehicles, two people," Jan said. "Are we missing someone?"

André looked first at Jan, then at the bodies on the floor. "How old would you guess them to be?"

"Mid-fifties," Max replied.

"I would have guessed sixty, at least. No matter. Look in the closets of the other bedrooms."

"No need to do that," Wini called from the door. "I think the third family member is here."

"One person?" André asked.

"Yes. A woman. In her early to mid-twenties. She just pulled up to the garage in a very expensive-looking sports car."

"Now we have three people and four vehicles," Jan said. "I hate these rich Americans."

The terrorists' vehicles were hidden in the garage, the huge doors closed and locked.

"She's trying to open the garage doors now," Wini called. "Now she's getting out of her car. She looks very haughty. I don't like her."

"Let her in," André said. "We'll welcome her with open arms."

"What do you mean?" Akal asked.

"She will be our ticket to New York City. First class all the way."

"A hostage, André?" Brigitte questioned. "That's risky."

"Why?" Max asked.

"We have two thousand miles to travel, that's why. Too many things could go wrong.

"Brigitte, go pack several changes of clothing for our guest," André ordered. "We want her to look presentable at all times."

"André—"

"Do it!"

Brigitte left the room.

Betsy Morrow opened the front door of her parents' home and stepped into hell.

"They've either switched vehicles or are holed up somewhere," John said. "And it may be both."

"You feel they're still in this area?" Don asked.

"I think it's a real possibility, but it's just a hunch."

"It's frustrating," Lana said. "Even if we saw them standing across the street, we couldn't do anything. I hate these cat-and-mouse games."

"Nothing out of New York City?" Mike asked.

"Not a word."

"So what do we do now?" Chris asked.

"We wait for them to make their next move."

"Is the president going to cancel any plans he has for this evening?" Martin Denning, President Kelley's Chief of Staff, was asked by his most trusted aide.

"No. He doesn't feel the situation is critical enough to alter anything."

"He might after reading this," the aide replied, handing his immediate boss a sealed envelope.

Denning's face tightened as he read the brief, typewritten message. "Lost them! Good God."

"That accident in Arizona was no accident."

"Obviously. I'll get this to the president immediately."

Denning was back in five minutes. "Nothing has changed. He won't alter his schedule."

"Not even his plans to visit New York?"

"Not at this time. It's too important an event. Millions of dollars of much-needed campaign funds are at stake."

The aide shrugged his shoulders and sighed.

"But he was highly irritated about the FBI and Secret Service losing the suspected terrorists."

"And?"

"He's ordered more agents onto the case."

"Does he know there are agents from half a dozen foreign countries in on this?"

"Yes. That's one of the reasons he got so angry. How could thirty or more highly trained agents lose a three-car caravan?"

"Easily, I suppose, when they're shooting rockets at you."

Betsy Morrow had never been so frightened in her life. She had screamed and cried and begged, and then vomited at the sight of her dead parents. That got her slapped around by the men and women who had invaded her home and killed her mother and father.

"You look like a Jew to me," André said, gripping her chin with a hard hand and painfully forcing her head back. "Are you?"

"I'm a Methodist."

"You're rich like a Jew," Hurran said, then spat on the carpeted floor. "Jews take care of other Jews. She's a liar. She's a kike, I'd bet on it."

"My parents earned their money just like everybody else: by working for it," Betsy said proudly. "Besides, I have several Jewish friends. Nobody gave them anything. They all worked for what they have . . . and worked hard."

"She's a damn Jew-lover," Brigitte said. "You have a Jew boyfriend, girl?"

Betsy did not answer, just glared at the woman. Her shock was gone. Now she was just plain mad.

"What is it with you people?" Betsy demanded, wiping the last of her tears from her eyes. "Who are you?"

"We are your captors," Wini said, an ugly glint in her eyes. She had taken an immediate dislike to Betsy. Betsy was a very pretty woman, while Wini bore a striking resemblance to absolutely nothing.

"You're cold-blooded killers. Why did you kill my mother and father? What did my parents ever do to you?"

"They grew fat while others withered and starved," Akal told her. "They flaunted their wealth, living in this expensive palace"—he waved his hand—"while others lived in cardboard boxes and ate out of garbage cans. They were pigs, greedily gobbling up everything in sight while forcing the more deserving to lick up the crumbs."

"What?" Betsy asked, thoroughly confused. "I don't understand any of this."

"Enough," André said. "We've lingered too long here. Get ready to move."

"Where are we going?" Betsy asked.

"To strike a blow for freedom," Brigitte said.

"Who are you people?" Betsy again asked. "And what in the hell are you talking about?"

"Freedom fighters," Max said. "Friends of all the oppressed peoples of the world."

"You're terrorists!" Betsy said.

"That is so typical of an American," Akal said. "Fat, lazy, and stupid."

"It's growing dark," Hurran called from a window.

"Load the vehicles," André ordered.

"What do we do with rich bitch's car?" Wini asked.

"Lock it up and leave it in the driveway."

"What are you going to do with me?" Betsy asked. "Just get out and leave me alone."

That brought smiles to the faces of the PLF group, especially to André, who seemed to be taking a great deal of pleasure from the exchange.

"Oh, no," Wini told her. "You're going on a trip, bitch. With us."

"No, I'm not!"

Wini slapped her, the blow staggering the young woman. "Learn this now, bitch: don't argue. Do what you are told to do, when you are told to do it."

"What about my mother and father?" Betsy asked, rubbing her cheek.

"What about them?" Akal asked. "Do you want us to linger while you arrange for an expensive funeral? Let them rot on the floor." He spat on the carpet, then looked at Betsy and smiled. "It will serve them right. I only wish we could dump them in a pigpen. That would be a more fitting end."

André took a pistol from his waistband and rubbed the weapon against Betsy's face. Betsy flinched at the touch of the cold steel. "Do what you are told and you'll live, Betsy. Fight us, try to escape, disobey orders, and I'll kill you. Do you understand?"

Betsy nodded. "I understand."

"Good."

Betsy cut her eyes to a clock. Her date was due to pick her up in one hour. They had made plans to go to a movie and have a late dinner. What if they were delayed here, and he showed up? She couldn't allow that to happen. If she wasn't here and her car was, Chuck would get suspicious and probably call the police. Yes, she was sure he would. They were informally engaged; everything but the ring and the date. Both sets of parents approved of the marriage, and each set liked the other. But if Chuck showed up here ahead of schedule—as he was prone to do, since he hated being late for anything—these nuts would kill him without hesitation. And Chuck could have a bad temper. He kept it under control most of the time, but he wouldn't be pushed and he hated lawbreakers. He was a couple of years older than Betsy, and arrow-straight in his thinking.

"All right," Betsy said. "I understand. I won't give you any trouble."

"Fine," André said. "You might live through this." He looked at the group. "Everybody ready to move?"

They were.

"Let's go!"

At seven-thirty Mike, who was taking his turn monitoring calls from the sheriff's department and the Phoenix PD, jerked open the adjoining door to John's room.

"We may have something, John."

John listened briefly and said, "Tell everybody to pack up. We're leaving. They've made their move. Tell me the rest of it on the road."

With the members in the second car listening on a cell phone, Mike explained. "A couple in a very expensive section of town were found murdered about an hour ago. Their throats were cut. It was really messy. Their daughter, Betsy Morrow, twenty-three, is missing. Three of their vehicles are gone—a full-size Ford pickup truck, a Ford Expedition, and a new Cadillac. The daughter's car is still at the house. The three vehicles the terrorists were driving were found inside the garage. Some of the daughter's clothing is missing."

"How do they know that?"

"From the man who called in the report, the daughter's fiancé, Charles Fordham."

"They took a hostage. I should have guessed they would. Damn! That really complicates matters."

"I just hope the Feds order a lid put on this," Jenny said.

"Oh, they will," John said. "But the question is: how long will it take the press to blow the lid off? If the press gets wind of this immediately and it goes print and broadcast, the terrorists will just switch cars and kill again . . . before they get out of the damn state."

"We going to stay on I-10, John?" Mike asked.

"Yes. The terrorists are probably in Tucson by now, or approaching the city. It's the logical route for them to take. It's been on the radio and TV and in the papers that there is heavy construction in progress on the other route. I-10 is clear and wide open."

"Tucson is home of the University of Arizona," Jenny pointed out.

"Yes," John agreed. "And they might have some sympathizers there. We don't know."

"I wonder why the parents were killed and not the daughter?" Mike questioned.

"She might have returned home after the killings and surprised the terrorists," John replied. "Or they might have planned the hostage taking."

"I wonder," Jenny said from the backseat, "if the gas or whatever they plan to use is already in New York City, and this group alone knows where it is, or how to use it?"

"Good point," John said, twisting around in the front seat to look at Jenny. "Only the terrorists know the answer to that. We're all operating in the dark."

Several cars pulled alongside them on the interstate and slowed. John and his team caught a quick glimpse of the passenger on the right hand side, front seat, of the lead car: Inspector Ballard. He gave them a scowl and then the car roared past.

"Your friend and mine," Jenny said with a grin, resisting an urge to give Ballard the middle finger.

"Yeah," Mike said. "I don't believe he was very happy to see us."

"We're going to have to be very careful about this," John said. "He could try to arrest us, or at least detain us. He certainly has the authority."

"He wouldn't dare," Mike said.

"Don't bet on that," Jenny said. "I told you about Ballard: he's right by the book. He'll never cross that line into any gray area."

Two more familiar cars roared past. The team recognized one of them as the vehicle driven by the Secret Service.

"Who was in that second car?" Mike asked. "It blew by so fast I couldn't tell."

"My ole buddy from the Company," John said. "Kemper."

"The parade has begun," Jenny remarked.

"I get the impression Kemper doesn't like you very much," Mike said.

"He doesn't like me at all," John replied. "Never has. Then when I beat him out of a Chief of Station position in Europe, he really turned up the dislike factor."

"Ballard and his bunch don't like me," Jenny said. "Kemper and his people don't like John. How many enemies do you have, Mike?"

"I worked for the IRS, Jenny," Mike said with a smile. "Everybody in America hates me."

Nine

As the team was approaching the outskirts of Tucson, John's cell phone rang. It was Control Central, and John did not have the foggiest idea where that was, although he strongly suspected it was somewhere in the Washington, DC, area. He had been advised not to ask, so he didn't. He put the phone on speaker.

The message was very brief. "The terrorists have been spotted. The information is coming your way by computer. Sending now."

"I've got it," Jenny said, just a few heartbeats later. "A nice map with it, too. Take I-19 south, Mike. We've got a ways to go yet."

"What I'd like to know is this: what do we do when we spot them?" Mike asked.

"Watch them," John replied.

"We don't try to grab the Morrow girl?"

"You know better, Mike."

"Just wanted to be sure."

"Are you going to tell the other agencies we've spotted the terrorists?" Jenny asked.

"How? I head a civilian security service. I'm not supposed to know anything about any terrorists."

"The Morrow girl is expendable, then?" Jenny asked.

"I don't like it, Jenny," John replied. "But for now, that's the way it has to be."

"If the press gets wind of this and breaks the story . . ." Mike trailed off into silence.

"There will be denials from the highest levels of government," John told them. "There is no threat of a poisonous gas attack on New York City. Bet on it."

"Governments never lie, they just deny," Mike said.

"That's about the size of it."

John stilled the ringing of his cell phone. He listened for a few seconds. "Any idea where he's gone?" he asked. Then: "All right, we'll keep our eyes open." He laid the phone aside and said, "Betsy Morrow's fiancé, Charles Fordham, has disappeared. His best friend told the Bureau Chuck packed a bag and took off."

"It's a foolish question, I know," Jenny said. "But I have to ask it—"

John held up a hand. "It seems that Chuck has a good friend who's a freelance journalist of some repute. Written several books that were well-received, and so forth. The journalist has a pipeline into the local PD. Either of you want to fill in the rest?"

"The journalist has also disappeared," Mike said. "Presumably with Chuck."

"Good guess," John said.

"The journalist's name?" Jenny asked.

"Scott Baker."

"I've heard of him," Mike said. "Read some of his articles. He's a good writer. Neither left nor right of center. So the local PD has an idea where the terrorists have gone?"

"Certainly looks that way."

"The field is getting even more crowded," Jenny said. "And the situation is becoming more tangled."

"Well, tangled is not exactly the word I would choose for this lash-up," John said. "What we have is this: Chuck wants his girlfriend back, the reporter wants a story, the police want a group of murderers and kidnappers—supposedly that's all they know about it—we want a gang of terrorists who are planning mass murder, and the Bureau, the Company, and the Secret Service want us to go away." John sighed. "I would very much like a drink right about now."

"How would you describe the situation, John?" Jenny asked.

"Fucked-up is the phrase that comes to mind."

"Goodness, John!" Jenny said with a laugh. "Such language!"

"Excuse me. That slipped out."

That got a laugh from both team members.

"Your exit is right up ahead, Mike," Jenny reminded him. "Stay on I-19 for about twenty miles. You'll exit off to the right. The road is not going to be a good one. The map doesn't show whether it's paved or not."

"OK."

John radioed back to the second car. "Chris, any sign that we're being followed?"

"Negative, John."

"All right. Stay with us."

On the twenty-mile drive to the exit, John sat in silence, wishing, at least part of the time, that he had a martini. Jenny longed for a cold beer. Mike wished for an icy cold Coca-Cola. All three tried to keep from thinking about what might happen when they confronted the terrorists. Soon enough the exit came into view.

"Three-quarters of a mile down this road, Mike," Jenny read from the detailed instructions she'd received by computer. "Take a turn to the left. Only house on the right."

"Pull over just ahead," John said. "Let's gear up from equipment in the trunk. No telling what we're going to be facing up ahead."

Armed with the best assault weapons on the market, and all wearing body armor, the six pushed on.

"Is this a dead-end road, Jenny?" Mike asked.

"Doesn't show it to be. It wanders off toward the east until I run out of map."

"There's the house," John said. "Drive on past, Mike." He

picked up the mic. "Chris, you people hold up where you are. We're going on ahead a few hundred feet."

"Ten-four, John."

"Would you look at the cars and trucks parked around there," Mike pointed out.

"It's a regular used-car lot," Jenny said.

"Yes," John said. "With a new Cadillac parked by the side of the house."

"Pull over and stop just around this curve?" Mike questioned.

"Yes. We'll leave the cars here."

"If they have any sense at all, they'll have a lookout," Jenny said.

"I'm sure," John said. "I doubt there is much traffic on this road. They're on alert right now. Bet on that."

"We're walking in blind," Jenny said.

"Can't be helped. I don't want trouble. I just want to make sure that's our PLF bunch. Then we'll back off and wait for them to move."

"Very charitable of you, John," Mike said. "But you know damn well as soon as they spot us they'll open fire. Figuring two to a vehicle, there must be at least fourteen people in that house."

"We've gotten lucky. It's the Tucson cell. I want a couple of those cell members. They probably don't know very much about the big picture, but it's worth a shot."

"And if we get any chance at all to grab Betsy, we take it?" Mike asked.

"Absolutely."

"I know what your orders are, John," Jenny said. "I read them off the screen, remember?"

"I have a free hand to change orders. That was part of the arrangement when I agreed to come aboard. If we get a chance to grab Betsy, we take it."

"Just wanted to be sure."

"Your headset working?"

"Yo, Chris," Jenny spoke into the tiny mic. "You copy?

"Five by five, Jenny."

"Working, John."

"Let's go."

The weapons they carried all had sound suppressors. No one among them was sure exactly what the terrorists had—except, of course, rocket launchers used in the attack back on the road.

The team walked slowly into the yard, on both sides of the house. No lights were showing, but they sensed the house was not empty. It was almost a tangible sensation hanging thickly in the air. There were no other houses within a mile or more of the suspected PLF safe house. No car lights were visible on the road leading past the house.

Chris and his people angled off toward the back of the house, to check on the vehicles. "It's our people, Jenny." The words were whispered into Jenny's ear. "At least it's the vehicles that were stolen back in Phoenix."

The front and back doors of the house suddenly slammed open and several people came running out, front and rear. Even in the darkness of night the team could see they were armed.

"Down!" John yelled, just as the dark was ripped with muzzle flashes. The whine of bullets lashed the air, reminiscent of dozens of angry bees.

Jenny was the first to return the fire. She knocked the legs from under one attacker, running with a stuttering automatic weapon. The person—in the dark it was impossible to tell if it was a man or woman—tumbled to the ground and thrashed about, screaming in pain and shock.

Chris and his team members sought cover and were pinned down in the backyard. Bullets clanged and slammed into the metal of the half-dozen or so vehicles parked in the rear of the house. They were unable to stop the group of people who reached a couple of cars and roared off into the night, bouncing across and kicking up a wall of dust in the field next to the house.

Mike crawled over to the person Jenny had brought down and dragged the young man behind cover. The team had a prisoner. Now if they could just get out alive to question him.

"Don's been hit!" Chris's words jumped into Jenny's ear.

"Don's down!" she yelled to John.

Over the stutter of gunfire, they all heard Don yell, "I'm all right! It just knocked the wind out of me. It didn't penetrate the vest."

One more vehicle roared out of the backyard, running without lights. It was a dark sedan; that was all anyone could determine in the night.

"That was the last of our bunch," Chris radioed. "I'm sure of it."

Jenny did not have time to reply or to call to John. The PLF sympathizers poured on the gunfire, and the team could do nothing but return it, which they did with brutal efficiency.

Two of the PLF cell went down and did not move. Another ran from the side of the house and Lana cut him or her down, sending the terrorist sympathizer sliding belly down onto the dusty ground. A yell and a solid round of cussing followed.

"Definitely a female," John muttered, as the gunfire from the PLF cell members tapered off. He motioned for Jenny to get the wounded young lady.

She nodded and crawled off under the protective cover fire of John and Mike. With both of them firing, the cell members at the front of the house were forced to keep their heads down as lead tore into the frame house and knocked chunks of wood out of it.

"Did you get my last transmission, Jenny?" Chris radioed.

"Yes!" Jenny panted her reply as she dragged the wounded young woman over to John.

"Yes, what?" John asked.

"The terrorists are gone with that last car."

"I expected that. Let's get out of here. Can that girl walk?"

"Yes. She isn't hurt bad. Just pissed off."

"Tell Chris to swing around here and get one of these prisoners."

"How about the Morrow girl?" Mike called, just a couple of seconds before gunfire once more began ripping the night as the cell members opened up.

John made the hard decision without hesitation. "She's on her own. We've got what we came for. Let's go. This area is going to be crawling with cops in a few minutes."

The team began backing out, slipping into the night, dragging the wounded PLF people with them.

Two minutes later the team was rolling, angling south for a few miles before picking up a highway that would take them to I-10.

"You goddamn fascist scum," the young woman PLF member cursed. She tried to take a swing at Jenny, and the former FBI agent smacked her.

"Watch your mouth, bitch," Jenny warned her.

"I'll never tell you anything, you capitalist whore!"

"Nobody's asked you anything, stupid."

"Who are you?" the young woman demanded.

"Santa Claus's elves," Jenny told her. "We came down from the North Pole to tell you you've been a really, really bad girl, and you're not going to get anything for Christmas."

"Smart-mouth bitch!"

"That's me," Jenny replied cheerfully.

"My leg hurts. I'm bleeding to death."

"No, you're not. The bullet just grazed you. If you'll hold still, I'll put a bandage on it."

"You pig bitch!"

"You're really a delightful young lady, aren't you?"

"Go to hell."

John had been talking with his team in the second car. The other PLF member's wound was more serious, but not life-threatening.

"How do we know the terrorists took I-10?" Mike asked.

"We don't. I just made a guess. If I'm wrong . . . well, we're screwed."

"Do we get kissed while we're getting screwed?" Jenny asked. "It's more fun that way."

John shook his head as he smiled. He was growing accustomed to Jenny's language . . . slowly.

"Power to the people!" the young lady prisoner suddenly yelled.

"I haven't heard that in years," John said.

"You'll never stop us!" the young woman shouted.

"Oh, put a sock in it," Mike said.

"You're Mexican," the young woman said. "I can tell. Why are you working for this fascist government?"

"I'm an American," Mike said. "And who says we're working for the government?"

"What's your name?" John asked her, twisting around in the front seat to look at her.

"I'll never tell you anything!"

"Back to that again," Mike muttered.

"Oh, you'll tell me," John said. "I can assure you of that. One way or the other."

"Go ahead! Torture me. That's what I expect you to do. I won't talk. Power to the people! Destroy the capitalist power-mongers."

"Good God! Do you promise to shut up if we beat you?" Jenny asked. "You're giving me a headache."

"Bitch! You brainwashed stooge of tyranny and oppression!"

"This could be funny if it wasn't so serious," Mike said.

"Does she have any ID at all?" John asked.

"A wallet in her back pocket, but her jeans are so tight I jut can't get it out."

"Rip the pocket if you have to," John said. "I want to see that wallet."

"I knew it!" the young woman hollered. "You're going to rape me!"

"Not even with Frankenstein's dick, honey," Mike said.

"Fuck you!" the captive hollered, then cut loose with a string of cusswords that awed them all.

When she wound down, Jenny said, "And you thought I had a bad mouth, boss."

"That was truly obscene," John agreed. "How about the wallet?"

Jenny opened the man's style wallet and laughed. "Visa, MasterCard, American Express, and about a dozen department store charge cards. And I'll bet you the bill goes to dear ole capitalistic daddy, right, Ms. Victoria Pardue?"

"Victoria?" Mike asked.

The young woman leaned back in the seat and folded her arms under her breasts. "I will tell you nothing," she said. "Nothing at all."

In the front seat, John smiled. He opened the glove box and took out a roll of heavy duct tape, handing it to Jenny. "Tape her mouth securely. Then her wrists, behind her." He radioed Chris. "What's the young man's name?"

"Neil Underwood."

"Did he tell you anything?"

"Not much. Except that he swore he'd kill us all if we harm the young lady with you. I think he's rather fond of her."

"Good. I was hoping that would be the case. Are you driving?"

"No. Lana is. Don's in the front seat with her."

"We may not need to do what I have in mind. We'll see. I'll be calling you on the phone in a minute. Get ready."

"Standing by."

John looked back at Jenny and motioned her to lean forward. He whispered: "How good an actress are you?"

"Fair, I reckon. I was in a couple of plays in high school and several in college."

"Pretty good screamer and moaner?"

"Oh, you bet. I can do that with the best of them. What do you have in mind?"

"Ms. Pardue all snugged down and secure?"

"Yep."

"OK."

John looked at Victoria. "Your young Mr. Underwood, Vickie. He just lost a couple of fingernails. . . ."

The young woman thrashed around in the seat and her eyes bugged out.

"They're going to work on his toes next. If that doesn't loosen his tongue, then we'll try a cigarette lighter on his penis. . . ."

Victoria really started squirming around at that. She grunted and kicked as best she could in the cramped space. She fought against the tape that covered her mouth.

Mike's eyes widened at that thought and he dropped one hand to his crotch and grimaced.

"Of course, Victoria," John told the young woman, "you could stop all of your friend's pain and disfigurement. You could if you wanted to. Tell us everything you know about the PLF's plans."

Victoria shook her head defiantly.

"I see a flickering light in the car behind us, boss," Mike lied, getting into the game. "I guess they've started with the cigarette lighter on the boy's privates."

"I'd hate to be in that car listening to his screaming," Jenny said.

All the fight abruptly seemed to leave Victoria, and she nodded her head several times.

"Remove the tape from her mouth," John said, picking up the mic. He spoke into the dead mic. "Hold up on the flame, guys. Oh, yeah? Well, that's his fault. We'll get him to a hospital as soon as Victoria starts giving us some information. Right." He laid the mic aside and looked back at Victoria. "Your friend is still alive, but in a lot of pain. If you want us to get him to a hospital, Vickie, start talking." *Good God,* John thought, struggling to keep a straight face, *I sound like something out of a bad movie!*

Jenny was not gentle in removing the tape, and Victoria was rubbing her sore mouth when the cell phone rang. It was Chris.

"John, the boy broke wide open when I told him we were torturing his girlfriend. I taped it."

"All right. Good. I'll get back to you in a moment." He clicked off and turned to Victoria. "Your boyfriend is in worse shape than we thought, Vickie. Start talking, and do it very quickly."

"Then will you take him to a hospital?" she spoke in a very subdued voice.

"Just as quickly as possible."

"You promise?"

"I promise that you both will be well-treated, Victoria, and you won't see us again."

"I hope you all die a horrible death. I hope you suffer and suffer."

"The longer you stall the more difficult your friend's wounds will be to treat, Vickie."

"All right. But I don't know very much. . . ."

Jenny clicked on the small tape recorder.

The next morning, the FBI task force handling the suspected terrorist threat against New York City received this message via a recorded telephone call from a person whose voice had been electronically altered: "Two members of the Peoples' Liberation Front can be found in a motel room at Lordsburg, New Mexico. I would suggest you go there immediately. By now the two subjects probably really need to go to the bathroom."

Ten

"That damned John Barrone!" Inspector Ballard blurted after listening to the message. "I told you he's the one who led the raid on that house outside Tucson."

"We have no proof of that. His Security Services is a legitimate business."

"That number is nothing but an answering service. Where are his offices?"

"The road. He and his team live in hotels and motels."

"That's nonsense, and you know it! He's tracking these PLF members."

"So are about a dozen or so other agencies, half of them foreign."

"We need to do something about that, too."

"Has Barrone interfered in any way with your investigation?"

"Not really. Not yet."

"Continue surveilling the PLF."

"I don't know where they are!"

Ballard's boss had a much better sense of humor than his inspector. Just before he broke the connection, he chuckled in spite of the deadly situation. "Why don't you make some sort of peace with John Barrone?"

"Why should I do that?"

"He probably knows where the terrorists are."

Ballard was furious as he turned to his team. "Barrone's

got a lot of stroke with some people in awfully high places. That has to be it."

"Orders, Inspector?" Special Agent Harden asked.

"Find the PLF."

"John, this is one very large organization," Lana said. "Why didn't the Bureau know of all these cells?"

"Hell, the Company didn't know about them, either. But in defense of my old agency, the Bureau is supposed to handle domestic matters."

"I think they were just moved into place," Jenny said. "Either that or they've been dormant for a long time."

"I tend to agree with the former," John replied, "for the most part. But not when it comes to the young people. They were recruited under a different organization and gently turned over a period of time."

The team was grabbing a bite to eat in a truck stop just outside El Paso, Texas, waiting for the phone call that would tell them where to change vehicles.

John took a bite of his sandwich and then a sip of tea. "But you can't really blame the Bureau; they're spread too thin, and have been for a number of years."

"Amen to that," Jenny said.

"All right." John pushed his plate away. "Here's what we have: Bob and his people have uncovered rumors of a college-based cell or cells sympathetic to the PLF in New York City and/or vicinity. Pretty good work on their part, considering they're operating alone. If we can believe what Victoria and her boyfriend told us, the PLF have cells in almost every major city in America. They're going to be switching vehicles more frequently than they change underwear. . . ."

At that, Don looked at the remnants of his chili-covered hotdog, grimaced, and pushed it aside.

"But we know the route they're taking—again, if we can

believe what was told to us. We have to follow it. It's pretty much all we've got."

"How many cars are we getting?" Chris asked.

"I requested two. I don't want Don behind the wheel unless it's some sort of emergency."

Don grinned. "What can I say? I'm accident-prone."

John answered his cell phone and listened for a few seconds. "On our way." He pushed back his chair. "Let's go, people. Our cars are ready."

The Bureau could get little information from those members of the PLF who survived the wild shoot-out on the outskirts of Tucson. They did learn that Betsy Morrow was alive and unhurt. No, the PLF members did not know who attacked them, except that they were sure it was agents of the fascist government of the United States.

"This is rhetoric right out of the sixties," one agent remarked. "My dad used to tell me about those days of the SDS and the Weathermen and the SLA. He said it was wild. Obviously those days are returning." He pointed to a message spray-painted on the wall of the living room:

DEATH TO THE FASCIST VULTURES OF THE UNITED STATES THAT SUCK THE BLOOD FROM THE POOR AND OPPRESSED.

"God help us all," another agent said, shaking his head after reading the message. "Where the hell do these people come from?"

"Every kid we've questioned so far is American," a third agent said. "Most from very comfortable, upper-middle-class homes."

Another agent walked up. "The attackers used 9mm automatic weapons. Brass all over the place outside. No semi could spit it out that fast."

"Did you get tireprints?"

"Yes. Two cars."

"Ballard is very unhappy about this. He's convinced that retired spook, John Barrone, is mixed up in this attack."

"What does Kemper say?"

"He agrees."

"Maybe he is. Maybe he's working for the kidnapped girl's relatives. Who knows? Come on, let's get busy. We've got a lot of work to do."

The terrorists made it as far east as a rest stop between Pecos and Odessa before one of their cars broke down. They didn't need a mechanic to tell them the transmission was shot. They gathered around the crippled car and looked at one another. Betsy was trussed up and lying on the backseat.

"Howdy, folks."

The words spun the PLF members around. None of them had heard the man approach.

"Y'all got troubles, I see."

"Nothing major, but thank you," André said.

"Nothing major?" The man shook his head. "You got transmission fluid durn near ankle deep under that car."

Akal was looking at the man's truck. A new king cab Ford long bed. And there was a gun rack in the rear window. Several rifles were in the rack. He cut his eyes to André, and knew that he had also seen the truck.

"Well, you're right about that, sir," André said. "I was just too embarrassed to admit we know nothing about cars."

"Most folks don't," the Texan said with a smile. "Me, included. Not when it comes to transmissions. I think the best thing for you to do is—"

He never got to finish his sentence. Akal had watched the last car leave the rest area, then walked up behind the stranger and cut his throat.

"Get him in the trunk of the car," André ordered. "Quickly, now."

The man was muscled into the trunk and the blood wiped up from the pavement.

"I'll check the truck," Jan said, just as a car pulled into the rest area. Jan was back in half a minute. "No keys in the ignition. The man must have them in his pocket."

"Goddamn it!" André cursed. "All right, people. Separate. Get a drink of water, go to the restrooms. Do something! We're tourists. Act like it."

The man and woman in the out-of-state vehicle did not stay long, and did not give the terrorists more than a perfunctory glance as they got drinks of water, went to the rest rooms, then pulled away.

The keys to the truck were quickly retrieved from the dead man's pocket and the trunk lid slammed shut. "Get the rich bitch out of there and lock up the vehicle," André ordered. "With any sort of luck at all it'll be many hours, maybe even a day or more, before anyone in authority gets curious and starts snooping around. Let's go!" He looked at the group; no one had made a move. "What is it, now?"

"We have a job to do, André," Akal said. "A very important job. We trained for months for this assignment. The girl is nothing but a drag on us. Why don't we just kill her and be done with it? She's more trouble than she's worth."

André ignored that. He fully intended to kill the girl, but not just yet.

"If you want to fuck her, André," Wini said, "then do so and get it over with. Then kill the spoiled bitch. If you don't want to be the one, I'll do it and be glad to. We're all tired of listening to her whining and having to take care of her."

"Don't be stupid!" André snapped. "And did you take her to the rest room like I told you to?"

"No."

"Then do it, dammit! I don't want her peeing or shitting in her pants."

"It's too risky," Brigitte said.

André stared at each member of his group, one at a time,

anger glinting dangerously in his eyes. After a few seconds he took a deep breath. "I see. When we reach our objective, are you going to question my orders there, too?"

Alain was the first to reply. "Of course not."

André nodded. "Very well." He walked over to the car and removed the ropes from Betsy's wrists and ankles. He pulled the young woman out of the backseat and shoved her toward the rest room area.

"I'll take her to use the facilities, André," Wini called. "Please?"

"Then get over here and do it!"

Wini hurried over and took Betsy into the ladies' section of the rest room building. André motioned for the others to get into the vehicles. "I'll take the truck," he called. "With Wini and the girl. Move. We'll catch up. And while you're driving, remember this: Don't ever question my orders again. If you do, I'll kill you and leave you by the side of the road."

André stood on the sidewalk and watched as the members of his team nodded in understanding. He watched as they got into their vehicles and drove away. He then looked up and down the interstate. Cars and trucks were zipping past the rest area. No one was pulling in. The rest area was unusually deserted. André touched the butt of the pistol tucked in his waistband, covered by his shirt. He then felt in his pocket for the keys to the crippled vehicle containing the body of the helpful Texan.

He was thoughtful for a moment, standing in the warm breeze of the West Texas day, then shook his head. "Not yet," he muttered. "Not yet?"

"Not yet what?" Wini asked, exiting the ladies' room, pushing Betsy along in front of her.

Betsy's face was impassive, but if her thoughts could have been read they would have frightened the devil.

"Never mind," André told her. "Quickly now, get the bitch in the truck and secure her."

As the two young women walked away, André made up his

mind not to kill Betsy just yet. She might still come in handy . . . even though she was a lot of trouble.

The breeze softened, and André grimaced as he smelled the stink of his own body odor. None of them had bathed for several days, and they all desperately needed to wash and change clothing. In Dallas they would have to clean up and put on fresh clothing. Never mind the risk. It just had to be.

But Dallas was hours away, and every mile was fraught with danger.

André walked over to the truck and drove away from the rest area.

"We did not mean to anger you," Wini explained, as they rolled onto the interstate and headed east. "It's just that we have two thousand miles to go and we're getting nervous."

"I know. Forget it. I understand. We'll have different vehicles when we leave Dallas. When we pull out we'll all be rested and refreshed."

"I long to be clean more than anything else," Wini said with a sigh.

André's mood lifted somewhat, and he chuckled. "I do understand, Wini."

Betsy began kicking on the interior and wriggling about until Wini looked back at her. "What do you want, bitch?"

Betsy jerked her head several times until Wini got the message. "She wants the tape removed from her mouth, André. Shall I?"

"Go ahead." The tape pulled off, André said, "If you try to scream or make any kind of trouble, Betsy, Wini or I will kill you. Do you understand that perfectly?"

"Yes. I won't cause you any trouble."

"What do you want, bitch?" Wini asked her.

"For you to stop calling me bitch, for one thing."

Wini laughed. "All right, how about rich bitch? Is that any better?"

"Not much."

"Tough."

"You wanted to kill me back there at the rest area, didn't you?"

"I still do. I hate rich bitches like you. And your rich parents."

"Why?"

"Change the subject, Betsy," André said. "Or I'll have Wini tape your mouth."

"I just don't understand you people."

"We could talk for months and you still wouldn't," Wini told her. "So just shut up and enjoy the ride."

"While I'm alive to do that. Right?"

André and Wini smiled.

Eleven

"I think we're on the right track," Mike said, his eyes on the computer screen. "A body has just been found in the trunk of a car at a rest stop on eastbound I-20."

"Where?" John asked. He was handling the wheel on this leg of the team's odyssey.

"Between Pecos and Odessa."

"Heading straight for Dallas," John said.

"Any other information?" Jenny asked from the backseat of the car.

"Nothing yet."

"There probably won't be any more," John said. "You can bet the Bureau will step in and put a lid on this. We know where they're heading. It's confirmed there's a cell in Dallas."

"They'll change cars there," Jenny said.

"We must be the highest paid bird dogs in history," Mike said. "Those goddamn people are leaving a trail of bodies all across the country, and we can't do anything but follow along and mop up the blood."

"What sex was the body in the trunk?" Jenny asked.

"I don't know. The report didn't say. Wait a minute. There's more coming in. OK. Male. Middle-aged. Local man. His new pickup truck was stolen. Shit!"

"What's wrong?" John asked.

"I'm losing the signal. No, I've lost it. It's gone."

"John," Jenny said. "If we're powerless to act against this

bunch of whackos, and we know where they're going . . . Ah, forget it. I know the answer. I'm just blowing off steam."

"I feel the same, Jenny, but all we can do is keep tracking their movements. What if New York City isn't the target? What if it's Chicago, or Atlanta, or Washington, or some smaller city—or even a small town?"

Jenny looked out the rear window. "That same damn car's been laying back behind Chris for miles."

"I've been watching it. But I don't know whether it's following us or just heading in the same direction at a slightly slower speed."

"It's going to be a long, very boring trip, I'm thinking," Mike said, trying to get comfortable in the seat. "I'm going to take a nap. Night all."

"You want to get in the backseat and stretch out?" Jenny asked.

"Can we do that without having to pull over and stop?"

"Sure. You mind, John?"

"Not a bit."

It got a little hectic for a few seconds, but the shifting around was completed without causing a wreck. The adjusting of the seat and resettling of the powerful laptop computer took longer. Finally that was accomplished.

"Reminds me of my kids when they were little," John said with a smile.

"I hate to tell you this, John, but I have to go to the bathroom," Jenny said.

John looked at her for a few seconds. "You just went back in that last town we . . ." Then he realized she was putting him on, and shook his head and sighed. Jenny laughed at the expression on his face. In the backseat, Mike chuckled.

"I figure we'd better laugh while we can," Jenny said. "When this seemingly endless pursuit is finally over, there'll be damn little time for laughs and not much to laugh at, I betcha."

"The thing that puzzles me still is what type of delivery

system they plan to use," John said. "I just don't believe it's going to be cyanide."

"Germ?" Jenny asked as she looked back at Mike. He was already asleep, snoring softly.

"I don't know, Jenny. I might be completely wrong in thinking it isn't cyanide. I just can't figure out how they plan to use it."

"Maybe we'll get lucky, John?"

"We'd better."

"We have a small problem, Mr. President," Martin Denning said, sitting down in the Oval Office.

"The terrorists?"

"Yes, sir."

"They slipped out of the noose again?"

"We really never had them back in. They've killed again, Mr. President. A rancher in West Texas. They cut his throat and stuffed him in the trunk of a car, then stole his pickup truck."

President Richard Kelley cursed softly. "We know for sure the target is New York City?"

"It looks that way, sir."

"Damn! Did those in custody add anything more?"

"Nothing. Ah, sir, about your speaking engagement in New York . . ."

"What about it?"

"Don't you think we should cancel it?"

"Absolutely not. I'll be well-protected there. I'll be in no danger."

"Sir, we're talking about poisonous gas being used. The threat is very real. I hope you'll reconsider."

"I won't, Martin. I'm firm on that. But I want every available agent on this."

"What about the press?"

"What about them?"

"If we start pulling agents in from all over the country to work on this, the press will be on it immediately. We'll have to tell them something. What do we tell them?"

President Kelley leaned back in his chair and sighed. "Well, we can't tell them the truth. They'd blow it all out of proportion and create panic in the streets. The press is one of the reasons I've decided to go ahead with plans to visit New York City. What about the CIA?"

Martin stared at him for a couple of heartbeats. "What about them?"

"Why didn't they uncover this plot? They're supposed to be on top of these things."

"They say the original plan was hatched here in America, and by law they can't work in the United States. So therefore they had no knowledge of it."

"That's crap, Martin. They've been working domestic since nineteen forty-eight, and have never stopped doing so. What's the real reason?"

The chief of staff shrugged his shoulders. "I guess they blew it, Mr. President."

"Oh, for Christ's sake, Martin, will you please knock off this 'Mr. President' crap! We've known each other since we were fraternity brothers at college."

Martin leaned forward and placed his hands on the president's desk. "Dick, listen to me. This terrorist threat is very real. This is no half-baked plan. I believe—"

Kelley waved him silent. "I know, Martin. I know. But I can't show cowardice in the face of it—"

"My God, are you worried about reelection?"

"Don't be ridiculous!" the president snapped. "I haven't made up my mind whether or not I'm even going to run."

"You can't mean that, Dick! You're just tired and worried. You—"

The president waved him silent. "Wrong on one count, Martin: I'm not tired at all. If I am worried, it's not for my own safety, but rather for the future of this country. I wanted to be the president of the United States for years. When I was elected it was the greatest moment of my life. You were there. You know. Now, after only sixteen months on the job in this thankless office . . ." He shook his head. "I don't know if I want to continue. And that is the gospel truth."

Denning leaned back in his chair and stared at his longtime friend. "Well, I'll be goddamned!"

The president smiled. "We just might know the truth or fallacy of that remark sooner than we would like, if the terrorists carry out their threat."

When his team rolled into Dallas, John decided it was time for a break. "Let's find a nice looking restaurant and stretch our legs and get something to eat. There's no point in wandering aimlessly around this city."

"Do we believe what Victoria told us about the route the terrorists are taking, or do we flip a coin to decide which route to take out of here?" Lana asked, only half kidding.

"I-30," John replied. "I'm betting they'll make another stop in Little Rock to switch vehicles again. That truck will be dumped here in Dallas . . . if it hasn't been already. Victoria's information has proven correct. I think the kid told us the truth, as much as she knew."

"Little Rock, Memphis, Nashville, Louisville, Columbus, Cleveland, and after that she didn't know," Mike said, shaking his head in the waning light in the restaurant's parking lot. "The PLF has a hell of a lot of supporters in America."

"Not so many," John countered. "Say eight or ten in each of those cities named. A hundred people coast-to-coast, not counting the main cell in New York City."

"And that could be anything from ten to a hundred people," Chris said.

"It won't be small, that's for sure."

"I'm hungry," Don said, looking at the restaurant. "I wonder if they serve good cheeseburgers in there?"

* * *

The stolen pickup truck was discovered just after 10:00 P.M. in the parking lot of a huge shopping mall. The hunting rifles were missing from the gun rack. There were no incidents of violence in that part of Dallas that could in any way be linked to the terrorists. They had dropped out of sight without a trace.

John checked his team into a motel and told them all to get a good night's sleep. There was no point in blindly beating the bushes trying to locate the terrorists; no one had the slightest idea where to even start looking.

"All we can do is head for Little Rock in the morning and hope for the best," John told his people.

John called in and was told the FBI had put every available agent on the case.

"Wonderful," he replied. "We're already falling all over each other out here. I just wonder how many more countries are going to be sending agents over here."

"The Dutch," he was immediately informed.

"The Netherlands? What in the world is their interest in this mess?"

"One of the terrorists is believed to be a Dutch citizen. Jan something-or-another."

"I thought he was from Belgium."

"No. There is a very good possibility he is a Dutch terrorist with a long and bloody criminal record. The Dutch have sent one of their top people in. Jost Van Liter. They asked permission to send him in, and it was granted. He is working with the FBI."

"Is the public going to be told about this threat?"

"There are no plans to do so at the present time."

"Is the president still planning to visit New York City?"

"Yes."

"That doesn't make much sense."

"The president is a politician."

"I suppose that's as good an explanation as any."

"You think further pursuit is a waste of time, don't you?"

"Yes, I do."

"Explain."

"There are at least nine teams from various agencies and countries on the tail of the PLF. Hundreds of FBI agents hunting down every lead from Texas to New York City. What good are we out here? We can't do anything if we do catch up with them except try to keep a loose surveillance on them—that, and irritate the hell out of the agent in charge, Inspector Ballard. You can bet the FBI is on high alert in every city known to have PLF sympathizers."

"You want to jump ahead in each city and check around?"

"Yes. But not spend a lot of time in each place—maybe half a day unless we turn up something solid. I think the best thing we can do is head on in to New York and get set up there. I have a lot of good contacts there, both in and out of the Agency, and both civilian and on the NYPD."

"You think you can find the PLF cell in New York City?"

John hesitated. "I think I have a good shot at it. A lot of my contacts are members of organized crime."

"I see. Well, I should have guessed that. All right, John. It's your show. Do what you think is best."

"I'll report in from all stops."

"Do that."

John left his room to get some ice—he'd bought a bottle of vodka, a small bottle of vermouth, and a jar of olives—and met Jenny in the hall. Her expression was one of disgust.

"What's the matter?"

"We all have to wash out some things and this motel doesn't have a washer and dryer for guests' use."

"Go across the street to that all-night store and buy what you need. Throw the dirty clothing away. That's what those credit cards are for."

"Oh. Neat! I hadn't thought of that."

"And get me some toothpicks, will you?"

"I beg your pardon?"

"Toothpicks, Jenny."

"You have something stuck around a tooth?"

"A martini, Jenny?"

She looked at him very strangely for a moment. "You have a martini stuck . . . Oh! You want toothpicks for the olives. Now I get you. Sure will."

John watched with a smile as Jenny bebopped on down the hall. The young woman had energy to burn. She was also incredibly strong for her size. Those years as a gymnast had toned and fine-tuned her muscles. John had also never seen the lady in a bad mood. Just being around her put him in a better mood.

John walked to the ice machine and filled his bucket. Don Yee was in the small room, leaning up against a snack machine, eating out of a bag of potato chips.

"I got hungry again," Don explained.

"I've never seen you when you weren't. My mother would have said you are a bottomless pit."

"She'd be right. Your parents still living, John?"

"No," John replied, filling his ice bucket. "They both died a few years back."

Chris appeared in the doorway. "I took a nap and now I'm not sleepy. Came to get me a Coke. What's the word, John?"

"Is everybody awake?" John asked.

"All up and restless," Chris said.

"Jenny just went across the street to buy some things. We'll meet down in my room in say, ten minutes?"

"Suits me," Don replied. "Got anything to snack on down there?"

John laughed at that. "I'm quite sure you'll bring something."

"I'd better stock up now," Don said, digging in his pocket for change.

"It's a wonder you're not fat as a pig, Don," Chris remarked.

"It's my metabolism. I burn it up as fast as I take it in. I'll pass the word to meet in your room, John."

John stood back and watched Don feed money into the snack machine. "You'd better get a bag to carry all that stuff."

"I'll help him," Chris volunteered. "That's the only way to ensure there'll be something left for the rest of us."

Lana joined the group standing in the hall outside the snack room. "Ballard and his FBI team want to talk to you, John. They're waiting in the lobby."

"Well, crap!" John said. "All good things come to an end, I suppose."

"How did they know we were here?" Don asked.

"I'll ask," John said, handing him the ice bucket and the entry card to his room. "See you all in a few minutes."

Twelve

"Before you ask, Mr. Barrone, I could tell you it was skill on the part of my people that led us to you," Inspector Ballard said. "But that would be a blatant lie. I was in the parking lot of that chain store across the street, checking for one of those vehicles the PLF used in getting away from that wild shoot-out in Tucson, when I spotted Miss Barnes coming out of this motel."

"I won't even ask what wild shoot-out you're referring to, Inspector Ballard. I haven't heard anything about it. I don't listen to the radio much. I prefer tapes of my favorite operas."

"Of course you don't know, Mr. Barrone." Ballard's words were thick with sarcasm.

"What do you want, Inspector?"

"To give you a bit of advice."

"Go right ahead."

"Don't interfere with this operation."

"What operation is that?"

Ballard waved that aside without comment. "You've been warned, Mr. Barrone. Don't force me to arrest you."

"Arrest me for what? What have I done?"

Ballard struggled with his temper for a moment. "I don't know who you're working for, Mr. Barrone. I don't really know if that is important . . . at this time. What I do know is this: you're somehow all tangled up in the assignment I'm working on. I won't have that. I absolutely will not tolerate any interference, and I certainly will not tolerate you withholding information . . . *any* information that might aid in bringing this investigation to a satisfactory conclusion. Is that understood, Mr. Barrone? Did I make myself perfectly clear?"

"Oh, yes, Inspector. It would be even clearer if I knew what you're talking about. Perhaps you'd be kind enough to enlighten me?"

Ballard's expression changed to one of disgust. "Barrone, you are a real pain in the butt!"

John laughed. "That's the same thing some people say about you, Ballard."

"I can just imagine who that is, too."

"Jenny? No. She just says you're a prick and lets it go at that."

Ballard's face turned a bright red and he balled his hands into fists. "That . . . bitch!"

"Now, now, Ballard. What's your hang-up with Jenny? Did you proposition her and she turned you down? Is that it?"

Ballard spun around and stalked out of the motel lobby without another word.

"I believe I hit a sore spot there," John muttered as he walked back to his room. He could not conceal his smile. John had developed a strong dislike for the inspector. Ballard was probably a good agent who did the investigative part of his job well, but he had a lousy personality. John had found nothing about Jenny that was anything short of delightful . . . except perhaps her language.

The team rolled into Little Rock and were checked into a motel by mid-afternoon. John called in and was informed by the mysterious voice on the other end—John no longer spent much time wondering who it was—that the terrorists had dropped out of sight without a trace, taking Betsy Morrow with them.

"We hope," John said.

"Betsy is, unfortunately, expendable in this situation," the voice informed John with absolutely no emotion. "As regrettable as that might be."

John offered no reply to that. In his long career as a field operative for the Company, he had faced this same situation many times, and liked it less each time. He did not hold even a modicum of sympathy for terrorists who placed innocent civilians in harm's way, no matter what their grievances. If found guilty for their crimes, terrorists should be executed as quickly as possible. John had held those beliefs for many years, and they had hardened with time.

When the voice on the other end finally realized that John was not going to offer any response to his statement of expendability, he said, "No need to call in until you have something of substance to report."

"Understood."

The connection was broken.

Spinning our wheels and accomplishing nothing, John thought, leaning back in the uncomfortable motel desk chair in his room. *What we are doing, and have done, for the most part, is a complete and utter waste of time.*

A knock on the door interrupted his sour thoughts. "It's your friendly Oriental-type person, John."

Shaking his head at Don's comment, John opened the door and Don walked in, eating out of a bag of corn chips.

"You just had lunch about two hours ago!" John said, eyeballing the huge bag. "You ate enough for three people. I thought the buffet manager was going to throw us all out."

Don ignored the comments about his eating habits. "I just intercepted a message from the state cops. A motorist called in, reporting seeing a young woman in the backseat of a late model Chevy. The girl appeared to be in some sort of distress. She fit the description of Betsy Morrow. The car was about fifty miles southwest of Little Rock on I-30. State cops are rolling now."

John made up his mind quickly. "We're not going to go

anywhere near that car. You can bet Ballard is close by, and he would just love to find us there. He would arrest us on the spot and come up with something to hold us for about seventy-two hours . . . or longer. He's just itching to nail me for anything."

"He sure hates Jenny."

"Yes, and I'm next on his hate list. Right now, let's keep a close ear to state police traffic."

"Jenny's monitoring police calls now. So we wait?"

"That's all we can do."

"I feel so helpless."

"Join the club."

"We've got one state cop following us," Jan said. "He's laying back. Just close enough to keep us in visual."

"There is no way the police can know we are in three cars," Hurran said.

"I don't understand how they found us," Max said. "Unless they struck our people in Dallas and one talked."

"That must be it," Jan agreed. "André is in the lead car, and we have no way of communicating. Dammit!"

"Can anyone spot planes or helicopters?" Hurran asked, looking out the window.

All three in the third car searched the sky as best they could. They could see nothing.

"This entire cross-country odyssey is idiotic," Jan said. "With a bit of planning we could have entered through New York. We could have completed our mission and been gone. It's stupid."

"We all know that, Jan," Max said. "And we are all in agreement. But it's pointless to debate it now."

"The police car has moved closer," Hurran said. "It's going to be up to us to do something about it."

"Without orders from André?" Jan questioned. "We are flirting with his wrath if we do."

"We're facing capture if we don't," Max countered. "And capture means failure. Think about that."

"Damn those people in Dallas for not providing us with cell phones!" Hurran said. "If we turn on our headlights, the rear lights will also come on, and that pig cop will know something is happening. But we must signal a warning to those ahead."

"I'll start using my turn indicators," Jan said. "The car ahead will notice."

"So will the pig behind us," Hurran said. "Then what?"

"Can't be helped. I'll take the next exit off the interstate and lead the pig into the country. Then we kill him."

"I like it," Hurran said. "I will be honored to kill the American bastard."

"The next exit is just ahead," Jan said, flipping on the turn signal. "Here we go."

André was driving the lead vehicle and did not see the turn signals come on. He drove past the exit and watched in dismay as the car behind him exited. He was slowing down when he saw the last car exit and caught a quick glimpse of the trooper's car as it exited right behind the car driven by Jan.

He knew immediately what they were planning and said, "I wish you much luck."

Brigitte had twisted in the seat in time to see the patrol car leave the highway. Wini was in the backseat with Betsy in the second car. Alain and Akal were in the front, Alain driving. "I hope they can pull this off," Brigitte said.

"They will," André said. "I have no doubts about that. Hurran is itching to kill an American—any American," he added. "And both Jan and Max will gladly give their lives to see that this mission does not fail."

"We go on?"

"Oh, yes. They know the location of the meeting place in the city ahead."

Jan drove down the blacktop road for several miles, Alain following close behind. The Arkansas State Trooper had radioed in what was happening. He knew nothing about any third car, and wasn't certain whether the car in the rear belonged to the kidnappers. He did know he wasn't about to let that middle vehicle with the girl in it out of his sight.

It can be a major problem when agencies don't share information, especially when a life-and-death situation is unfolding.

The trooper came around a curve in the road and found himself looking at two men, both of them armed with automatic weapons. He had just a couple of very fast heartbeats to react. He couldn't leave the road because it was a high drop-off on both sides of the blacktop. He couldn't stop, for that would mean certain death. He chose the only option left him: he floored the gas pedal and roared toward the terrorists just as they opened fire.

The windshield of his unit was spider-webbed and pocked with the impact of lead. The trooper scooted down as low as he could in the seat and gritted his teeth and held on to the wheel as he raced past, the bullets clanging into his car.

Both Hurran and Akal jumped to one side to avoid being run down and continued pouring the lead into the car.

The state police vehicle went into a sickening sideways slide and then flipped over onto its side, then onto its top. The sounds of grinding metal on the roadway became mixed with hissing steam from the radiator and breaking glass and plastic as the unit finally came to a halt. Although he was belted in, the trooper's head had banged against something, several times, and the blow knocked him out for a moment. When he awakened, with a terrible headache, he was upside down and bleeding in a car that was virtually destroyed. His seatbelt was holding him in, and he couldn't get the release button to work. He was stuck. But he was alive, and that was a lot more than he had hoped for a few moments back. He struggled to free himself but the release button was jammed.

"Well, shit!" the Arkansas highway cop hollered in total frustration.

"Something's happened," Chris said. "There hasn't been anything but normal traffic for over ten minutes."

"They're using cell phones or they've got a dark frequency," John replied.

A few more minutes passed and the high-powered little scanner suddenly erupted with traffic. After listening to a variety of 10-codes and cryptic conversations the team was able to piece together most of what happened.

"That is one lucky trooper," Lana observed.

"And the PLF bunch made it to another safe house," Mike said. "Where they'll change vehicles and take off again."

"While we sit here with one thumb up our ass and the other one in our mouth, waiting for someone to holler 'switch,' " Jenny added.

John gave her one of his very pained glances, which had no effect at all on her. "What an intriguing analogy," he said, his tone martini-dry.

"I thought so," Jenny said brightly.

John looked at her and sighed with the patience of a long-suffering parent.

"But it does sum up the situation rather well," Don remarked. "Don't you think?"

"That trooper didn't know anything about the kidnappers' real mission," Lana said. "If he had, it would have been handled very differently."

"So what do we do now, John?" Chris asked.

"Nothing. We know their next stop is Memphis. We just tag along."

"You can bet Ballard is at the scene of the ambush," Jenny said with a smile. "Looking around for us, hoping we'll make an appearance."

"I sure hate to disappointment him," Don said. "But right now there are more important things to tend to."

"What?" John asked.

Don looked at him and smiled. "Getting something to eat. I'm hungry."

Thirteen

André walked out of the bedroom of the safe house several miles outside Little Rock. He zipped up his trousers, then jerked a thumb toward the closed door behind him. "She's all yours, Jan. If you want her."

"How was it?" Jan asked.

André waggled a hand from side to side. "So so. I got a few grunts from her, and that's about it. She certainly is no blushing virgin."

"American whore!" Akal spat out the words. "No American woman has any morals."

Brigitte and Wini had taken their baths and were asleep in another part of the old farmhouse. The couple who had lived in the house for years had died, and the place was being rented until a buyer could be found.

Jan laughed at his fellow terrorist. "Then when it is your turn, Akal, you may take her like a dog."

"I shall. But first I will give her the beating she deserves." He cut his eyes to André. "If you have no objection, André?"

André shrugged his shoulders. "I don't care what you do, Akal. Just don't beat her so hard that she's crippled. She's enough trouble as it is."

Jan rubbed his crotch and grinned. "I will get a response from her. I assure you of that."

Akal ignored the boasting. "I won't cripple her, André. I

promise you that. But she will know humility when I am through."

Jan walked into the bedroom, closing the door behind him.

André looked at Max and Alain. They both shook their heads. Alain said, "You know that rape holds little appeal for me, André."

André smiled. He knew that Alain and Brigitte were lovers, and if Alain screwed the Morrow girl, Brigitte would cut his balls off and stuff them in his mouth.

Max said, "I'll pass as well, André."

Max was bisexual, with a slight preference for boys over girls. Akal was the only one in the group who showed any contempt for homosexuals. Sexual orientation made little or no difference to the rest.

André went into the kitchen, where members of the tiny cell of PLF supporters in Little Rock were seated around the kitchen table, having coffee. André noticed two were missing. They were standing guard outside.

"Any news of the incident today?" he asked.

"The pig is alive. He was not seriously injured."

"Too bad." André poured a mug of coffee and stepped outside to stand in the backyard and smoke a cigarette. Only a few moments passed before Jan stepped out to join him. André glanced at him. "That was quick."

"The bitch is not cooperative at all, but Akal will get some response from her. He will beat it out of her."

"Akal is a little strange in his sexual requirements . . . if you know what I mean."

"I do. But no stranger than Wini. She wanted to watch Akal . . . ah, do his thing."

"They do make quite a pair."

Conversation was interrupted for several moments by Betsy's muffled screams and Wini's laughter. André and Jan exchanged glances.

"I believe it's going to be a very long night for Betsy," Jan said.

* * *

"It's confirmed," the mysterious voice told John. "The target is New York City."

"How was it confirmed?" John asked. John had spent half his adult life in the intelligence community and was wary of any unverified information.

"The Canadian SIS broke up a plot to poison the water supply of a local bottled water company in Toronto. They were part of the PLF, and one of them broke."

"Good enough," John said.

"I'll send you the entire transcript of the interrogation by computer. It will be encrypted."

John knew better than to ask how his people got the news, much less how they got a transcript. "I'm sure it'll be interesting reading."

John's team left early the next morning. They drove through Memphis without stopping and headed for Nashville. Even before receiving the information about the Toronto incident, John had made up his mind about bird-dogging the PLF: it was over. John and his team were helpless to do anything even when they had the terrorists in visual. It was a waste of time.

"Too bad we don't have time to stop and take a tour of Graceland," Don radioed to the lead car as they rolled through Memphis. "I really got into Elvis."

Jenny grabbed the mic. "Forget it. Now if it were the Stones, that's another story."

"You have no taste for talent," Don fired back.

"Personally, I always liked Narvel Felts," John said. "That man could sing."

"Who?" Jenny said, a second before Don's voice bounced out of the speaker.

"Narvel Felts. The man has been around for a while and is just as good, maybe even better than ever. He's really big over in Europe. Folks over there really do appreciate authentic rock and roll."

"What do you think the Stones play?" Jenny asked, then named about a dozen groups that John had never heard of.

"Did you say the Rotten Returns?"

"No!"

"Well, whatever you said, most of those groups must play rock. But you can bet it isn't rock and roll. True rock and roll died decades ago."

Before Jenny could launch into a protest, Mike, who was handling the computer and monitoring another radio in the backseat, said, "Hold it, guys. Something coming in. Well, I'll just be damned."

"What is it?" Jenny asked.

"The FBI in New York just found a cache of toxins and arrested six people. They're saying the threat is over."

John was quick to speak. "They're saying that, but they don't believe it."

"That's in case the press finds out?" Jenny asked. "Strange they would release something like that before the press even knows anything about it. I never heard of the Bureau doing that."

"It may be for the benefit of the terrorists who have Betsy," John said. "Or the press has gotten wind of the threat, and are sitting on the story."

"Or it's for us," Mike opined.

John thought about that for a few seconds. "That's a possibility, Mike. But a slim one. We'll just have to wait and see what develops."

"We planning on spending the night in Nashville, John?" Jenny asked.

"I don't know. We'll stop when we get tired. But not hungry," he was quick to add. "Don would have us stopping every hour."

"He bought a big bag of chips, three Cokes for his ice chest, some sort of sweet rolls, and several candy bars last time we stopped," Mike said.

"My mama would say he has a tapeworm," Jenny said.

Lana's voice popped through the speaker. "Did you folks copy that dispatch about the toxins found in New York and those people arrested? What did you make of it?"

John told her the possibilities that had been discussed, and after that conversation waned as they all settled in for the drive to Nashville on Interstate 40.

They arrived in Nashville with hours of daylight left and decided to push on to Louisville.

"No point in checking into a motel now and just killing time doing nothing," John said, pulling into a gas station to turn the wheel over to Jenny.

"Hey!" Don stuck his head out of the window of the rear car. "Let's find a place to eat. I'm hungry."

Betsy had slept most of the way since leaving Little Rock. Akal had beaten her and then raped her, and then beaten her again because she was not more responsive. She was not severely hurt, but she ached all over—especially her butt, where Akal had whipped her with a wide leather belt. Wini had watched and laughed and made sexual suggestions as to what Akal should do next . . . which he did, causing more pain.

All during the rape and beatings Betsy had made up her mind that she was not only going to survive this kidnapping, but she was going to kill Wini if at all possible. Akal was nothing but a semi-educated savage, but she knew from listening to the others talk that Wini had graduated from some university in England and took advanced studies in Paris. There was no excuse for her behavior.

André and Jan's attack on her had not been merely a sexual assault, but an act of power and control.

But it didn't work, you bastards, Betsy thought. *And it never will.*

"Thank you again for not marking her face," André said to Akal as they pulled out of a gas station just outside of Nashville. They had decided against stopping in both Memphis and

Nashville, choosing instead to drive as long as they could; they hoped to make Louisville just after dark. They were only an hour behind John and his team. Akal and Hurran were riding with André, Hurran in the backseat with Betsy.

"No thanks needed," Akal replied. "I just want to take her again as soon as we get to a safe place. I know a way to make the rich American bitch beg for mercy."

André did not ask what Akal had in mind. He knew. Akal was more than a little warped in his sexual appetites.

"To hell with you, you unwashed perverted camelfucker!" Betsy blurted.

Akal cursed and twisted in the seat to strike her, his hand balled into a fist.

"No!" André shouted. "I forbid it. We are in heavy traffic and that would draw attention. It's only words, Akal. Words cannot hurt you. Control yourself."

Akal glared at Betsy. "Soon, bitch. Very soon. I will make you scream and beg for mercy."

"When hell freezes over, you stinking bastard!" Betsy fired right back.

"Bah! We shall see," Akal said, turning around to once more face the front.

"Terrorists," Betsy said. "Cowards. Every damned one of you. That's all you are."

"Be careful, girl," André said. "You are very, very expendable."

"No, I'm not," Betsy replied calmly. "You need me for insurance. The police are not going to use lethal force against you as long as I'm alive. That's not the American way." *At least I hope it isn't,* Betsy thought.

"You would be wise to shut your rich, spoiled mouth," Akal told her.

"Fuck you, shit-eater!"

André was forced to hide a small smile. The young woman might come from a rich family, but she was long on courage.

She knew which strings to pull on Akal to get him all worked up, and she wasn't at all shy about pulling them.

Akal cursed her hotly and long. Betsy laughed at him all during the raging outburst.

"Enough, both of you," Hurran said. "You're giving me a headache."

"Sheep-fucker hasn't got enough dick to make me beg for anything, except maybe relief from the tickling," Betsy said.

Akal acted so swiftly André did not have time to shout a warning. He twisted in the seat and slapped Betsy hard on the side of her face, then brought his hand back and backhanded her on the mouth, bloodying her lips.

"Brave son of a bitch, aren't you?" Betsy said, blood leaking from her mouth. "Just as I said: cowards."

"That's enough!" André shouted. "Both of you. Hurran, clean her up. Do it quickly. We can't have traffic all around us and the girl with blood leaking from her mouth. Do it!" He met Betsy's eyes in the rearview mirror. "And you, girl, had better learn this now: the PLF is international in its ranks. From many countries—"

"Especially the Middle East, Frenchman," Betsy said.

"Very good, girl," André complimented her. "I don't recall anyone telling you my country of origin."

"Your accent. I studied in Paris for a year."

"Did you now? My, my."

"Yes. My father's older brother is buried in France. He gave his life during World War Two."

"How noble of him to give his life so rich Americans could continue their exploitation of small nations."

Hurran had wet a cloth from a bottle of water and was wiping the blood from Betsy's mouth and chin.

"You're as dumb as Akal," Betsy said.

André laughed at that. "Oh, I think neither of us is dumb, Betsy. We just have higher ideals than you."

"Ideals? You have to be kidding! Killing innocent people is idealistic to you?"

"She has been hopelessly brainwashed by her money-hungry, Jew-loving parents," Akal said. "You're wasting your breath talking to her."

"My God, you people must kiss a picture of Hitler every night before you go to bed," Betsy said.

"He had some good ideas," André said. "He just got too ambitious and greedy, that's all."

"Incredible," Betsy muttered. "Good ideas? What good ideas?" The bleeding had almost stopped, but her lips were beginning to swell and ache.

"The obliteration of the Jews was a grand idea. It was really a shame he didn't succeed. He had such a good start. But we will, given enough time."

Betsy had no more to say. André and his little band of screw-balls were all flaky. She leaned back in the seat and wished she had some Tylenol or aspirin. She was really beginning to hurt . . . *all over more than anywhere else.* She remembered the old saying with a small smile.

"Why are you smiling, girl?" Hurran asked. "Is it that you find us so amusing you smile in the face of death? Or are you just insane?"

"Speaking of crazy . . ." Betsy allowed that to wander off into silence.

"Do you pray?" Hurran asked.

Betsy opened her eyes and looked at the terrorist. "Of course I pray."

"Shut up!" Akal said. "I'm tired of your stupid mouth, girl."

"Blow it out your ass, ratface."

Again André was forced to hide his smile. The girl was brave, no doubt about that. And she was right about them not killing her. She was vital insurance, and she knew it.

"Why don't you go to sleep?" André asked her.

"I'm not sleepy. I just hurt all over. I would very much like some aspirin."

"We don't have any," André said. "But if you promise to be quiet, I will stop and buy some for you."

"I know a way to shut her filthy mouth," Akal said.

"You're talking to me about filth?" Betsy came right back. "That's absurd coming out of your mouth, camel jockey."

André sighed and pulled deeply from both his patience level and pool of common sense. "I wish both of you would settle down and stop this nonsense."

"How would you like to suck something?" Akal asked Betsy. "I can give you a mouthful."

She laughed at him. "You couldn't give a sparrow a mouthful, midget dick."

"That's it!" André shouted. "Both of you shut up! I'm weary of this. There is a rest area up ahead. We'll stop and put the girl in another vehicle. That will settle matters."

"Suits me," Betsy said.

"Bitch!" Akal muttered.

"Asshole," Betsy popped right back.

"Why don't we stop at some sort of convenience store?" Hurran suggested. "We'll get some aspirin to give the girl."

"Just a few miles ahead," André said. "Will that shut your mouth, girl?"

"Yes."

"Wonderful."

John and his team were just finishing a snack and stretching their legs at a fast-food place just off the interstate. They had been there about forty-five minutes.

John looked up just as André pulled into the parking lot.

Fourteen

John's people were spread out all over the place. Some in the rest rooms, some walking around the parking lot, others looking at books in the rack.

The team members had studied pictures of the terrorists, and John immediately recognized André and quickly got into his car. He sat behind the wheel and watched as two more cars pulled in and parked side by side in the area closest to the exit. Jenny stepped out of the restaurant just as the terrorists in the second and third cars stepped out. Jenny looked up and momentarily froze at the sight. Those in the first car remained in the car, the windows rolled up.

Jenny walked over to the car and got in beside John. "You see them?"

"Oh, yes. Indeed I do."

"Did they see you?"

"If they did, I was just another traveler."

"Do we make a try for Betsy?"

"No. That isn't our job."

"So here we go again, playing bird-dog."

"Looks that way. But they've been driving as long as we have, and they're just as road-weary. They'll probably stop in Louisville at a safe house. We might get a chance to expose another cell. Get on the horn to Control. I want a change of cars waiting for us in Louisville."

Jenny made the call, brought Control up to speed, and was

told the arrangements would be made. They would be contacted in a few minutes about where to make the switch.

Jenny broke the connection and said, "I just caught a glimpse of Betsy. So we know she's still alive."

"I don't believe they'll kill her until right before they put their plan into operation, or just afterward. She's insurance. By now, the feds have surely passed the word up and down the line about her."

"Let's hope, on both counts. But I wouldn't count on the latter. And, for whatever good it will do us, I've got their tag numbers."

"Nothing's happened inside the place, so our people are playing their cards close."

"While we're playing cat and mouse, I have a question."

"Ask."

"What if they start shooting right here in this parking lot?"

"We return the fire."

Two couples with several kids in tow came out of the restaurant with John's team right behind them.

"Oh, boy," Jenny whispered.

"Our people are staying cool," John said.

"Cool, John?" Jenny looked at him and grinned.

John smiled. "That word was in vogue long before you were born, kiddo."

"Oh, boy," Jenny said. "Look, the mice are walking up to the cats."

Several PLF members were now within touching distance of John's people.

Neither group gave the other more than a passing glance as they walked past each other. Mike got into the backseat of John's car while the three remaining members walked over to their car and got in.

"Talk about blind luck," Mike said, closing the door.

"Jenny, tell the others to pull out now," John said. "We'll stay here until the mice pull out and bring up the rear. Maintain the speed limit."

Jenny got on the radio and gave the orders. They watched as Lana pulled out onto the interstate and disappeared. A couple of minutes later the PLF members exited the restaurant, got into their vehicles and drove out of the parking lot, heading north on Interstate 65. John waited a full sixty count before pulling out behind them.

"As soon as Control notifies the feds," Mike said, "Louisville is going to be crawling with all sorts of agents."

"You can count on that," John said, reaching over and turning on the car's radio. The words spewing out of the speaker chilled them all.

". . . manhunt is under way nationwide for a group of terrorists who murdered a man and woman in Arizona and took their daughter hostage. . . ."

"Oh, shit!" Mike said.

". . . suspects are believed to be part of an international terrorist group called the Peoples' Liberation Front. They are believed to be responsible for the deaths of dozens of people in several countries. This reporter has learned that the PLF is planning some sort of attack in New York State, probably in New York City, in the borough of Manhattan. . . ."

"It's going to bust wide open now," Jenny said. "Who in the hell leaked all that?"

"Doesn't much matter now," John replied as the network broke for a commercial. "What matters now is how the White House responds. And right now they're in a quiet panic trying to figure out what to do."

"I just bet they are," Mike said. "I'd like to be in the war room right now listening."

"I've got a rough draft of your response."

"Telling the people there is no danger?" President Kelley asked.

"Well . . . ah, yes," the advisor said.

"Lies," the president said. "Dammit, I hate to lie to the American people."

Maybe you shouldn't run for another term, his chief of staff thought. *Takes a son of a bitch to sit in the Oval Office, and you, old buddy, are too damn honest.*

"It isn't a real lie, Mr. President," an aide said. "I mean, the FBI is sure to catch these terrorists."

"Really?" Kelley responded. "Well, where were they last sighted, just moments ago? Kentucky, wasn't it? They started in California, goddamn it! They've traveled about two thousand fucking miles, killed a couple of people, kidnapped a young woman, and shot up an Arkansas trooper's car. And goddamn it, they're still out there, Peter."

Peter looked at Martin Denning for help.

Before Denning could speak, the president held up a hand, silencing him. Then he held up a file folder. "This is the top secret file on the PLF, gentlemen. The CIA sent it over by special courier about an hour ago. Nice of them. Gentlemen and lady"—he nodded his head at the lone woman in the office, Alice Parker, a very senior aide who had been with him since he was a senator, almost as long as Martin Denning— "the PLF is no ragtag bunch of stars-in-their-eyes, slogan-spouting amateurs. They're an international group with cells in almost every country in the world. And they've got cells up the kazoo here in the States."

"Mr. President—" George began.

Kelley cut him off. "Be quiet. I'm just getting started." He looked at the Director of the FBI, Anthony Harris, and waved the file folder. "Tony, you've had time to scan this report. Did the Bureau know this?"

Director Harris shifted in his chair. "Not to that extent, Mr. President."

"Why not?"

"Well . . . the Company and the Bureau don't always share information."

"Why not? Goddamn it, the CIA predicted a terrorist attack

against New York City by this very group several months ago. Didn't you take it seriously?"

"Frankly, no, Mr. President."

"Why not?"

"Our own intelligence people couldn't confirm any part of that report."

President Kelley drummed his fingers on the desktop and stared at the director for a moment. When he spoke his voice was low and controlled. "Would you agree that it has now been confirmed?"

"I would say so, yes."

"Marvelous," the president muttered darkly, obviously highly irritated.

"We've got to respond to the news report very soon, Mr. President," Denning said, hoping to defuse what could quickly turn into a bad scene between the two men. Denning knew only too well that Richard Kelley possessed a hot temper that could explode without warning. "Before there is panic in the streets."

"And that panic could quickly spread," Alice added.

"Tony, I suppose when the first canister of poisonous gas kills a few hundred people you just might admit the CIA one-upped your people," Kelley remarked, not quite ready to let go.

Director Harris didn't respond. He held his tongue and stared at the president.

"Give me the rough draft of what you think I should tell the American people," Kelley said. He met the eyes of every person in the room. "Then I'll decide if it's what I should say."

"We should make up a song about bird-dogging," Jenny said, looking out the window. The three-car caravan of terrorists was about a mile ahead, with half a dozen other vehicles between John and the team's prey.

"If I recall," John said, "something along those lines was recorded—back in the late fifties, I think it was."

"You were just a little kid back then, John," Mike said. "We know how old you are."

"But I've always liked fifties music," John replied. "The ballads and the rock and roll."

"You have a large collection?" Jenny asked.

"Quite extensive, yes. Up to about sixty-one or sixty-two. I was working on getting as much of it as I could on CD."

"Beats what's currently in vogue," Mike said. "Most of it is pure crap."

"I'll certainly agree with that," John said.

"Oh, some of it isn't that bad," Jenny said. "Ricky Martin is cute."

"Who?" John asked.

"Subjects signaling to exit off into a rest area," Don radioed from the lead car. "Instructions?" That put an end to the discussion of modern music.

"Do not exit with them," John told him. "We'll all pick them up a few miles on. We know where they're going."

Fifteen minutes later the three cars carrying the terrorists and Betsy Morrow passed John on the interstate, and the boring job of bird-dogging resumed.

"Just think," Jenny said, a decidedly wistful note in her voice. "Only fifteen hundred miles to go."

"But we'll be either laying well back, miles ahead, or well on our way to New York City," John told her. "We'll let the feds have it."

"Sure suits me," Mike said from the backseat.

"When they were within a few miles of Louisville, John radioed in to Control and told them they were breaking off surveillance in Louisville and asked if the feds had been notified.

"Yes," the voice replied. "They have the terrorists in visual."

"We're out of it as of now," John said. He did not want

Ballard to spot them . . . once in New York City, John didn't care.

The team exchanged cars on the outskirts of Louisville—for two new Ford Expeditions—and then checked into a motel for some much-needed rest.

"I hope we can keep these vehicles for the duration," Chris commented over dinner. "With that third seat out, we've got all sorts of cargo room."

"I'll pass along your request," John said, then added, "They are nice rides, aren't they?" Then he frowned as his eyes roamed the room.

"What's the matter, John?" Lana asked.

"Kemper from the Agency just walked in. Damn!" he said, pushing his plate away. "Here he comes."

Fifteen

The CIA man walked over to the group, pulled out a chair, and sat down. He smiled at John.

"Do join us, Kemp," John said.

"Thanks, I believe I will." He glanced over at John's plate. "I'm hungry. Is that steak good?"

"Very good."

"Do finish your meal. Don't let me interrupt."

"Thanks so much."

"Small world, isn't it, John? I never dreamed I'd see you in Louisville."

"Coincidence can be very strange."

Kemper's eyes met John's level gaze. "Bullshit," he said softly.

"Actually, it's a porterhouse." John cut off a small piece and held it out. "Want a sample before you order?"

Kemper smiled and took the small bit of steak with his fingers and ate it. "It is good. I'll follow your suggestion. This time." He waved a waitress over and ordered his dinner. After she had poured his coffee and left, Kemp said, "Ballard is going to be very unhappy about you being here, ole buddy."

"He'll get over it."

"Don't be too sure of that. Ballard doesn't like you very much."

"I'm heartbroken about that. How'd you know I was here?"

"You spent over two decades as a spook, and you're asking me that?" Kemper grinned. "We have our ways."

"Very amusing. Remind me to laugh later."

"You're crowding your luck. Ballard is just aching to arrest you."

"Tell him to take two aspirin and get some rest. The aching will stop."

Kemper laughed softly. "Now who's being funny? I'm not kidding, Johnny Boy. Ballard hates you, and he really hates Miss Barnes here." He looked at Jenny. "What did you ever do to him, Miss Barnes?"

"I wouldn't kowtow and kiss his royal ass."

Kemper blinked at that. Then he grinned. "Yeah, that would certainly do it. Ballard sure thinks he's something special."

"Didn't you chase a cell of the PLF all over Europe?" John asked.

"You know I did. And you know I got a couple of them, too."

"I think perhaps it's you who should be careful," John cautioned. "Maybe this bunch knows you're after them."

"Now how would you know about the PLF?"

"It was on the news, that's how."

"How would you know they're in this area?"

"Call it a lucky guess."

"Sure. I'll do that, John. The PLF doesn't frighten me. They're a pack of hyenas, nothing more."

"I pulled some time in Africa. You ever seen a hyena fight?"

"Truthfully, no, I haven't. Why? What difference does that make?"

"It makes a lot of difference. They get a lot of bad press. But a hyena is a damn tough critter. They have very powerful jaws. Back one into a corner, and they're ferocious animals."

"Level with me, John. What do you know about the PLF? This particular bunch, that is?"

"Nothing specific about this bunch. Only what I hear on the news."

Kemp sighed and leaned back in his chair. "The powers that be are not happy about you getting involved in this affair. Surely you must realize that."

"I'm—rather, we—are not involved in anything that concerns the agency."

"Sorry, but I'm going to have to call your hand on that. I just don't believe it, and I don't think you expect me to believe it."

John smiled and shrugged that off. "Tell the boys and girls back at Langley not to worry about it."

"I will. Count on it."

"I have no doubts about that."

Both Don and Lana stood up, Don saying, "We're going to walk around a bit." He patted his stomach. "I know you won't believe it, but I'm stuffed."

"You're right, I don't," Mike said. "But you did eat enough for three people."

Don and Lana threaded their way past the tables in the dining room and exited out the lobby.

"Interesting group you have here," Kemper said. "Naturally, I ran a check on them. You want to know how I got the prints?"

"Not particularly, but I'm sure it was legal. And I'm sure Ballard had something to do with it."

Kemper smiled. "All ex-government agents. All abruptly drop out of sight for weeks and weeks. Not a trace of any of you can be found—and we looked for you, John."

"I'm sure."

"Where were you?"

"On vacation."

"Well, you certainly have the tan to prove it, ole buddy. And I must say, you have never looked fitter."

"Thank you."

"You must have gotten some exercise on your, ah, vacation, right?"

"Sure. Why not? Man gets middle-aged, he'd better start taking care of himself." John gave Kemper a hard look. "You could use some sun and exercise yourself. You're getting pale, and you've picked up a few pounds. That's not good for a man your age."

"Don't worry about my health, John. The doctors say I'm in good shape."

"Glad to hear it."

"I think I'll join the others outside," Mike said. "How about you, Chris?"

"Yeah," the former FBI sniper said. "Walk off some of this meal. How about you, Jenny?"

"Oh, I'll stick around here, guys. You have fun taking in the night air. Besides, Mr. Kemper here might have something to say about me. I wouldn't want to miss that."

Kemp's steak came and he smiled and dug in while the waitress refilled John and Jenny's coffee cups. After a moment, Kemp waved his fork and said, "I'm going to say this one more time, then I'll drop it: for your own good, you and your bunch had better back off."

"I don't know what you're talking about."

"Suit yourself, ole buddy. Just don't ever say you weren't warned."

"You're the one who'd best heed a warning, Kemp," John replied.

"What do you mean?"

"You're on the PLF's hit list, remember? Do I have to keep reminding you of that?"

"And I told you that pack of crud doesn't worry me." He cut off another piece of steak and popped it into his mouth.

"It's going to do a lot more than worry people if just one of them gets to that poison they have cached in New York City," John said.

Kemp laid down his knife and fork and took a sip of coffee. "John, you and your bunch might be up to your knees in this— for whatever reason—but there are a few things you still don't know. And I'm going to violate all sorts of security rules and tell you. Not because you're such a good pal, because you sure as hell aren't. I don't like you, never have, and you don't much care for me. But you're in this game, so it's only fair you know what you're up against. We know for a hard fact this bunch has some poisons with them—enough to kill a lot of people. We uncovered that even before they left their training base in the desert."

"What kind of toxins?"

"We don't know. We don't even know for sure that it's toxins. Could be a nerve agent, or a general poison such as hydrogen cyanide. It might be some of all three."

"What about the delivery system?"

"We don't know that, either. What we do know is that this group is well-financed with cells all over this nation. It's taken them years to get everything in place."

"How much does the president know?"

Kemper sighed and pushed his plate away. "Probably not as much as he should. I'm a field agent, John. I'm not privy to those types of high-level briefings."

"So this threat could well be something along the lines of a plague, right?"

"Could be. We just don't know."

"Could this entire chase be a ruse? Could the target be Detroit or Chicago or Washington, DC?"

Kemp shook his head. "No. It's New York City. That we know for a dead bang certainty."

"Is the use of troops being considered?"

"I rather doubt it."

"Let me see if I understand all this," Jenny spoke. "Certain government agencies have known for some time this danger was coming. But nothing was done about it, probably because of the restrictive policies the United States government has in place about assassinations. Am I on the mark so far?"

"So far, so good, Miss Barnes," Kemp replied.

"The lives of thousands, perhaps millions, of people, Americans, are now in danger because of the mumblings of a bunch of candy-ass politicians and bed-wetting liberals, right?"

"Ah . . ." Kemper paused and chuckled. "Well, that's basically correct."

"Jenny doesn't care much for liberals," John said, signaling the waitress for more coffee.

"I never would have guessed," the CIA man said. "I can see why Ballard could form a dislike for the young lady."

"Screw Ballard. All this mess with the PLF could have been prevented, is what I'm trying to say," Jenny finished it.

"Well, yes and no. We could have taken out a lot of cells of the PLF. But another group would have stepped up and into their place, in a month or six months or a year. And the PLF members that remained would be more determined than ever to strike against America. We're going to get hit hard here in America. And that isn't a prediction or a guess: that's a hard cold fact. Every analyst agrees on that point. All we can do is try to prevent it on a day-by-day basis."

"That's the same song and dance I used to hear from people in the Bureau," Jenny said.

"But it's true, Jenny," John said. "Kemp's right. There is no easy fix. For all the good we've done in this world, and all the billions and billions of dollars we've given away, we're a nation hated by many."

"And the list is growing," Kemp added.

"Yes," John agreed, adding, "unfortunately."

The waitress filled their coffee cups and left, walking away as though her feet hurt, which they probably did.

Outside in the parking lot, part of which faced the dining room, a car horn started honking, followed by the howling of a car alarm system.

"Somebody bumped up against a car," Jenny remarked. "Probably some kids."

"I hate those damn car alarms," Kemp said. "I know cops who don't pay the slightest bit of attention to them."

"They annoy me," John said. "And I don't know of *any* cops who pay attention to them."

The honking and electronic howling continued unabated for

another half-minute, which seemed more like half an hour to the people in the dining room.

"Damn!" Jenny said. "I wish somebody would go out there and turn that thing off."

"Probably parked the car in the lot and went off to a movie," Kemp said.

"It should turn off automatically in about a minute," John remarked. "I hope."

Several of the patrons in the dining room had gotten to their feet and, obviously annoyed, were looking out the huge window that faced the parking lot. Several of them, men and women, were softly cursing under their breath. Others were looking around for someone to blame for the noise.

"Well, by God!" one man said belligerently. "I've had all of this I can stand. That noise is giving me a headache. I'm going to see about this.

"Do that," the woman with him said.

"Unless it's his car, what does he think he's going to be able to do?" Jenny questioned.

"It'll make him feel better," John explained. "Just the illusion that he's going to do something."

"I could go out and shoot the car," Jenny suggested, a hopeful note to her voice.

"That's not a bad idea," John replied. "But the police might frown on that."

The annoying noise ended abruptly, and a collective sigh went up from the diners.

"Thank God," Kemp said. Then he grinned. "Maybe one of your people crippled the damn thing, John?"

"Could be."

A sudden flash, followed immediately by a deafening roar, ripped from the parking lot. The huge window blew inward, sending thousands of pieces of glass all over the diners. Any who were standing were immediately knocked to the floor by the blast, many of them bleeding from cuts, all of them stunned by the heavy concussion.

The parking lot was eerily lit by flames from several automobiles, which blazed brightly in the early night. Gas tanks suddenly began blowing, sending more metal debris flying.

A hood from an automobile came sailing into the dining room. It bounced from table to table, and the hot and twisted heavy metal finally came to a smoking rest not far from where Kemp, John, and Jenny were sprawled on the floor.

The explosions ended, leaving a strange silence in the large dining area for a moment. Then sounds of moaning and crying began.

John crawled to his knees and looked around at the mangled wreckage and injured men and women and several children.

Jenny crawled over to join John. "Accident?" she whispered.

"I doubt it."

Kemp crawled over, his face cut and bleeding. "I think the PLF just sent us a message," he said.

"Well, it was certainly received," John replied, getting to his feet.

"The guys outside?" Jenny said, standing up.

"I wouldn't want to make a guess," John told her, holding out a hand to Kemp, helping the man up.

The dining room was dark, the power knocked out by the heavy blasts. The sounds of screaming sirens were drawing closer. Within a few seconds the night was illuminated by red and blue spinning lights. Running and shouting figures could be seen and heard. In the lights from the emergency vehicles and the still-burning cars and pickup trucks, the parking lot resembled a war zone.

"Let's get out of here," Kemp said just as a half-dozen more EMT and police vehicles screamed into the parking lot. "I'd rather not be found here. And Ballard is sure to come snooping around in a few minutes."

"You'd better take off," John told him as old survival instincts took over. He jerked a thumb toward a side door. "That way. I haven't seen you."

"Thanks. I owe you one." The CIA man limped away, vanishing in the growing and cluttered confusion of the dark and wrecked dining room.

"Let's go see what's left of our team," John said.

"And hope for the best," Jenny added.

"Are you all right?" John asked. "I can't tell in here."

"I'm OK. You?"

"I'm still navigating. Come on. Watch where you step. Don't stumble over something and break a leg now."

John and Jenny made their way outside and stepped into a scene of burned metal and broken bodies.

Sixteen

Outside, John and Jenny found the rest of their team, and they were not in good shape. Don was cut up and had a sprained ankle. Lana's head had been cut in several places by flying metal. She was bleeding profusely and her right shoulder was dislocated. Mike's left arm appeared to be broken, and Chris was unconscious.

John waved a couple of EMTs over, then he and Jenny backed out of the way and let the emergency people go to work.

"I think we're going to be on our own for the rest of this op," John said when they were out of earshot of the injured team members.

"Looks like it. All four of them are going to be out of commission for quite a while."

John nodded and walked back over to where his team was being readied for transport to a local hospital. He knelt down beside Mike and spoke just loud enough for Mike to hear him. "Jenny and I are out of here ASAP, Mike. We can't afford to have Ballard detain us. You know our contact point in New York. When you all get ready to travel, we'll meet you there."

"OK, John. Both of you take care, and we'll see you in a few days."

John smiled. "Sure, Mike. A few days." *More like a few weeks,* he thought.

John and Jenny waited until the EMTs informed them what

hospital the team members were being taken to and then pulled out, emergency lights flashing.

"Pack up, Jenny," John told her. "We're out of here. I'll settle up at the front desk. Meet you at the SUVs. We'll transfer the equipment at the pickup point, leave one of the vehicles, and advise Control what's happened and that we're going on alone."

"We're taking just one vehicle?"

"Yes. Any objection to that?"

"No objections. I'll be ready to go." She paused, and then said, "John?"

"Yes?"

"Don't forget your toothbrush."

John laughed, and the two parted in the torn and smoky night.

Twenty minutes later they were on their way. The two SUVs had been parked on the opposite side of the building and had escaped any damage. They left the spare Ford Expedition at a parking area and got back on the interstate.

"We'll travel for a couple of hours and then stop at the first decent-looking motel," John told her.

"Oh my, John," Jenny breathed, leaning over close to him.

"What?"

"Alone at last!"

John shook his head and told her, "Behave yourself. Go to sleep."

"Impossible. I can't behave myself. That's not in my nature. And I'm not a bit sleepy. But I'll try."

"Do that."

She was asleep in five minutes.

The lights burned late in the Oval Office. President Kelley had addressed the American people and downplayed the alleged terrorist threat. He hadn't blatantly lied . . . he just didn't lay out all the known facts. And Kelley felt rotten about it.

He hated his job. Even though his job approval rating was very high and he was practically a shoo-in for reelection, he wanted out. But he knew he couldn't do that. He had to serve another term. He had to see something locked in place.

Kelley's chief of staff sat with the president, drinking seemingly endless cups of coffee. Denning finally stood up and stretched. "You did what you had to do, Richard," he told his friend. "If you had told the American people any more, you would have run the risk of creating panic."

"I don't belong in this job, Martin. I hate it."

"You've done a fabulous job. The majority of the voters love you. Don't ever forget that."

"The majority of the American people don't have a clue about what is really going on," Kelley said sourly. "And you know it. We campaign on half-truths and sound bytes and alleged wrongdoing by our opponent. We tell the voters we won't raise taxes and won't do this and won't do that and won't do the other thing, and then juggle facts and figures and do exactly what we promised not to do." He slowly shook his head. "Speaking quite frankly, Martin, the job sucks, to use a popular kids' expression."

"It's the way it is, Richard."

"Doesn't make it right."

"But it's necessary and practical. And, to speak frankly, that's the way politics has been in America for two hundred years. You can bitch about it until your last day in office, but you're not going to change it, Richard."

"I just live with it, right?"

"That's about the size of it, yes."

"What happens if the worst-case scenario comes to be in New York, Martin?"

"There will be panic in the streets. People will die. Then life will go on. There will be all sorts of finger-pointing, and we will stand straight and tall and steadfastly deny blame. Certain third world nations that harbor terrorist groups and encourage terrorism will become even more hated. The press will have a field day until the next tragedy comes along. There is no paper trail, Richard. There is nothing that leads to the White House."

"I'm supposed to take comfort in that?"

"Yes."

"Hundreds, perhaps thousands, of Americans dead in the streets, and all I'm supposed to say is, 'I'm sorry. We did the best we could.' "

"That's about it. Jesus, Richard, if the worst should occur, what do you want to do, sit outside the White House in rags and pour ashes over your head? You want to use the expressions of the young? Well, here's one: get real."

The president of the United States looked at his chief of staff. He had to continue playing the role of being in a box. But he knew he couldn't order the terrorists stopped until they reached their cache of . . . whatever the hell kind of deadly gas or toxins they planned to use. The gang of malcontents had to be found and stopped and the deadly materials destroyed.

"Dammit!" the president said.

"We've got another problem, Richard," Denning said. "Albeit a small one."

"A small problem would be delightful. What is it?"

"John Barrone."

"Who the hell is John Barrone?"

"A retired CIA man. He seems to be working the trail of the PLF members—"

"Along with the Dutch, the French, the Germans, the Canadians, the British, the Israelis, and God only knows who else," the president said sarcastically. "Oh, I forgot our own people, didn't I? The FBI, the ATF, the Secret Service, about a hundred or so thousand highway patrol, local cops, and sheriff's deputies who all still don't know the full story, because that would jeopardize national security—or some such bullshit as that—but are nevertheless looking for these people with blood in their eyes, and are prepared to shoot it out like a reenactment of the O.K. Corral. Good God, Martin, this is the biggest fucking lash-up since Vietnam."

"Every agency is doing the best they can, Richard."

"Well, it isn't good enough! How many people do we have working the New York City area?"

"Several thousand."

"Like looking for a needle in a haystack."

"Worse than that, I would imagine. Richard, there is no paper trail connecting this office with the PLF's threat to kill New Yorkers."

He held up a folder. "What about this report from the CIA?"

"That report was issued several months ago, and does not specifically mention New York City."

"It sure as hell does."

Denning smiled. "In that copy only, Richard. With that in mind, I would suggest you destroy it. Right now."

"How did you arrange—" He frowned and waved a hand. "Never mind, I don't want to know. It's better if I don't. I'll shred this document personally."

"Good. Once that is done, we're in the clear one hundred percent."

"But Americans are still going to die."

"Maybe. Maybe not. Whatever tragedy might develop, it isn't your fault. Cannot be blamed on you."

"That doesn't give me much consolation, old friend. Have you finalized the plans for my New York visit?"

"Richard—"

"No!" The president spoke sharply. "I've told you repeatedly, I have to go. And I think you know why."

Denning looked at his boss for a few heartbeats. "Oh, come on, Rich! You can't mean that! You just can't! I forbid it, by God."

"You forbid it, Marty?" Kelley grinned at his friend. "By what authority do you forbid it?"

Denning ignored that. "You're insisting upon going to show how damn brave you are, Rich. That's not using good sense."

"I'm going to New York City to show the American people that threats of terrorism will not bring this nation to a halt."

"I'll ask the Secret Service to forbid it!"

"They've already tried it. I'm going, and that is my final word on the subject."

"I can insist that your guard be doubled."

"Do that. I don't care. They'll just be falling all over each other."

Denning stood up. "I'm going home. I hope you'll change your mind by morning."

"I won't. So make plans. Pack some spare underwear in case we get trapped in the city."

"You think that's funny?"

"I assure you I don't feel that way at all. But it is a possibility."

"More than you might think."

"We have one week to stop these terrorists, Martin. Seven days."

"That gives me time to change your mind about going."

President Kelley laughed and waved a hand. "Good night, Martin."

As soon as his chief of staff had closed the door behind him, Kelley opened a desk drawer and pulled out a phone. He punched out a number that was answered immediately.

"Thanks for taking care of that little paper trail."

"No problem, sir."

Kelley hung up, punched out another number and said, "Tell Barrone to find and kill those PLF members ASAP," the president of the United States said. "Defuse this situation immediately. The kidnapped girl is totally expendable."

Seventeen

"We've had several excellent opportunities to ace this bunch of terrorists without regard to Betsy's safety," Jenny said after receiving the liquidation order from Control Central. "And each time we were told to hold off. Now this comes in. What's going on?"

"Someone had a change of heart. But they waited too long," John said.

"You think the terrorists are on their way to New York non-stop?"

"You bet they are. And they won't be stopping at any more safe houses. That's too risky for them now. They know that somebody talked and their route has been compromised."

"And we do . . . what?"

"Head straight for New York City. We'll take turns at the wheel, stopping only for fuel and food."

Jenny turned the interior light on and looked at the map. "You think the PLF has changed routes?"

"You bet they have. And so will we. Plot it out, Jenny."

She studied the map for a moment. "Pick up Interstate 80 up here in Ohio and take that straight to New York City. I think that's the best route."

"Does this highway connect?"

"No. Follow this to 76, then 76 to 80 at Youngstown."

"Good enough. Bump our team in the Big Apple and tell them we're on the way."

That quickly done, Jenny said, "What about Betsy's boy-friend, Charles, and his reporter friend—what's his name? You think they've given up?"

"Scott Blake is his name. No. They haven't given up at all. I think they've been tagging along, listening to news stories and adding them up. Now I'd make a bet they're on their way to New York City."

"The Big Apple is going to be crowded."

"A classic understatement, Jenny. We're going to be falling all over each other, probably annoying the hell out of each other. Ballard will be sure to try to arrest us if we get too close to him."

"Manhattan is a big place, if I remember correctly."

"You've been there?"

"Just a couple of times for a visit." She looked at John and grinned. "I got lost."

"It's easy to do."

"You worked out of there, right?"

"A few times. Just remember that streets run east and west and avenues run north and south." He smiled. "Usually."

"Oh, thanks a lot. Usually?"

He laughed. "Just be careful in Wall Street, Chinatown, SoHo, TriBeCa, and the Village. Other than that, you'll be fine."

"I'll hold your hand all the time, Daddy."

John sighed with the patience of an experienced father. "Go back to sleep, Jenny."

"Yes, Daddy. Hey, are you sure you don't want me to drive?"

"You can take over the next time we gas up." He looked at the 'miles to go before fill-up' monitor. "It'll be a while. Get some sleep."

"I'm going to be ready for a snack the next time we stop," she warned him.

"Me, too. Go to sleep."

"And a pit stop," she added.

"Go to sleep!"

"Will you tell me story before I go night night?"

"All right," John surprised her by saying. "How about the story of a very nice FBI agent named Ballard and a mean little girl named Jenny who was forever tormenting him—"

Jenny made a gagging sound and said, "Forget it. Wake me in a couple of hours."

The motel guests had been moved to another place and the bombed-out motel closed while investigators went to work. When Ballard checked the guest registration and found John's name he gritted his teeth. Libby Carson and Special Agent Harden wisely stayed a few steps away from Ballard and said nothing.

Henry Thompkins, of the British MI6, who was working with the FBI, knew nothing about Ballard's intense dislike for Jenny Barnes or of his suspicion of John Barrone. "Whatever is the matter, Inspector?" the Brit asked. "You look positively grim."

"What?" Ballard said, looking up. "Oh, nothing, Henry. Well, frustration, I suppose."

"I know the feeling well, old man. We've been dealing with the IRA for decades. Sometimes the frustration makes a chap want to take the law into his own hands, doesn't it?"

Ballard cut his eyes to the MI6 man, wondering if there was some hidden message behind the words. He couldn't tell. "To be honest, Henry, yes, it does."

"Quite," the Brit said.

Jacques LaBlanc of the French DGSE walked up. Henry gave him a look of utter disdain and turned his back to him. The two men did not like each other, and made no effort to disguise that dislike.

Ballard tugged deeply at his level of patience and sighed. He had been told that this operation was one of international cooperation. However, the FBI man had seen little of that thus far.

And it didn't appear to be getting any better.

Ballard didn't know what he'd do if any more agents showed up; they were already falling all over each other, and so far accomplishing nothing. Ballard's orders remained the same: track the terrorists to New York City and do not endanger the kidnapped young lady.

Odd orders, to Ballard's way of thinking.

"The terrorists did not approach the known PLF safe house," an agent said, walking up. "We found their vehicles abandoned on the south side of town."

"And they are where now?" Ballard asked, already sensing what the agent's answer would be.

"We lost them."

Ballard remained silent, clenching his fists and taking several deep breaths, calming himself.

"But another small problem has arisen," the reporting agent said.

"What?"

"The kidnapped girl's boyfriend and the reporter are threatening to hold a news conference."

"So? That's their right. What can they say that would hurt us?"

"They claim to have more knowledge of the planned terrorist attack against New York City. They're preparing to say the president lied in his speech to the American public—that the citizens of New York City are in terrible danger."

"Where did they get this new information?"

"The reporter won't say. Says he has the right to protect his sources."

"They're bluffing," Jacques said.

"I don't think so," Ballard told him.

"Then arrest them and detain them in the interest of national security," Henry Thompkins suggested. "If they are allowed to spread rumors about a terrorist attack, the city will go into a panic."

"He's right about that," Jacques said. "For once."

"I've got to call in for orders," Ballard said. "Damn!" He wanted to use some stronger profanity, but he took his new-found born-again Christianity very seriously, and he held his tongue. He knew he'd been backsliding of late, and that had to stop. He didn't want to end up sounding like that vulgar slut, Jenny Barnes. "Did you go to the hospital and speak to John Barrone's people?"

"Yes. They told us nothing of substance. Before we could question them further, the doctors made us leave."

Ballard nodded his head and the agent walked away. Ballard looked around him. The forensic team had been flown in and were busy at work; there was nothing left for him to do except call in for instructions. Thompkins had walked off in one direction and Jacques had walked off in another. Ballard sighed. On top of everything else he had a couple of foreign primadonnas to contend with.

"Lord, give me strength," Ballard muttered, looking heavenward.

Stopping only for gas, sandwiches, and soft drinks and coffee to go, John and Jenny made the seven hundred odd miles to the outskirts of New York City by mid-morning of the next day. Neither one was overly fatigued from the drive, but both could use a shower and a change of clothing.

"We going into the city today?" Jenny asked.

John shook his head. "Not immediately. We'll find a nice motel, check in with our people and see what's going on, if anything, then clean up and get something to eat."

"Then go into the city."

"No. Then we'll arrange to turn in this vehicle and draw a new one."

"Then we'll go into the city."

"Right. But only so far. We'll find a parking garage and cab it from then on."

"It won't take Ballard long to find us. You know he's tracking us by credit card usage."

"Let him. We've broken no laws, and haven't interfered with any ongoing investigation. Besides, we'll only be here in New Jersey for this one night. Then we'll move into a safe house in the city."

"Let's find that motel. I long for a hot soapy soak."

"You want me to stop somewhere so you can get some bubble bath?"

"That would be awfully sweet of you, John."

"Right." John's reply was very dry. "The very first chance I get."

Two hours later, after baths and something to eat, the two drove into Manhattan. By early afternoon they were reunited with the rest of the team in a brownstone in a quiet residential part of the city.

Over coffee, Bob Garrett unfolded a detailed map of the city and brought them up to date.

"We believe one part of the cell is headquartered somewhere along here," Bob said, his finger tracing an area a few blocks from the river. "One of my friends on the NYPD has a good snitch who finally turned up something solid."

"One part of the cell?" John questioned.

"Yes," Bob said. "You want to take it, Paul?"

Paul Brewer leaned forward. "I was walking back here from the market the day before yesterday when I spotted a young lady parking a very expensive automobile. It was a new Jag and it was a beauty, but the car paled against the lady. She was light chocolate, class all the way. Well, naturally, I paused for a moment and pretended to do something else while all the time I was looking at her. Then damned if this scruffy-looking young man doesn't suddenly get out of the backseat. He's carrying something wrapped in a blanket, something long and heavy—"

"Weapons?" Jenny asked.

"I'd bet on it. Well, I straightened up and walked on, but kept an eye on the unlikely pair. They go into this brownstone and I walk on to the end of the block and call for some new eyes. We've kept a loose surveillance on the place ever since. Lots of coming and going by some very interesting-looking people. We got some pictures, and two of the visitors are known sympathizers of the PLF. No warrants out on them, but they're heavily involved in the movement."

"Right under our noses," John said, leaning back and taking a sip of coffee. "And the Bureau's made no move against them?"

"We haven't seen the Bureau, John," Linda said. "Not at this location. They're all over the first area we pointed out, but not around here."

"We haven't seen a single person from any agency here," Al said. "And Control provided us with photographs of every one of them working this operation."

John set his cup in the saucer on the coffee table and leaned back in his chair. "Either we're dead wrong about the people in this location or you've found a deep cell the Bureau doesn't yet know about."

"Do we tell them?" Paul asked.

John cut his eyes and watched as Jenny shook her head in a very emphatic no. "No. Not yet. We watch and see what happens. We"—his eyes again briefly touched Jenny—"can't be more than a few hours ahead of the bunch we've been bird-dogging, if they're not already here. We're going to take a chance—when and if one presents itself—to grab Betsy Morrow. If we blow it, the young lady is history."

"I hope we can pull it off," Bob said. "We got the same orders you did, John. And I don't like the idea of this girl being tossed to the lions. Although," he was quick to add, "it might come to that."

"You let any US enforcement agency in on this, and they've got to play it by the rules," Jenny said. "I think that terrorists worldwide have got to be shown that the US will treat them ruthlessly, that we'll play their stinking game low-down and dirty. What was that expression in the movie: mad-dog mean? That's the way I believe we've got to play it."

"I agree," Linda said.

John nodded, thinking that he really wouldn't want to have any of the women in the team angry at him. "Have any of you picked up anything about the type of poison or toxins the terrorists plan to use?"

"Not a thing," Al said. "At least that part of the plan was not thrown together. That appears to have been very well-thought-out."

"Except for putting the terrorists ashore on the west coast," Bob said. "Whoever thought that one up wasn't thinking too clearly."

"Or maybe was," John said. "It's certainly made a lot of supposedly skilled investigators run around in circles accomplishing absolutely nothing."

The team members were silent for several moments, all of them shifting restlessly in their chairs. Paul Brewer was the first to break the uncomfortable silence.

"It all sounded so easy a few weeks ago," the former Border Patrol agent said. "Just put a ragtag bunch of terrorists out of business. It all appeared to be pure black-and-white, with no gray areas at all. But things sure turned hazy real quick."

John stood and began pacing the room. He stopped at the windows facing the quiet street and looked out. "Then let's give some thought to blowing the smoke away," he said.

Before anyone could question him on particulars, Linda held up a hand. "Hold it!" she said, pointing to the TV set. She rose from her chair and walked over and turned up the sound.

"Dozens of shoppers in the midtown area were rushed to area hospitals a few minutes ago after inhaling what appears to have been some sort of poisonous fumes," the announcer said. "The store was immediately closed while teams of investigators from state, local, and federal agencies suited up in emergency gear, preparing to enter the department store."

"Let's go to work," John said. "Rumor has just turned to reality."

Eighteen

The police had evacuated the entire block around the department store and cordoned it off. Hundreds of people were milling about in the crisp fall air. Dozens of ambulances were moving in and out of the police blockades. Some in the crowd were still weeping, or looked as though they had been. Others looked angry or confused.

"Let's circulate and listen to the talk," John told his people. "Split up and see what we can pick up."

The team wandered off, stopping at the fringes of small groups to listen to the people.

John heard one man say, "I was just stepping off the elevator when I felt something crunch under my shoe. Then the door closed behind me. Jesus Christ! Everyone who remained on that elevator was taken to the hospital. Some of them are not expected to live. God! What the hell is going on in this city?"

"Have you reported this to the police?" someone asked.

"Not yet. The cops haven't talked to me yet."

Jenny heard a woman say, "I went in the little shop in the lobby of my building to buy some cough drops and I couldn't get waited on. I looked over the counter and the salesman was on the floor. He was dead! It was terrible."

"Did you touch him?"

"God, no. His face was all dark. His tongue was sticking out of his mouth, and it looked black. I've never seen anything like that."

"How awful for you!"

"Not as awful as it was for the man on the floor," Jenny muttered and walked on.

Bob heard, "I knew the president was lying the other day. I just knew he was. You know as well as I do that the FBI or the CIA or somebody knew something like this was going to happen. They have spies all over the place. Lying goddamned politicians. You can't trust any of them."

"Well, if we had elected a real liberal instead of a half-ass one he wouldn't have lied."

"You two guys ought to get married," Bob muttered, and walked on.

Some sort of nerve agent that shuts down the entire system, John thought, as he walked along, pausing occasionally to listen to people talk. *And it's fast-acting and deadly in high enough concentration.*

John caught Jenny's eyes as she stood in the middle of the block and motioned for her to join him. "Find the others," he told her. "Let's get out of here."

"You know what this stuff is?"

"Nerve agent. Tabun, Sarin, Soman, GF, or VX. Whatever the name, it's fast and deadly in high concentration. That's enough for me."

"I'll find the others."

Several blocks away, the team gathered at a bar and took a table at the back of the room.

"Anyone hear anything concerning the fatality count?" John asked.

"I know it's going to be grim," Linda said. "I saw a lot of sheet-covered bodies on stretchers."

"Several dozen or so, so far," Paul said. "Most of them caught in elevators."

Linda picked it up. "Delivery system is tiny glass vials. So far, that is. Somebody steps on them, releases the nerve agent, and it's all over."

"Terrorism has hit America in full force," Al said, pausing

until the waiter had placed their drinks on the table and walked away. "And it's ugly."

"You think the bunch we've been bird-dogging made it here ahead of us?" Jenny asked.

"Maybe. It's possible the local cell got edgy and jumped the gun."

"Either way, John," Bob said. "What's next for us?"

"We hit the cell close to us tonight."

"Stupid damn fools!" André raged at members of the local cell. "You have jeopardized the entire mission."

"You were out of contact for twenty-four hours," the local cell leader replied. "We thought you had been captured. We felt it was best to go ahead."

André waved his hand in dismissal and frustration. "No point in belaboring the point. It's done. Now we must proceed without letup."

"When and how?" he was asked.

"Now. Immediately. Grand Central Terminal." He looked at his watch. "We have time to get there if we hurry. How? In every way we know how. Scatter vials in rest rooms, and in the main corridors and walkways. Let's go."

"What about the bitch you've dragged along?" a cell member asked accusingly.

André stared hard at the questioner for a few seconds, a local college student with some very strange ideas concerning freedom and government's role. "We'll keep her alive for a while longer, Beth. You have some objections to that?"

The young woman dropped her gaze under André's very direct and intense stare. She had never met André until an hour ago, but she knew his worldwide reputation and his penchant for cold-blooded killing, and was more than a little afraid of him. "No, André. None at all."

"Very good. I'm so pleased my orders meet with your approval. You and Wini will take her to the safe house. Wait for us there. We should return shortly after dark." He stood up. "Let's go, people. We have work to do."

Ballard and his people had been flown into the city as soon as they received word about the terrorist attack. Ballard had also been informed that John Barrone and Jenny Barnes had checked into a motel in New Jersey.

"Up to his neck in this," Ballard said. "But who's paying him, and why?"

Questions that had no answers . . . yet. But Ballard was determined to get those answers, somehow.

"Thirty-nine people dead," Special Agent Harden said, adding, "so far. Dozens in the hospital. Some of them not expected to live."

The agent in charge of the New York office walked up. "We're ready to move, Inspector."

Ballard looked at his watch. "An hour and a half until the exodus from the city begins." He paused, a thoughtful look in his eyes. "The tunnels will be crowded. However, I don't think we have to worry about them . . . yet. The delivery system they're using would not be effective there. But Grand Central Terminal is quite another matter." He met the gaze of the agent in charge of the New York office. "Wouldn't you say so, King?"

Agent King muttered a profanity under his breath. Ignoring Ballard's frown at his cursing, he said, "Yes. There will be thousands of people going through there. Good God, the death toll could be staggering!"

"Let's go," Ballard ordered.

André and his people were dressed at the height of fashion, blending in perfectly with the trickle of people now beginning to move toward Grand Central Terminal for the commuter ride out of the city.

André and his team all carried briefcases, just like thousands of other people now beginning to leave their office buildings. But instead of containing spreadsheets and reports, their brief-cases contained hundreds of tiny vials of the world's deadliest nerve gas. The contents of André's briefcase were somewhat different from the others. It contained a small pressurized tank; the trigger for the tank was located just under the handle. When the trigger was pushed, the time-operated mechanism on the tank would open in sixty seconds and begin releasing the deadly nerve agent.

André was quite pleased with himself. He could not contain a small smile as he strolled along. This would be the greatest coup ever for the PLF. What a blow for the oppressed people of the world, what a magnificent glorious strike for freedom. Of course, many of those who would die a horrible suffocating death this day would be men and women who were at the low end of the economic scale, many of them working two jobs and struggling to make ends meet, but that couldn't be helped. It was unfortunate, even sad, but at least death would relieve those people of their burden of endless toiling for their rich masters in this fat and bloated nation.

There would be children among the dead, but André chose not to dwell on that. They would only have grown up to be slaves of the capitalist system like their parents. Certainly death was preferable to that.

André and his PLF team were now two blocks away from Grand Central. The foot traffic was picking up as office build-ings began emptying of people.

André felt a glow begin to build within him. He always experienced that warm radiance when a worthy goal was about to be reached. It was a good feeling. He slowed his pace to further enjoy the sensation.

It was almost sexual.

If the truth be known, André was just about as goofy as a road lizard. Had he not been found and recruited by the PLF, he would probably have been a serial killer, maiming and torturing without reason, taking human life simply for the bloody thrill of it.

Across town, John paused in his fieldstripping and cleaning of his .45 autoloader, thinking. Where would the PLF strike next? And when? Would they try two attacks on the same day, within hours of each other? He cut his eyes to the television set, the volume turned down low. Over thirty people dead, the news reporter was saying, and so far, the NYPD and FBI had not released the name of the chemical used in the terrorist attack.

In the few hours following the attack, the city had calmed down somewhat, but many workers were still on edge, anxious to get home to safe refuge in the suburbs.

Taking the train.

Damn! John thought. *Penn Station. Or, more likely, Grand Central Terminal. Of course. Thousands of people heading through there on their way home.* He quickly assembled his .45 and called for the other members of his team.

He stood up to face his people. "I think Grand Central Terminal might be next on the terrorist's hit list. I hope I'm wrong." He glanced at his watch. "Bob, does the Bureau have people there, do you know?"

"I haven't picked up anything on the computer about it."

"I would almost guarantee they do," Jenny said. "Ballard's a jerk, but he doesn't miss much."

"Let's go, people."

"Are we going to warn the Bureau about our suspicions?" Linda asked.

"How?" John replied. "We're not supposed to be involved in this matter."

"How about Betsy?" Bob asked.

"She'll have to wait. You all know what the terrorists look like. If you spot one in the terminal, start shouting and pointing. That will spook them and put them on the run. Let's go, people."

"If any PLF member is carrying a suitcase or briefcase, that's going to spook me, too," Jenny said.

"When you stop yelling and pointing," John said, "just hold your breath and run."

Nineteen

Betsy opened her eyes and tried to bring everything into focus. She blinked several times and shook her head, and finally the room ceased its tilting and spinning and settled down. Her captors had given her a shot that had knocked her out, slamming her into very quick and deep unconsciousness. The last thing she remembered was André saying that should keep her out for hours.

Betsy lay very still for several more minutes, trying as hard as she could to make some sense out of things. Slowly, one jagged and jumbled piece at a time, her full memory began returning.

Betsy swung her legs off the bed and placed her feet on the floor. She sat there for a moment, feeling her strength and coordination returning.

She took stock of her surroundings. The bed, a dresser, a small, single-bulb brass lamp, and a door she presumed was locked.

She rose from the bed and stood up—unsteadily at first, then her balance returned. She walked over to the dresser and removed the shade from the lamp, then unscrewed the bulb and pulled the plug from the wall. She wound the cord around the narrow part of the base so it would not dangle. The lamp was heavy for its size, and would certainly put a dent in someone's head.

Which is precisely what Betsy planned to do if she got the

chance. Wini's head, preferably. Of all her captors, Betsy hated that twisted and warped bitch more than any of them.

She found her sneakers under the bed and slipped them on. She felt grimy and longed for a hot bath. She couldn't remember the last time she'd had a bath or a change of clothing. She was determined to make a break for freedom if the opportunity presented itself . . . and she was also determined to somehow press for that chance.

Betsy went to the door and pressed her ear against it, listening. She could hear the very faint sounds of a television set, but nothing else. She tried the doorknob. Locked. She glanced again toward the window. No chance of escape there; the window had outside bars.

"Now what?" she muttered.

Then she heard footsteps. She stepped to one side and waited. "Come on in, you bastards," she whispered. "I have a surprise for you."

Someone stopped just outside the door. Betsy waited, gripping the heavy brass lamp.

A key rattled in the lock and the door swung inward. A young woman stepped into the room and paused for just a couple of seconds, looking at the empty bed.

"What the hell?" Betsy heard the young woman say. Then she stepped clear of the door and turned, presenting her face clearly to Betsy.

Betsy swung, and the base of the brass lamp connected solidly with the side of the young woman's head. She hit the floor without making another sound.

Betsy closed the door and knelt down, quickly searching the young woman for a weapon of some sort—a knife, a gun. Nothing. Betsy's father had taught her how to shoot, both rifle and pistol, although she had not fired either in several years.

"Damn," Betsy whispered, standing up. "Now what?" She looked down at the young woman on the floor, whose forehead was bleeding and beginning to swell. "Good," Betsy said. "I hope you die, you bitch."

She was startled by the viciousness in her thoughts and voice. Betsy had never been a violent person, and avoided the more violent movies and shows on TV. Then she shook her head and said, "I'll kill you all if I get the chance."

She opened the door cautiously and looked out into the hall. Empty. She stepped out, still gripping the lamp. The sounds of the TV were louder now—some talk show; the audience was laughing. Betsy peeked into the living room. Wini was sitting on the sofa, eating from a bag of chips. Betsy began slowly slipping up behind her. Just a few more steps . . .

Wini suddenly turned and her mouth dropped open in shock and surprise. "What the hell!" she blurted, spraying the air with bits of potato chips. "Where's Beth?"

Betsy swung the lamp.

Wini threw up an arm, and the lamp caught her on the forearm. She yelped in pain and fell off the couch onto the floor, but recovered quickly and lunged to her feet, looking around her.

Betsy followed her eyes to a sub-machine gun lying on a table. "Go ahead," Betsy told her. "Try for it. But if you fire that weapon, you'll see how fast the people on either side of this place call the police."

"You rotten rich bitch!" Wini hissed at her. "I'm going to get my wish to kill you!"

Betsy laughed at the woman. "Come on, you terrorist whore. I'm going to beat your brains out."

Wini jumped at Betsy and Betsy sidestepped and swung the heavy lamp base, striking Wini's shoulder and bringing a gasp of pain. Wini staggered under the blow and backed up; that move placed her between Betsy and the front door.

"Beth!" Wini called.

"Beth is out of it," Betsy told her. "I caved her damned stupid head in."

"She's dead?"

"She was alive a few minutes ago, but she's bleeding all

over the floor. The same way you're going to be in a few minutes."

Wini suddenly ran at Betsy, so fast Betsy did not have time to swing the lamp. The two women went to the floor, cussing and swinging, Wini with her fists, Betsy with the lamp. Betsy won that round by slamming the lamp base against Wini's side and back again and again until the woman yelled in pain and rolled away.

Betsy was on her feet first and kicked Wini in the belly. Wini grunted in pain, but managed to grab Betsy's ankle and hold on, finally bringing the young woman tumbling down to the floor. Betsy lost her grip on the lamp.

Wini smiled in triumph as the lamp went clattering off to one side. Betsy cooled that smile with a fist to Wini's nose. Wini yelped as her nose was suddenly bent to one side and the blood began to flow.

"God'am you, 'itch!" Wini slurred, unable to breathe through her broken nose. "I'm gonna 'ill you!"

Betsy's reply was another fist to Wini's face, the blow striking her on the side of the jaw and jarring her head back, banging hard against the floor.

Betsy crawled to her knees and was about to rise to her feet and make a run for the front door when Wini clamped a hand around an ankle and twisted hard. Betsy grunted in pain and kicked back several times. The third kick scored when it smashed into Wini's face. This time her mouth took the brunt of the kick, and Betsy's sneaker mashed her lips. The blood began dripping, joining the flow from her broken and bent nose. Wini cursed her until she was breathless.

Betsy struggled to her feet and then dropped on Wini, knees bent. Her weight landed on Wini's stomach and all the fight went out of the terrorist. She screamed in pain, tried to stand up, and then fainted away.

Betsy got to her feet and staggered across the room, almost out of steam. The wild fight with Wini, the long, semi-drugged ride across the nation, the beatings and rapes, and the lingering effect of the powerful shot she'd received hours before had just about sapped her strength.

She managed to make it to the table and leaned against it for a moment, trying to control her labored breathing and calm her racing heart.

"Goddamn you!" a voice called from the archway leading to the hall.

Betsy looked up. Beth was standing there, blood still dripping down her face. She was holding a long-bladed butcher knife.

Beth cursed Betsy as she lurched out of the hall and into the living room.

Betsy's hand fell on the Uzi sub-machine gun and looked down for a second. She knew it was an Uzi because of their popularity in the movies and television shows. *Funny,* she thought through a haze, *this group hates Jews but uses a Jewish-made weapon. How strange.*

"You're dead, bitch," Beth said. "I'm going to cut you bad, make you hurt before I kill you."

Betsy stared at the woman for a few numbing seconds, and then her hands closed around the Uzi. She had never fired a sub-machine gun in her life, had no idea how to make it work except to point it and squeeze the trigger.

"It's over, Beth," Betsy said. "Wini's hurt bad, and so are you. Give it up."

Beth cursed her and took another step toward her, the knife held menacingly. It looked very sharp.

Betsy raised the Uzi. It was surprisingly light. Actually it was a machine pistol—a mini-Uzi with the folding metal stock removed. It weighed about six pounds with the full twenty-five round magazine.

"Don't come any closer, Beth. I mean it. I don't want to kill you, but I will if you force me."

"You don't have the courage, bitch." Beth took another step.

Betsy raised the mini-Uzi and moved her finger to the trigger. "Stop, Beth. I mean it. Put down the knife."

Beth laughed at her.

Betsy squeezed the trigger. Nothing happened. The weapon wouldn't fire.

"You stupid bitch." Beth laughed, taunting her, and moved closer.

Betsy's fumbling fingers found a switch and pushed it. She leveled the mini-Uzi again and squeezed the trigger. The muzzle exploded in a fury of automatic fire. Betsy held the trigger back and tried to control the weapon with one hand. She failed miserably as the weapon started climbing up and right, and the 9mm rounds tore into Beth. Starting at Beth's hips and moving upward, Betsy shot the young woman all over the place. The entire episode took no more than two seconds.

Beth was knocked backward by the impacting lead. The last six or eight rounds struck her in the face and tore off her jaw. She was dead when she was driven against the wall and slid downward, to land on her butt in a mess of blood, bits of bone, and tiny bits of gray matter from her shattered brain. She was still gripping the butcher knife.

Betsy laid the mini-Uzi on the table and stood for a moment. She felt sick to her stomach and fought back an almost uncontrollable urge to vomit. "Oh, Jesus," she whispered. "Oh, Jesus."

She looked over at the still-unconscious Wini. Blood was leaking from the woman's mouth and nose. Betsy wondered if maybe she'd broken something when she knee-dropped on her. Not that she cared one little bit.

When she felt she had enough strength to make it to the front door, Betsy pushed away from the table and staggered toward the foyer. She was so tired and weak she thought she might faint. She stopped to rest along the way, leaning against the wall, a chair, and finally a small table in the foyer.

She managed to unlock the front door only to find herself facing a door of iron bars. "Oh, shit!" Betsy said. "I forgot, this is New York. Fourteen damn locks on every door."

She had to return to Wini and go through the woman's pockets, searching for the key. She found a ring of keys and returned to the barred door, fumbling around until she finally found the right key.

Betsy stepped outside and took a deep breath of fresh air. Nothing had ever felt so good as that breath of freedom. She took a hesitant step before exhaustion finally caught up with her, and then she tumbled down the steps to the sidewalk.

She lay on the sidewalk, too exhausted to move. A few seconds after she landed on the concrete, an NYPD car rounded the corner and came to a halt. Two officers got out cautiously and approached her.

Betsy looked up at the cops and said, "I'm Betsy Morrow. The woman who was kidnapped in Arizona . . ."

"Jesus Christ!" one officer said. "It's her, all right. I'll call it in."

"Listen to me," Betsy said. "Please listen to me. There isn't much time."

"Time for what, lady?" the cop said. "Just relax, you're all right, now. You're safe."

"You've got to get to Grand Central Station, Terminal, whatever it's called. . . ."

"What about it, Miss Morrow?"

"That house there," Betsy said, cutting her eyes. "The one with the open door. Terrorists are using it as a safe house. Bodies in there."

"Get SWAT here, right now!" said the cop who was kneeling beside Betsy.*

"Grand Central . . ." Betsy said. "The PLF is planning an attack there. Right now. During rush hour. Some sort of nerve gas. There's about a dozen of them."

"Holy God!" the cop said.

Betsy struggled to sit upright on the sidewalk, despite the cop trying to hold her back. "Let me up, dammit!" she said. "Thank you."

*SWAT. Special Weapons & Tactics

"You should lie back, Miss Morrow. Are you hurt?"

"No. Just pissed off, Officer."

The NYPD cop smiled. "I think you're going to be all right, Miss Morrow."

Betsy pointed to a new Jaguar parked at the curb. "That car belongs to one of the PLF. A very pretty black woman."

The street was rapidly filling up with police units and ambulances.

"Goddamn!" a cop called from the foyer of the brownstone. "Bodies in here."

"One's still alive," Betsy said. "Winifried is her name, I think. The dead girl is named Beth something-or-another."

"The FBI is here," a cop said.

"Wonderful," the officer kneeling beside Betsy said, his voice dripping with sarcasm. "We can all go home now. Everything is under control."

"Knock it off," a plainclothes detective told him.

"Screw you," the cop muttered.

Betsy managed a smile. "Could I have a drink of water? I'm really thirsty."

"I think we can arrange that, Miss Morrow."

"Read her her rights, just in case," the detective said.

"Her rights?" the uniform questioned. "For Christ sake, *she's* the one who was kidnapped. Her rights? All her rights have been violated."

"You can say that again," Betsy said.

"Just in case," the detective said patiently. "We don't know what happened in there." He jerked a thumb toward the brownstone. "Do we, Nick?"

"Oh, hell," Betsy said. "Read me my rights and get me out of here. I want a long hot bath and a change of clothes."

"It's for your own good, Miss Morrow," the detective said.

"That's what my mother used to say when she made me eat all my green beans," Betsy said.

The detective laughed. "Forget it," he told the uniform he'd called Nick. "Get her in an ambulance. Ride with her. Go with them, Officer Foster," he said to a female officer. "And phone in."

Betsy smiled. "Just like E.T."

She sighed with relief when she stretched out on the gurney and was loaded into the ambulance.

"Any hospital preference, Miss Morrow?" the uniform asked.

"Oh, not really. I don't know New York City. But one with a bathtub, thank you."

"The FBI wants to ride along," Officer Foster said, holding the door open.

"Close the door," Nick said. "If they can't find the hospital on their own, we're all in trouble."

Foster allowed the door to close and the ambulance wailed off. "You're going to get your butt in trouble with the FBI, Nick. You got a lousy attitude toward them."

"I don't have a lousy attitude, Foster. I just don't like those that I know, that's all."

"They don't like you because of that damned survivalist group you belong to, Nick."

"It's my right to belong if I want to, and I want to."

"What's the name of it, Nick?" Betsy asked. "I'd like to join."

Twenty

John and his team taxied to within a couple of blocks of Grand Central Terminal, then walked the rest of the way.

"What happens if we see Ballard?" Jenny asked as they approached the terminal.

"Ask him yourself," John replied, halting the parade almost directly in front of the station. "He's standing right over there, looking at us."

Jenny turned and looked squarely at Ballard, scowling at her. She stuck out her tongue at him. "His attitude sure hasn't changed any," she remarked.

"I asked for a report on him," John said. "He's a good agent. And stop that!" he told Jenny, taking notice of her antics.

"Here he comes," Jenny said. "All puffed up and full of self-righteous indignation."

"Well, hello there, Ballard," John said, before the inspector could say a word. "How nice meeting you here."

"You've got some explaining to do, Barrone," Ballard said. "I want to know what you're—"

A call from another agent spun Ballard around. "The Morrow girl's been found, Inspector. She's all right, and being taken to a hospital here in the city."

"I want her guarded around the clock," Ballard said.

"Being done, sir. The NYPD is taking care of that."

"I want *us* guarding her, Wilson. Got that?"

"Yes, sir."

"Fine." He turned back to Barrone. "You shouldn't be here, Barrone. This area is dangerous."

"Tell that to these hundreds of people, Ballard."

Before either of them could say another word, the street was filled with NYPD cars, officers jumping out.

"What in the world . . . ?" Ballard said.

The Agent in Charge of the New York City office ran up. "Betsy Morrow told us the PLF is planning an attack here at the terminal," he panted. "We believe they're here now. Inside the terminal."

Hundreds of people were streaming into the terminal, hundreds more milling about inside.

"Good God!" Ballard said. "Get your people inside the building. You know what the terrorists look like. Find them."

The agent hesitated. "What is it?" Ballard demanded. The agent shook his head. "Move, man!" Ballard turned to John. "Get out of here." Then he was off, pushing his way into the huge terminal building.

"Where're the rest of our people?" John asked.

"Inside."

"Let's join them."

"This is really going to irritate Ballard."

"If things go wrong, none of us will be irritated for very long."

"What a cheerful thought."

The news of Betsy's freedom had hit the airwaves. One of the local PLF members signaled André, who was standing about fifty feet away. She walked over to him.

"What is it?" André demanded.

"The Morrow girl is free. The safe house has been compromised."

"Wini?"

"I don't know. The news flash just said that one person is dead, the other badly injured."

"Get out of here. Right now. Get on a train, any train, and

get clear. Find your way back to . . . the alternate house. Move!"

"What about you?"

"I'll meet you there. Don't go near the warehouse. For sure that's being watched. Get out now! Abort the attack."

The word was passed to André's people and they all got clear in the confusion and crush.

André paused, pretending to read a newspaper. He scanned the crowd. There were uniformed police everywhere he looked. And he knew there must also be dozens of plainclothes officers working the crowd. *Hopeless,* he concluded. *Goddamn these American cops,* he silently raged, *and goddamn Betsy Morrow.* He realized that he should have killed the young woman long before they reached the city.

André put a hand inside a pocket of his topcoat and wrapped his fingers around a grenade. He smiled. Well, he could still cause some damage and get away in the confusion, perhaps even activate the tank inside the briefcase.

He slipped the grenade from his pocket and pulled the pin, keeping the grenade close to him and holding the spoon down as he walked toward a heavy crowd of people. He walked right past a police officer, so close he could have reached out and touched the man or shoved the minibomb down the bastard's throat. He smiled at the thought. He had another grenade in his other topcoat pocket. He would save that one.

André released the spoon and tossed the grenade underhanded into a knot of people. It struck one man on the leg. André turned and walked calmly away.

"What the hell?" the man hollered as the heavy grenade hit his leg. "Who the hell is throwing things at me?"

I am, you American asshole, André thought with a hidden smile. He continued walking.

"That's a fuckin' grenade!" the man hollered. "Run!"

Just as the last word left the man's mouth the powerful grenade blew, hurling shrapnel for yards around.

The man who yelled lost parts of both legs and he was

ripped open from crotch to throat, his intestines peppered with hot metal. He would die before emergency personnel could get him to a hospital. A woman standing closest to the mini-bomb when it exploded was literally blown apart, bits and pieces of her scattered all over the place. A man caught a piece of shrapnel in the temple and died on the terminal floor. Another lost part of his jaw and collarbone. A dozen more people were seriously hurt.

André pushed the trigger of the tank holding the deadly nerve gas and dropped it, joining the others in a wild run toward the outside. Those panicked people behind him stepped on the briefcase, smashing it and kicking it off to one side. It landed under a vendor's station and slipped out of sight. The stiff wire leading to the trigger was bent and the valve only partially opened, releasing just a tiny invisible hissing of deadly gas.

A crying and nearly hysterical teenage girl was pushed and shoved hard by the panicked crowd and fell down, her face just inches from the hissing spray of nerve gas. Within seconds the girl started having difficulty breathing, and her legs began jerking. Heavy mucus began building in her lungs and nose. She began coughing up a black substance, and within a minute she was unconscious as her respiratory system began totally shutting down. In another minute she was dead, her dark and swollen tongue sticking grotesquely out of her mouth.

A police officer knelt down to aid the girl and noticed the briefcase under the vendor's stand. He got down on all fours to shield her from the wild stampede of humanity, and within seconds he was unable to rise. He was dizzy, and having trouble breathing. In another ten seconds he collapsed to the floor, nearly unconscious as he took the full load of the tank of deadly nerve gas.

Once outside, dozens of people who had been jammed up close to the vendor's stand as they tried to get out of the terminal began getting dizzy, feeling sick, and having difficulty breathing. The EMTs were staying busy and calling for more help.

Two elderly men collapsed and died in front of the terminal. One cracked his head on the way down and his nose was flattened, the blood gushing from his still erratically beating heart.

A young street punk—who had either seen one too many blood-and-guts movies or recently sniffed some chemical he shouldn't have been sniffing—saw the man fall and the blood spurt. He immediately put two and two together. After several agonizing seconds of mental straining, he came up with five, which was about normal, considering the level of attentiveness and the intelligence quotient of many in the public school system in America. "Somebody's shooting at us!" he screamed.

Hundreds of people on the sidewalks and in the street panicked. It became a mob scene as people began running wildly in all directions, fleeing in sheer terror. Several dozen people suffered injuries ranging from cuts and bruises to compound fractures and severe head traumas.

The street punk who started the near riot found a purse on the sidewalk and looked inside. His eyes bugged out, and he strained his brain to use much of his entire vocabulary by saying, "Oh, wow, man!" Then he wandered off in search of the nearest video parlor, where he could satisfy his mental capacities with heavy and heady stimuli such as a video game titled something like: Spaceman Warrior X Takes a Dump After Annihilating the Entire Population of the Planet Zargon.

John Barrone and his team had retreated to the safety of two blocks away and stood in the crowd watching the panic.

"I didn't hear any gunfire," Al said.

"There wasn't any," Paul replied. "Someone just shouted fire in a crowded theater."

The team watched as the NYPD began pushing people back and setting up portable barricades. HAZMAT teams began suiting up and cautiously entering the terminal.

"They just found something," Jenny remarked. "Or they suspect something."

"I don't believe all those people who are collapsing out here are doing so because of fright," Linda said. "Something was released into the air inside that terminal. Something besides a grenade . . . if that's what it was."

"And not a single member of the PLF was captured," Jenny said.

"Maybe this was their grand finale," Bob said. "Maybe they're through."

"You really believe that?" Paul asked.

Bob shook his head. "Unfortunately, no, I don't. It was just wishful thinking."

"I sure would like to talk to Betsy Morrow," Al said. "Five minutes would do it."

"You can forget that," John told him. "The Bureau has her covered with a blanket of guards. Everybody going in and out of that hospital is being checked. And unless she's hurt bad, she won't be there for very long. You can bet plans are being made right now to move her."

"So where does that leave us?" Paul asked.

"Free to move around unrestricted, with no rules or guidelines," John told him. "And no one to report to or take orders from."

"And right now?" Jenny asked.

"We find PLF members and deal with them."

"With extreme prejudice?" Bob asked.

"I believe that is the term used," John said. "Let's go to work."

Twenty-one

"One of my buddy's snitches came through," John said. "He gave us the names of several people who are big supporters of the PLF. One in particular I want to talk to before any of the others. Guy lives over in Brooklyn. Josh Parnell. Part-time professional college student and self-proclaimed anarchist."

Forensic teams were still working in the brownstone where Betsy had been held. John and his people had quickly moved to another location in the East 80s, before any of Ballard's people could spot them in the area. If that had occurred, John would have had a lot of explaining to do, and he might have ended up in custody.

Two more vehicles had been provided for John and his team: Ford sedans. John still marveled at how easily Control had arranged things, and mentioned that to the team members riding with him over to Brooklyn.

"I think this network of people took a long, long time to get into place," Al said. "But how it was done without somebody talking still puzzles me."

"Twenty-five years ago," John replied, "when I first joined the Company, it was still a lot like this organization we now work for. We had a close-mouthed network of people worldwide. The Company still does, of course, to some degree, but not like it used to. And nothing at all like this outfit."

"What happened?" Paul asked.

"The paper clip counters took over. The press was allowed

to snoop everywhere, and most couldn't keep their damned mouths shut . . . couldn't be trusted. I wouldn't trust a reporter now if he or she swore to secrecy standing in the middle of a bible factory."

"Of course not," Jenny said, and John smiled as he handled the wheel of the sedan, knowing how Jenny felt. "How many do you know who even believe in the Bible, or God, or Jesus? I haven't found very many. Liberals have ruined this nation. I don't understand how anyone can call themselves a Christian and a liberal. The two are at opposite ends of the spectrum."

John vocally stepped back in before Jenny could really get wound up. "It was the combination of a lot of things that virtually tied the hands of the Company . . . and cost a lot of good men and women their lives."

Both Al and Paul smiled. They knew John was attempting to muzzle Jenny before she expounded even further. But it was a long ride over to Brooklyn, for the traffic was unusually heavy for this time of evening, and despite John's best efforts, both knew Jenny was not about to shut up.

Al tried to change the subject. "Won't the FBI be watching this Parnell person?"

"They haven't been. Seems as though no one takes this guy seriously. He's been blowing off at the mouth since he was about fifteen. He's twenty-five now. All he's done thus far is talk. His parents finally threw him out of the house a couple of years ago. Of course, he might be under surveillance now. We'll just have to see. If he is, we'll go to the next person on the list."

"Does he live in the city?"

"No. Up in the Bronx. He's a skinhead."

"Oh, that's wonderful," Paul said. "What a lovely bunch of people."

"What's his name?" Jenny asked.

"Johnny Stomper."

"I beg your pardon?"

"Johnny Stomper. That's what he goes by. His real name

isn't known. Came in here about five years ago to recruit, and did fairly well. They have a club in the South Bronx area."

"How many members?" Al asked.

"Twenty or so. They stay in constant trouble with the police."

"I'm a Christian," Jenny said. "I may not act like it at times, but I am."

Both Paul and Al rolled their eyes. John sighed.

"I don't go to church as often as I should. But I do go, and I believe in the Bible."

"I think we all do, Jenny," John said.

"When the Bible says we shouldn't do something, I try not to do it. I don't always succeed, but I do try. Except for my language. When the Bible condemns something, that's the way it should be."

Al, Paul, and John said nothing.

"This country's gone to hell in a big bucket of puke," Jenny said.

John grimaced. "You do have such a marvelous way with words, Jenny."

"Thank you. I'll ignore the sarcasm. But it's true. And you know it and believe it. If you didn't, you wouldn't be working for this organization."

"I'm forced to agree with you, Jenny," John said, handing her a slip of paper. "Now look for this street, please."

"You can't take every word in the Bible literally, Jenny," Paul said.

"I don't. People have to use common sense when applying the Bible to day-to-day living. But following the teachings in the Bible isn't that difficult. Turn here, John."

The second team car was right with them, several car lengths behind.

"The address is just up ahead," Jenny said. "And would you look at that van parked across the street from it? How damn obvious can you get?"

"They—local, state, or federal—want Parnell to know he's

being watched," John said. "OK, then. Forget Mister Parnell. We'll find Johnny Stomper."

"Won't he be surveilled, as well?"

"Maybe not. I was told that he's very low on the list. We'll see."

They drove a few miles in silence. "Has anyone given any thought to our first assignment being a bust?" Jenny asked. "I mean, exactly what have we accomplished? The way I see it, nothing."

"We haven't accomplished much," John agreed. "At least not yet. But we have learned to work as a team and we've found that we all get along. Control knew there would be feds all over this case when they handed it to us. I personally believe it was done as a test."

"We've picked up a tail," Jenny said.

"I know," John said. "They swung in behind us as soon as we left Parnell's block. But I don't think it's Ballard's people."

"Why not?" Al asked.

"The car. From what I can see, it's not in good shape. We may have a pack of punks behind us."

"We're sure in a good neighborhood for it," Paul observed.

"This is the worst section," John said. "Some of these streets can be very dangerous."

"Worse than parts of DC?" Jenny asked.

"East Berlin wasn't as bad as those sections of DC. As a matter of fact, as I recall it was probably safer." He glanced in the rearview mirror. "I think the punks are getting ready to make their move. They've gotten between us and the others, and another car is moving up behind Bob and Linda."

The older model car pulled alongside on the deserted street and a young man yelled, "Hey, pull over. We wanna talk to you, man."

"How original," Al said. "Do you suppose he wants to discuss some deep philosophical point?"

"Somehow I doubt it," John said, ignoring the young man.

"You deaf, dude?" the young man yelled. "I said pull over."

John stepped on the brakes and the car containing four young men shot on past, then braked and pulled over to the curb.

"You're really going to stop?" Paul asked as John nosed over to the curb.

"I don't like punks," John replied.

Bob and Linda pulled in right behind them, the second carload of young men behind them.

"We're boxed in," Al said.

"We won't be for long," John said, reaching inside his jacket and pulling out his .45 "I assure you of that."

"This is a side of you I didn't know about, John," Paul remarked.

Jenny had taken her 9mm out of the special pocket of her shoulder bag.

John stepped out of the car, keeping the door between himself and the four, tough-looking young men, all of whom appeared to be in their early to mid-twenties. "You boys got a problem?" John asked.

Behind him, Bob and Linda had gotten out of their car and were facing four other young man, approximately the same age of those now facing John.

There were no private homes or apartment buildings along this stretch of ill-lighted street, just dark warehouses and old boarded-up buildings.

"Naw, you got the problem, old dude," said the rougher looking of the quartet facing John. His eyes narrowed as Jenny, Al, and Paul stepped out of the car. Then he laughed. "What a bunch of pussies, right, guys?"

The others with him grunted their replies in something akin to the English language. John had heard clearer phrases from aborigine bushmen on the edges of the Kalahari in Africa.

"What did your cretinous friends just say?" John asked. "And in what language?"

"You 'bout a smart-mouth old dude, ain't you?" said the spokesman of the group.

John offered no reply.

"I axed you a question, dude!" the young man said. "You better answer it if you know what's good for you."

"Oh, my," John said. "He's frightening me terribly. I might faint from fear at any moment."

Jenny laughed and said, "Me, too. I'm trembling from fright. They're all so menacing looking."

"An' that's a smart-mouth cunt, too," tough boy said. "I don't like her."

"Fuck you," Jenny very bluntly told him. Before the street tough could respond, she turned around and looked at Bob and Linda. "You guys having any sort of understandable dialogue with your pack of peckerheads?"

"Not much of a one," Linda said. "But I think they want our cars and our money."

"What did you say to me, bitch?" the punk hollered. "Hey! What did you say to me?"

Jenny looked at him in the dim light of the lone street lamp. "I guess I'm going to have to spell it out for you, numb nuts. . . ."

"She called me a peckerhead!" one of those in the other group said. "Peckerhead?"

"Well, she called me a numb nuts," tough boy said. He rubbed his crotch and grinned at Jenny. "I betcha my nuts ain't numb, baby. And I guess I'm just gonna have to show you. I think you'll like that, baby."

"When pigs fly," Jenny told him.

"You boys move your damn cars and leave," John said, his voice calm in the tense situation. "And I would suggest you do that immediately."

"Oh, my, my!" tough boy said, putting one hand on his hip and waving the other in a very dainty feminine gesture. "We must do that immediately, boys. Immediately! What do you all think about that?"

The other toughs laughed and made some very crude and obscene suggestions and gestures.

"Where the hell is a cop when you need one?" Al tossed out the question.

"You can forget all about the cops, dude," tough boy said. "They made their drive by here a few minutes ago. They won't be back for at least half an hour. We know the routine, don't we, guys?"

"Yeah," one of the guys in the second group said. "We sure do. And don't nobody live around here, neither. So let's get to it: you people start emptying your pockets and purses on the hood of the cars."

"I don't think so," John told him.

"Man, you must be crazy!" said the street tough facing John. He reached into his pocket and pulled out a pistol. "Now, by God, you gonna do what you're told or you gonna die, fool!"

John shot him.

The big slug slammed into the young man's chest and knocked him back, turning him to one side and sitting him down hard on the concrete. The street tough looked down at his chest and said, "Shit!" Then he died.

"Kill them crazy motherfuckers!" one of the gang of toughs shouted, jerking out a pistol.

Jenny put a hole in the center of his chest with a 9mm hollowpoint, and the street tough suddenly found himself on his butt in the street, hollering for his mother.

Two of the street toughs who had driven up in the second vehicle jumped in their car and roared away, tires squealing on the pavement and the rubber smoking on the road.

The gunfight was over in less than half a minute, the curb-side littered with dead and dying punks.

"Lousy motherfuckers," one dying street punk said.

John ignored the profane comments as he shoved his .45 autoloader back into leather and said, "Let's go. We still have a lot of work to do."

There would be no prints from the team found on any of the brass that shone dully in the dim light, for the team wore thin surgical gloves when handling rounds, wiping them clean before filling magazines.

For a few moments, no mention was made of the brief firefight as the team drove away. None of the team members had any use at all for street punks.

They all knew that many of the New York press types would make a big deal out of the shooting, some of the reporters verbally pissing and moaning and waving damp hankies about the terrible and tragic loss of young life. The physical and monetary agonies of their victims and the rap sheets of the punks would probably not be mentioned.

Certain big-mouth talk show hosts would once more climb on the verbal bandwagon and restart their tiresome and ill-thought-out dialogue about gun control, most of them blatantly choosing to ignore the Constitution.

More than one Washington politician, hoping to pick up a few votes from the socialistic left wing, all filled with resolve and self-righteous indignation, would march up to the podium to make long-winded speeches about gathering up all the guns from law-abiding citizens . . . but never offer any workable suggestions about how to disarm the nation's thousands of criminals and keep them disarmed, or to keep them away from knives, axes, tire-irons, and other types of instruments which could be used to assault law-abiding citizens.

All of the team members knew that once the bodies of the street punks were found, the major TV networks would spend many boring hours on the subject of violence, with many so-called experts expounding their haughtily given theories—most concluding that the majority of the fault lies with guns, only a small part lying with the person who pulls the trigger, leaving the impression that a hunk of metal with a hole in it has a brain and is capable of coming alive, picking a target, and killing without a human hand guiding its actions. Almost no one will say that at least part of the fault just might lie in the nation's rapidly declining morals, lack of discipline among kids, a heightening mood of "if it feels good, do it" pervading the movies and television.

"I think abortion has something to do with the wave of lawlessness in this country," Jenny said, breaking the silence.

John cut his eyes toward her for a heartbeat. "You don't believe in abortion?" he asked.

"In cases of rape or incest or to save the mother's life, sure," Jenny said. "I don't like this idea of women going in for an abortion because a baby might interfere with their social life, though, or it might hurt their chances for a promotion on the job, or they're just not ready to have a baby yet. Well, dammit, why didn't they think about that before they went out and fucked somebody?"

John again grimaced at Jenny's bluntness. He was getting used to it, but slowly.

"Whatever happened to morals in this country?" Paul questioned. "I know that my parents were very strict. I came from a very disciplined background. When my brother got hooked on drugs it almost destroyed my parents. We all worked to get him clean." He paused. "It didn't take. John knows what happened to that son of a bitch who sold him the drugs. I was straight with the organization people when they contacted me, and I know John read the full profile in my jacket."

"You killed him?" Al asked.

"I beat him to death with my fists," Paul said tightly. "And I'm glad I did. I would cheerfully hang every goddamn drug dealer in America. I would take great joy in fitting the noose around their necks and personally tripping the trap door."

A few minutes later, John hooked up with the interstate loop that would take them to the Bronx.

"Johnny Stomper," Al mused. "Anybody want to make a guess how he got his name?"

"I'm not sure I want to know," Jenny said.

"He's a bad one," John said. "He's fast and strong as an ox. And yes, he likes to stomp people."

"One thing about this new job of ours," Paul said. "We get to meet such delightful people."

Twenty-two

"I don't care who you are," the federal marshal told Charles Fordham. "You can't see Miss Morrow."

"We're engaged to be married!" Charles struggled to keep his voice at a normal level.

"Congratulations, son. But you still can't see her."

"This is ridiculous," Scott Baker said.

A very tired Ballard was standing a few yards away in the hospital corridor, listening to a special agent from the NYC office tell about the bodies found in the street in a bad neighborhood in Brooklyn. He held up a hand, silencing the young FBI agent, then walked over to Fordham and the reporter.

"She's sleeping right now, Mr. Fordham," Ballard explained. "I assure you she's all right. Just exhausted."

"If I could just look in at her," Charles pleaded.

Ballard hesitated for a few heartbeats, then nodded his head. "All right. You may open the door and look in. But that's all. Not a word, understand?"

"Yes, sir. Thank you."

Ballard put his hand on the reporter's chest. "Not you. You stay here." He waved Charles on through, and the federal marshal stationed in front of the door stepped to one side but kept a wary eye on Betsy's boyfriend.

"I would like to interview you," the journalist said to Ballard.

"Sorry," Ballard said. "But no. Any comments concerning the kidnapping or the tragedy that occurred at Grand Central

Terminal will have to come from the Special Agent in Charge of the New York City office."

"But you're the agent in charge of a special antiterrorist team out of the Washington, DC, office, aren't you? The two incidents are connected, aren't they?"

Ballard did not reply, just stared at the young journalist. If looks could kill . . .

"People are still dying from the attack at Grand Central," the journalist pressed. "What type of nerve gas was used, Inspector?"

"I have no comment at this time. Now if you will excuse me, I have work to do."

Ballard signaled the federal marshal at Betsy's door to end Fordham's brief visit, and the door was closed. Ballard walked away and slipped out an exit door to avoid the crush of reporters in the hospital lobby. Baker did not follow the FBI agent, choosing not to press his luck at that time.

Ballard and members of his team drove to the scene of the shooting in Brooklyn. Libby Carson was working with the NYPD's HAZMAT team at Grand Central. Other FBI and NYPD personnel were still working at the brownstone where Betsy had been held.

John and his team were slowly driving past the rundown building in a very bad section of the Bronx that served as the headquarters for the local skinhead group.

"I guess someone's in there," Jenny said. "The lights are still on."

"I was told Stomper lives there," John replied. "We'll circle the block."

"I sure as hell wouldn't want to leave a car unattended in this area," Paul remarked. "I've seen better looking neighborhoods in the slums of Tijuana."

"I haven't seen a cop," Al said.

"Nothing here for them to patrol," Jenny said. "A couple of

blocks of buildings scheduled to be torn down. I read in the paper that many sections of the Bronx were being restored."

"I always thought it was worse than this," Paul said. "Isn't this where Fort Apache was supposed to be?"

"Fort Apache?" John questioned.

"It was a movie about a police station. I thought it was in this borough. Maybe not. Car just turned the corner up ahead. Looked like he was in a hurry."

"I noticed that. And wondered about it."

"What are we looking for?" Bob radioed from the second car.

"Just checking things out," John told him. "When we do park, you stay a couple of car lengths behind us and stay in your car. Keep a lookout."

"Will do."

John completed his circling of the block and pulled in, parking about twenty-five feet from the front door of the slum building. Just as he was about to open his door, the night erupted in an enormous cacophony of sound and fury and flames. The front of the old building was blown all over the street . . . along with what looked to John to be the lower half of a human body. The concussion rocked the car and debris rained down, cracking the windshield in several places and denting the hood.

"Holy shit!" Jenny shouted.

"I agree wholeheartedly," Al said. "I think our Mr. Stomper is finished."

"Yes, and somebody finished him," John replied.

"Bob and Linda are signaling they're OK," Paul said.

"Let's get the hell out of here," John said. "We don't want to be here when the police arrive." He cranked the car and pulled out, making a U-turn. The street in front of what was left of the old building was blocked with debris. The second car pulled in behind them and they sped off.

It did not take the emergency vehicles long to respond, roaring by John and his team on the other side of the wide street.

"What now?" Jenny asked.

"Couple more names on the list. The first one is Marilyn Benson. Lives over in Queens."

"Back across the bridge," Jenny said. "We're sure seeing a lot of New York at night."

"We'll take a different route this time. Just for luck, among other reasons."

"Somebody is making sure about any loose lips," Al said.

"That's why I would like to get to this Benson woman tonight. She might not be alive in a few hours."

The team saw the flashing emergency lights before the apartment complex where Marilyn Benson lived came into view.

"Too late," John said. He thumped the steering wheel with the heel of his hand. "Dammit!"

"Maybe it's just a Peeping Tom call," Jenny said. "We can always hope."

"Right," John said. "But would you like to place a small wager on that?"

"No, I think I'll pass," Jenny said.

John took a chance and parked half a block away from the police cars, cut his lights and engine, and waited. Bob and Linda pulled in behind him.

"You have a ready answer for the cops when they haul us out of this car and ask what the hell we're doing here in the middle of the night?" Jenny asked.

"Have you taken a good look at that packet of cards you were given back at the training base?" John asked.

"Yes. What are we now?"

"Let's be bounty hunters," John said with a smile. "From the Successful Bail Bonding Company."

"Who are we after?" Paul asked.

"Pick a name."

"Melvin Fornortner?" Jenny suggested.

"Try again."

"Tony Scarpetti," Al said.

"That's good enough. From Los Angeles. He's a bad one. Bail jumping on a robbery charge. Tell Bob and Linda."

That done, Jenny asked, "Do we have papers on him?"

"We'll just have to bluff our way through that one, if we're asked."

"Looks like they're bringing out a body," Paul said. "Yeah. There it is."

"Somebody has been real busy tonight," Jenny said. "If that's Marilyn covered with the sheet."

"I'll walk up and listen," Al said. "OK, John?"

"Go ahead." He smiled. "We'll bail you out if they decide to lock you up."

"I'm touched by your caring." Al walked up to the knot of police and stood for a few minutes. One police officer turned and stared at Al for a moment, then said something to him. Al nodded and slowly walked away. He paused by the car just long enough to say, "No names. But it was a woman. I heard one officer say she was in her late twenties. Pick me up at the end of the block, around the corner." Al walked on.

The cop who had spoken to Al watched him for a moment longer, then turned away.

John pulled out, turned around in a driveway, and headed out toward the corner of the block, the second car right behind him. He paused just long enough for Al to get into the back-seat.

"It looked as though it was a messy killing," Al said, as John pulled away. "The cop didn't tell me. I saw the blood-stained sheet covering the body."

"She must have put up a struggle," Paul said. "One more on the list, John?"

"Yes. He's a real maybe. Some Nazi-worshipping nut who calls himself Adolph Hammerschmidt."

"You've got to be kidding!" Jenny said.

"No. He's got a small following. But growing. Lives out on Long Island."

"What's his real name?" Paul asked.

"Larry Morgan."

"Figures," Al said. "But I can't understand why all of a sudden anti-Semitism is on the upswing."

"It's pure undirected hate, Al," John answered. "All kinds of hate. It's all over America and growing daily. Once these anti-Jewish groups find someone who hates but really doesn't know why, they direct it. Jews traditionally support liberal causes. Millions of Americans dislike ultra-liberal causes and programs. But most, thank God, don't align themselves with Hitler-loving groups."

"But those who do align with groups who sling terms around like Zionist Occupied Government—ZOG—can be extremely violent," Al said.

"Exactly. And so is Larry Morgan, aka Adolph Hammerschmidt. He's reportedly killed several people. One thing I don't understand, Al: You would have made a fine field agent. How come the Bureau kept you poring over ledgers and dealing with white-collar crime for ten years?"

"It's what I wanted to do, and I enjoyed it for several years. But when I got tired of it and tried to get into a different section, the answer was always no."

"Well, you're sure in a different section now, ole buddy," Paul said. "Even though we haven't exactly been a ball of fire on our first assignment."

"Let's hope our next job will be slightly less complicated," Jenny said. She reached over and clicked on the radio, keeping the volume down until the news came on.

"In five days President Kelley will arrive in New York," the newscaster said. "His press secretary said at a press conference held today that the tragedy at Grand Central Terminal only heightened the president's determination to visit our city. President Kelley will not allow terrorists to dictate his travel plans. The president will—"

John clicked it off. "There it is, people. That's why all loose ends are being knotted up. That's the terrorist's next target."

"The president?" Jenny asked.

"Or the hotel where he's staying, or the hall where he's speaking. We've got our work cut out for us, people."

"And five days to get it done," Al added.

Twenty-three

A very sullen and scared Larry Morgan sat on the edge of his bed and stared at the men and women who had crowded into his bedroom and rousted him out of a deep sleep.

"You need to change your underwear, fellow," Jenny told him. "Don't you ever take a bath?"

"Screw you, bitch!" Larry muttered.

John stepped closer and slapped him hard with an open hand. The blow shocked the man and left the side of the neo-Nazi's face red.

"I'll sue you," Larry aka Adolph mumbled, rubbing his stinging face.

John slapped him again, twice, and that really got Adolph's attention. With a tiny trickle of blood leaking from one corner of his mouth, he said, "I ain't done nothin' to you people. I don't even know none of you. What the hell do you want?"

"Information, Larry," John told him.

"My name is Adolph," the neo-Nazi insisted.

"Your name can be crap-head as far as I'm concerned," John said. "But you'll tell me what you know about the PLF or you can make your peace with whatever God you worship."

"I ain't never heard of no PLF."

"You're a liar, Larry." John looked at Paul with a wink that Larry could not see and said, "Work on him, Paul."

Paul reached down with one big hand, grabbed Larry's T-shirt, and jerked him off the bed. With a seemingly effortless move, he slung the neo-Nazi across the room. Larry crashed against the wall and slid to the floor. On his ass, he shouted, "I'll kill you, you damn nigger bastard."

"That was the wrong thing to say, Larry," John told him, shaking his head.

"Goddamn Zulu!" Adolph/Larry yelled. "You keep this fuckin' bush ape away from me!"

Paul moved toward the man and Larry began kicking with his bare feet. Paul grabbed one of his ankles and began dragging the man across the floor. Larry was cussing and shouting all sorts of dire threats. He lost his undershorts as he was dragged around and around the room. His T-shirt was in rags, having been nearly torn from him when Paul jerked him off the bed. Larry started yelping as his bare ass began picking up splinters from the wooden floor.

"You'd better talk to me, Larry," John said.

"I ain't got nothin' to say to none of you assholes!" Larry shouted. He once more began kicking with his bare feet. "Get away from me, you goddamn gorilla!" he shouted at Paul.

Jenny reached into her purse and came out with a disposable cigarette lighter. "Hold him down and let me barbecue his pecker with this," she said, flicking her Bic a couple of times. The flame danced from the lighter. "I bet I can get him singing like a bird."

"You keep that crazy bitch away from me!" Larry yelled. "Goddamn you all!"

"That's a good idea," John said. "Hold him down, boys. And put a gag on him. This is going to be painful. I don't want the screaming to wake any neighbors."

Adolph/Larry's home was located near the end of a road on the outskirts of a small town. The chance of anyone hearing any screaming was remote, but John's words were having a very dramatic effect on the neo-Nazi. Adolph/Larry was turning pale and beginning to tremble.

"Somebody get me some tweezers so I can find his dick," Jenny said.

Larry really started hollering and cussing at that. "You crazy whore!" he shouted.

"And something to catch the blood when it starts squirting," Jenny added. "This is going to get messy."

"Won't the flames seal the wound?" Linda asked.

"Yeah," Jenny said. "But I'm going to have to cut off any badly burned part and cauterize it. And if I do it wrong, he won't be able to pee. Then I'll have to cut off some more. That's when the blood will really start squirting."

Larry was listening wide-eyed and open-mouthed to all this. "Oh, shit!" Larry shouted. "Now, you just wait a damn minute here."

"Why should we?" Jenny asked, flicking her Bic.

Larry's eyes were on the tiny flame. He groaned in fear. "Well, maybe I have heard about this PLF thing."

"Hold it," John said. He looked down at the naked and very frightened neo-Nazi. "Then you'd better start telling me all you know."

"Who are you people?"

"Talk to me, Larry."

Al had turned on a small tape recorder.

"I guess I better do that. Them people ain't never done nothin' for me."

"Now you're being smart," John told him.

"Can I have my pants, please? It's embarrassin' bein' nekkid an' all in front of these women."

John found a pair of khaki pants and a shirt on a chair and handed them to the neo-Nazi. He waited until the man was dressed before saying, "Take it from the top, Larry."

"Huh?"

"From the beginning."

"Oh. Right. Well . . ."

It took a good hour to get all the information out of the neo-Nazi. John had to back him up and start him all over again several times. Just as Larry/Adolph was getting started on his first telling, Paul went into the kitchen to make some coffee and was appalled at the mound of dirty dishes piled in the sink and large roaches scurrying for cover all over the place when the lights were clicked on. Paul also found signs of mice droppings in various places in the kitchen.

"Good God!" he muttered.

He found the coffeemaker and rinsed it out with hot water then filled it up with cold tap water, found the coffee, and fixed a pot. Then he had to wash out all the coffee cups he could find. He looked around through all the mess in the cupboard and spotted the sugar. Larry at least had enough sense to keep the sugar in a jar with a lid on it. He opened the refrigerator and found an unopened container of milk. He checked the date, then carefully smelled the contents. Still good.

Linda wandered into the kitchen, stopped cold in her tracks in the doorway, and said, "Oh, my God! What a filthy mess."

"You should have seen the roaches," Paul said.

"I wish you hadn't told me that. I *hate* roaches!"

"I rinsed out the coffeepot and the cups," Paul assured her.

"You don't mind if I do it again?"

Paul smiled. "Not a bit. Watch out for the mice crap by the sink."

"Oh, God!"

"It's better than finding rat crap."

"I suppose."

The coffee cups rinsed once more, Paul and Linda filled them with fresh brewed coffee, found a big platter that would serve as a tray, put the sugar and a small glass of milk on it (after carefully rinsing out the glass, which had once held grape jelly), and took everything into the bedroom. Linda was glad to get out of the messy kitchen. In the bedroom, she took pity on the bedraggled and still very frightened neo-Nazi and asked, "You want a cup of coffee, Larry?"

"That's very kind of you. Yes, I sure would appreciate it, ma'am."

"Let's go over it again, Larry," John said, after the man had fixed his coffee. "From the top, and take it slow."

When Larry hesitated, Jenny smiled at him and flicked her Bic. That got him going quickly.

It was four o'clock in the morning and three pots of coffee later before John was certain Larry/Adolph had told them everything he knew. Al clicked off the recorder.

"What the hell difference does it make?" Larry tossed out the question. "President Kelley ain't nothin' but a damn commonist, anyway. The country would be better off without him."

"Commonist?" Linda asked.

"Communist," John said.

"Oh. Kelley? He's a good man."

"The hell he is. He loves niggers and Jews and queers," Larry said.

Paul sighed.

The team had been taking turns standing watch on the small front porch. Jenny opened the front door and called, "I think we've got company, gang. Two cars of them."

"Now you know why I wanted your story on tape, Larry," John said.

"Huh? They ain't gonna kill me. I'm one of their most loyal members."

"Sure, you are, Larry," John said. "So were Johnny Stomper and Marilyn Benson. And I'll make you a bet Josh Parnell won't live another twenty-four hours."

"Marilyn wasn't nothin', nohow. I never did like that uppity bitch."

"I bet she wasn't real thrilled with you either, Larry," Al said.

"Huh? Who cares? I asked her to gimme some one night, and she laughed in my face. I should have stomped her fuckin' head in right then and there's what I should have done."

"You're a real twenty-first century man, aren't you, Larry?" Linda asked.

"I get by," Larry/Adolph said just as John cut the lights in the bedroom.

"How many, Jenny?"

"Three or four to a car."

"Sure it's not the Bureau or ATF or the state police?"

"Not unless they've started driving Lincolns and Cadillacs."

"Bob, you and Linda take Larry and the tapes and get gone from here," John said. "If we don't link up again, take Larry to Ballard."

"And what story do we tell him as to why we have Mr. Adolph?"

"Make up something. Hell, I don't care. He'll know you're lying, anyway. What's important is to confirm the PLF's plans to attack the president during his visit to the city."

"That's right," Larry said. "It was a crazy plan from the git-go. Get me outta here. If that's the PLF out there they come to kill me."

"Go!" John said.

Linda, Bob, and Larry went out the back door. John, Jenny, Al, and Paul made ready to hold off the PLF, giving the second team time to get clear of the house.

"This group sure is in bed with some strange people," Paul remarked.

"And not at all hesitant in getting rid of them," John replied.

"Our bunch made it to the car," Al called from the back of the house. "They're ready to go."

"It's going to get wild here in a minute," Jenny said. She smiled as she felt the weight of a Fire-Frag grenade in the right hand pocket of her hip-length leather jacket.

"At the first hostile move from our visitors," John told her, "you toss that grenade."

"You got it, boss."

"They're still in their cars," Paul said. "Wait! The interior light from the lead car just came on. Four people in that car. They're getting out. Looks like three men, one woman. They're all armed with what look like machine pistols. Mini-Uzis, I think. They have sound suppressors on them."

"It's going to be a relatively silent fight," John said. "Unless you toss that grenade, Jenny." John paused for a heartbeat. "Jenny?"

"Right here."

"Use that grenade to cripple one of their vehicles. That'll give us a better-than-even chance of getting out of here. But don't toss it until we're ready to bug out. Understood?"

"That's a great big ten-four, boss," Jenny replied lightly.

John smiled at that response as he stood in the darkness of the frame house.

"Here they come," Paul said. "Four circling to the rear of the house. The others getting out of the second car. Four of them. All armed. Two men, two women, it looks like."

"Paul, get to the rear and help Al," John ordered. "You and me in the front, Jenny."

"We can handle it," Jenny said.

"I'm sure," John replied with a smile.

"Adolph?" the call came from the front yard. "You and your friends stand easy. We need to talk."

"I don't believe they know about our people in the rear," Jenny whispered.

"Yeah? The same way you talked to Johnny and Marilyn?" John called.

"That isn't Larry," a woman's voice drifted out of the darkness.

"Who are you?" a man called. "Will you identify yourself, please?"

"Polite fucker, isn't he?" Jenny whispered.

"I swear I'm going to wash your mouth out with soap," John returned the whisper. "That's a European accent. We're friends of Larry," John raised his voice. "We're here to see that he stays alive. Why are you armed?"

"Only as a precaution," the man called. "Are you also armed?"

"Of course," John said. "But only as a precaution," he added, only slightly sarcastically.

"Step out on the porch," a different voice called. "We're your friends, Adolph."

"I think you'd better leave," John said. "Just get out and leave us alone."

"Send Larry out."

"Get ready," John whispered to Jenny. "Here it comes."

"Send Larry out or we're coming in to get him!" The voice had changed, and was now harsh and demanding.

"I have a better idea," Jenny called. "Why don't you go somewhere, drop your pants, bend over, and have someone pound sand up your ass!"

There was a long silent pause, then the voice yelled "Go!" out of the night. "Take the house. Go, go!"

"Fire!" John yelled, and automatic gunfire opened up from all sides of the house.

Two of the PLF members went down in the front yard, cut down by 9mm fire. They tumbled to the ground and did not move.

"Toss it, Jenny!" John shouted.

A few seconds later the grenade exploded near the second car, blowing off the front tire, shattering the windows, and pocking the metal with shrapnel.

Al gunned the car and tore out of the side yard with Linda and Larry in the back seat. The car jumped a ditch, and fishtailed when it hit the pavement. Al straightened it out and went roaring up the deserted street.

"Cripple their second car!" John called.

He and Jenny each poured a full magazine into the tires and the sides of the second car parked almost directly in front of the small house. The punctured rubber caused the car to sag to the left with an audible thudding sound, and a small fire was started under the hood as the 9mm rounds blew through metal and severed the automobile's fuel lines. The radiator was hit and punctured and steam began hissing out the front, mixing with the smoke from the fire.

A couple of the PLF members had either been hit by shrapnel or the concussion of the exploding grenade had slammed them hard to the ground. One was not moving at all, and the other one was trying to get to his or her knees when John swung his weapon and burned a few rounds in that direction. The PLF follower slumped to the cool ground and kissed the earth for the last living time.

"Let's get out of here," John called. "Go, people, go!"

"What about you, John?" Jenny called.

"I'll make it. You people get the hell gone. Now move, dammit!"

"Screw that," Paul said. "We all go, John. Now come on, man. Get the lead out."

"I gave you all an order!" John yelled. "Now goddamn it, obey it! Move."

Jenny pulled away from her window. "Let's go, folks. The boss gave an order. Move!"

John had noticed where the keys to Larry/Adolph's pickup truck were. As soon as the others had cleared the back porch and were in the car, John burned another clip into the night and ran into the bedroom, grabbing up the keys from the dresser.

He ran out the back door and knocked a man spinning off the porch. John kicked the man in the head and made it to the pickup.

It wouldn't start. John tried again and again. Finally the engine caught and John dropped the pickup into gear and headed for the street. He turned right at the first street to avoid the emergency vehicles that were screaming up the road, lights flashing and sirens blaring, only a block away.

He made it to the highway and settled back for the drive into the city. The wind whistled through the several bullet holes in the front and rear glass of the truck. John clicked on the radio and found a station that was playing music that he could at least tolerate, if not really enjoy. He smiled as the thought entered his mind that Ballard was going to be very unhappy with him.

Twenty-four

John caught a few hours' sleep while the others took turns guarding Larry/Adolph. After a cup of strong coffee helped him shake the sleep from his brain, John placed a call to the local office of the FBI and asked to be patched through to Inspector Ballard. It took some doing, but he finally got through.

"Barrone," Ballard said, "I am really becoming very weary of you. I—"

"Be quiet and listen, Ballard. I want you to meet me at the Cloisters in a hour. I have a defector from the PLF, and he has some very interesting information for you. He has had no part in any of the attacks here in Manhattan or the kidnapping of the Morrow girl. He wants immunity from prosecution in exchange for his cooperation."

"Are you serious, Barrone?"

"Believe it."

"I can't promise anything. You know that."

"But I want your word that you'll try."

"You'd take my word?"

"You're an insufferable prick, Ballard, but you're an honorable prick. Yes, I'll take your word."

Ballard paused for a few seconds, then said, "I give you my word I'll try, Barrone."

"That's good enough for me."

"Did you have anything to do with all the shooting last night, Barrone?"

"What shooting?"

"You're a terrible liar."

"One hour."

"Where at the Cloisters?"

"Just outside the entrance, southern end."

"I'll be there. But I won't be alone."

"Neither will I," John told him, then hung up. He turned to his team. "Let's go."

"I don't want to go to prison," Larry said.

"I don't think you will," John told him. "But you're going to have to level with the Bureau."

"I don't like them damn people."

"That's all right, Larry."

"Huh?"

"They don't like you, either."

Ballard had several of his people lead Larry away and he listened to a few minutes of one of the tapes John gave him. "The president of the United States, Barrone? The PLF is going to try to kill the president? You really believe that?"

"Yes, I do. They're all suicidal. They'll die for their so-called 'cause' in a heartbeat."

"Why would they trust their plans to a loser like Larry Morgan?"

"They didn't. Further on in the tape he'll tell how he got that information. It's very interesting. Larry is a sneaky bastard, but he's not stupid. Although he certainly gives that impression."

"Who are you working for, Barrone?"

"A bail bonding company. We're here looking for a bail jumper."

"Crap!"

"Check it out."

"Oh, I have no doubt that it's probably legitimate, Barrone. But it's still crap. I have a hunch you and your team are nothing more than high-priced vigilantes."

"And you're going to do what about it?"

Ballard looked at the tapes Barrone had given him. "For the time being, nothing. But don't get in my way and screw up this investigation."

"I have no intention of doing that."

"I suppose it finally had to happen," Ballard said, looking off into the distance.

"What?"

"It's been rumored for some time now, several years at least."

"What are you talking about?"

Ballard met Barrone's eyes. "A top-gun group of people who hunt down and destroy criminals. Funded by a group of some of the world's wealthiest people. We maintain a file on all the rumors." He shook his head and frowned. "It's named Death Wish. I don't know who came up with that. But it certainly fits, don't you agree?"

"I have no idea what you're talking about, Ballard."

Ballard smiled very knowingly. "Of course you don't. So allow me to bring you up to date. That is, if you're interested."

"Go right ahead. It's a pleasant enough day, considering the season. And we're both dressed warmly against the chill."

"We first got wind of the group about five years ago. A number of companies, worldwide, began reporting small losses. Nothing significant; a million here, a million there. But it puzzled the IRS. You know how inquisitive those people can be."

"Don't get me started on the tactics of the IRS, Ballard."

"Yes. Your file is quite clear on that point. You are under the impression that the people's hatred of the IRS will be one of the primary reasons for the second civil war in this nation."

"That's correct."

"And you still believe that?"

"I do. That and any draconian type of gun control."

"I agree with you. This nation is heading for a world of trouble." Ballard again looked at the tapes John had given him. "But right now we have something else to worry about."

"Yes. President Kelley's plans to visit this city."

"He won't change his mind."

"Then we have four and a half days to find the PLF and put them out of business."

"We? So you admit you are working on this PLF matter?"

"Of course not, Ballard. I'm speaking strictly as a concerned citizen. But my people will help, you can count on that. If you need us, just call on us."

"That's very civic-minded of you."

"Thank you. May I ask a question?"

"Ask."

"News reports say one member of the PLF was taken from that brownstone alive after Miss Morrow escaped. Has that person given up any information?"

"You know I'm not at liberty to comment on that."

"All right. How is Miss Morrow?"

"She's doing well."

"She was not seriously hurt?"

"No."

"The attack at Grand Central Terminal?"

"What about it?"

"How many dead?"

"I can't comment on that, either."

"What type of gas was used?"

"No comment."

"How can we work together if you won't share information with me?"

"We're not working together, Barrone. Put that thought out of your mind."

John laughed softly in the late fall air which was rapidly turning colder. "Very well, Ballard. However, if I discover anything that might help you, I'll get it to you."

"After you and your, ah, team—for want of a better word—check it out, of course."

"Oh, if we have time, Ballard. We're here chasing a bail jumper."

"How could I forget that?"

"I hope the tapes will be of some help."

"They will certainly be closely reviewed."

"See you, Ballard."

"Oh, I'm quite sure of that," the FBI agent replied very, very drily.

John turned to leave. Ballard's voice stopped him. "Yes?" John asked.

"Now, about that wild shoot-out on Long Island last night—early this morning, actually. You wouldn't by any stretch of the imagination know anything about that, would you?"

"Sorry, no. First I've heard of it."

"I thought that would be your answer. The house was rented by your Larry Morgan."

"Really? How odd. Was anyone hurt?"

Ballard smiled. "I'm not at liberty to divulge that information."

"I certainly understand, Ballard."

"Larry Morgan just looked you up last night and volunteered all the information on these tapes?"

"Actually, no, he didn't. We found him."

"Of course, you did. How about that bombing over in the Bronx?"

"Bombing? Heavens no, Ballard."

"I see. Well, then, how about a shoot-out in Brooklyn?"

Barrone shook his head. "I haven't heard anything about that either. But my goodness, it certainly was a violent night, wasn't it?"

"I have to say that you're quite an accomplished liar, Barrone."

John smiled. "You think I had anything to do with any of those incidents you mentioned? Prove it."

"When this New York problem is resolved, I'm coming after you and your people. And I'm going to put you out of business."

"Thanks for the warning."

"Good day, Mr. Barrone."

"Good day to you, Mr. Ballard."

John watched Ballard walk away and thought: What an asshole!

Twenty-five

After the late-night shoot-out on Long Island, John's friends and acquaintances on the NYPD and in the New York underworld could dig up nothing on the PLF's whereabouts. It was as if the PLF had dropped off the face of the earth. He still had friends in the CIA's dark office in New York City, but did not call them. He did not want to get them into trouble with DC.

"The PLF is making their final plans," John told his team with only two and a half days left before the president's visit. "They'll be pulling out all the stops on this one."

"John," Jenny said, "you know the Secret Service and the Bureau will have every available agent surrounding the president on this visit. Also every New York City cop and New York State cop they can pull in. How in the hell does the PLF figure they can get to the president?"

"Maybe with a rocket along the way," John told her and the rest of his team. "The president is vulnerable in a lot of ways to people who don't care if they survive the assault. And the PLF members don't care. As long as they can strike a blow for their damn cause, whatever the hell it is."

"But you think the hotel is where they'll try?" Linda asked.

"I think they'll try something there," John replied. "*What* is anybody's guess."

"I guess we'll find out in about forty-eight or so hours,"

Bob said. "But you know damn well we won't be able to get inside that hotel."

"Or maybe anywhere near it," Al added.

"Oh, we can get close to the hotel," John said. "If that's what we decide to do."

"I presume you have some other plan?" Paul asked.

"Yeah, John," Jenny said. "Maybe you would like to let us in on it?"

"Actually, I don't have a plan," John admitted. "But think about it: what good could we possibly be inside that hotel? There're going to be several hundred agents from all over the world prowling those expensive halls. We're not guests, and there is no way we can register as such. The hotel is booked solid, and has been for months."

"And? So?" Paul questioned.

"So we'd better put our heads together and come up with something," John told them. "For I am fresh out of ideas."

"Are you going to see your kids while we're in the city, John?" Jenny asked.

John was standing by the window of the safe house when Jenny tossed the question at him. He turned and looked out at the street for a moment before replying, his back to the team. "No," he finally said. "My kids and I don't really get along."

Jenny got up and walked over to him, putting a hand on his arm. "Are they going to see the president while he's in town?"

"I doubt it. This affair is a thousand dollars a plate. They might go down just to see him enter the hotel. I really don't know."

"I was under the impression they were big supporters of President Kelley."

"They are. At least I think they are. We don't discuss, or we didn't discuss, politics the last time I saw them."

"When was that, John?" Linda asked.

John smiled sadly. "Six months ago."

"Your idea or theirs?" Paul asked.

"Theirs," John said without hesitation. "They never liked the idea of my working for the Company. Not since they were teenagers and became interested in politics."

"What the hell do they know about the Company?" Bob asked.

"Nothing, really," John replied. "Except what they read in the newspapers."

"Which amounts to a big zero," Jenny said.

"Yes," John agreed. "For the most part." He sighed. "Well, this isn't getting us anywhere, people. My kids are all grown up and on their own. Let's get back to why we're here. So far we've spent a lot of the organization's money and haven't accomplished very much."

"Except get rid of a number of PLF supporters," Paul said. "That's something."

"Groups like the PLF are never short of volunteers," John replied just before he headed into the kitchen for a cup of coffee.

"Millions of people in these five boroughs," Linda said. "And we're looking for maybe twenty, twenty-five people. Talk about your needle in the haystack."

"What if President Kelley isn't the real target?" John asked. "What if it's the crowds that will be around the hotel, hoping to get a glimpse of the president, or what if it's a popular night spot in the city? Or maybe some sort of a church event, a social, or something along those lines?"

"But Larry told us it was the president," Paul said.

"Why would the leadership of the PLF tell a minor player like Larry anything?" John came right back.

"Unless it was deliberately planted false information," Al said.

"Yes," John agreed. "Let's kick that around and see what we come up with."

"But they went to Larry's house to kill him," Linda pointed out. "And they did kill Johnny Stomper and the Benson woman."

"And Parnell has disappeared," Bob pointed out.

"The PLF is tying up loose ends," John said. "That's all. They may try to pull something at the hotel, but I'm going to bet the president isn't their primary target."

"So the hotel will be only a diversionary target?" Jenny asked.

"Maybe," John said. "Let's talk about it."

"What else do we have to kick around?" Paul asked. Then he answered his own question: "Nothing."

John pointed at Linda. "Get some sort of city guide that outlines events scheduled for this week. And pick up a couple of newspapers. Bob, you go with her."

"We're gone." They grabbed their coats and were out the door.

"We can find the local access channel on TV," Jenny said. "Or whatever they call it up here. We might get lucky and pick up something there."

"Good idea."

"The Empire State Building is always a tourist attraction," Al said. "Maybe there?"

John shook his head. "Heavily guarded. Besides, the wind is fairly strong on the observation deck. Gas would be ineffective there. Good thought, though."

When Bob and Linda returned, each with an armload of newspapers and weekly events guides, the team spent the next several hours poring over them . . . and came up with dozens of events and weekly and monthly meetings and gatherings.

John finally tossed his guide to the floor and leaned back in his chair. "Damn," he said. "Take your pick."

"Pages of them," said Paul.

"And not one of those events will be guarded," Bob said. "It's hopeless."

"Same with the TV," Jenny said, getting up and turning it off. "More meetings than I could keep up with. The PLF could strike at any of them."

After a moment of silence, Al spoke for the entire team when he asked, "Now what?"

"We do the only thing we can do," John replied. "We keep our eyes open and wait for the PLF to make the next move."

"I bet Ballard is so frustrated he's about to lose his religion," Jenny said. "This is one time, the first time, actually, that I really feel sorry for him." She paused and added, "And for the people of this city."

"What about that member of the PLF who was taken alive after Betsy escaped?" Paul asked. "The one with the cracked ribs and busted-up insides. That Winifried something or another. Has she said anything?"

John shrugged his shoulders. "I don't know. Control can't find out. They've hit a stone wall there. But I doubt if she has. She's hard-core PLF, for years. Any information she has will go to the grave with her."

The doorbell ringing startled them all. "What the hell?" John muttered.

"I'll get it," Jenny said.

"I'll back you," Al said, standing up and pulling his autoloader from a shoulder holster.

Jenny was back in half a minute, shaking her head. "You're not going to believe this, John."

John looked up as Kemper from the CIA, Jacques LaBlanc from the DGSE, and Henry Thompkins from MI6 were escorted into the room. Al was right behind the trio, a puzzled look on his face.

John chuckled. "Well, well, boys. Small world, isn't it?"

The three spooks shook hands with John. LaBlanc smiled and said, "Henry and I agreed to stop disliking one another until this operation is over . . . but it definitely is quite an effort on our part."

The Brit smiled, but it was strained.

"What's up, Kemp?" John asked.

"Cooperation between us, John. If you feel like it."

"Ballard isn't included in this?"

"We didn't approach him with the suggestion," Henry said. "Ballard is a good solid man, but he does tend to play his cards rather close to the vest."

"And right by the rule book," Jacques added. "The three of us don't object to bending a few rules occasionally." Jacques' command of English was nearly flawless, with only a slight hint of an accent.

"Sit down," John said. "Let's lay it all out on the table and see what we've got."

A small army of federal agents had gathered in New York City: FBI, Secret Service, ATF, federal marshals, members of an elite unit from the State Department, and dozens of other men and women in civilian clothing who looked, acted, and carried themselves like military personnel.

They had but two jobs: (1) protect the president of the United States and his wife and (2) find and either arrest or destroy the PLF—in the minds of many of the feds gathered: preferably the latter.

But Ballard nixed that first off. "We will, of course, return any hostile fire. That goes without saying. But regardless of how horrendous these acts of terrorism are, we will not—repeat, *not*—violate the very laws we are here to enforce. I want that understood. We have two days to find the PLF. Let's do it."

Actually they had slightly less time than that.

Miles away, in New Jersey, André sat in a comfortable chair in the apartment and smiled in satisfaction . . . occasionally he softly laughed out loud. Everything was working out perfectly. Finally, it was down to hours. The PLF would show the people of America, and especially the people of New York City, just how vulnerable they really were.

André had no interest in attacking the president of the United States. The man was too well-guarded. Besides, getting rid of the president would mean only that the number-two man, the vice president, would step into the Oval Office. Nothing gained there. No big deal. That would accomplish nothing. But killing hundreds of people, showing the stupid slaves of big business how unprotected they were, how uncaring their masters in the corporate towers were . . . that was something.

The attack on Grand Central Terminal was a mere appetizer . . . the main course was yet to come.

André smiled.

"So you're convinced the president is not the target?" Kemper asked.

"It would have to be a suicide attack," John replied. "My God, there are hundreds of federal agents in the city. The PLF wouldn't stand a chance."

"But you'll admit they are, quite probably, suicidal?" Jacques asked.

"Yes," John admitted. "To a degree. But think about this: they ran after the attack on Grand Central fizzled. They could have killed hundreds more, but they didn't. Does that mean Grand Central wasn't their primary target?"

"Several schools of thought on that, old boy," Henry Thompkins said.

"And one of them brings us back to President Kelley," Kemper said.

"Or something bigger," John countered. "Something grander, grander in the minds of the terrorists, that is."

"The president is due to arrive Friday afternoon," Thompkins said. "He will speak Friday night . . . God willing," he added.

"I personally believe the terrorists will strike before then," John said. "Maybe during the day on Friday."

"Where?" Jacques asked.

John looked at him. "Somewhere in the city. Other than that, I have absolutely no idea."

"Assuming you're correct," Kemper said. "That brings it down to a matter of hours."

"Yes."

"What's the weather forecast for the next couple of days?" Thompkins asked.

"Cloudy and cool, with a brisk wind and forty percent chance of rain possibly mixed with sleet," Jenny said.

"That certainly lets out the use of gas anywhere outside," Jacques said.

"Yes," John said. "But I also do not believe they will use gas again."

"Oh?" Kemper questioned. "But the Agency was sure, as I'm sure were your people, whoever they might be, that chemicals were to be the primary weapon."

"They might still be," John replied. "But I'm not so sure."

"I might ask you to explain that," Kemper said. "But who can explain a hunch?"

"Thank you," John told him.

"I tend to agree with John," Thompkins said. "Gas is too smooth. Terrorists like lots of blood and gore. Frankly, the use of gas surprised me."

"André likes plenty of gore," Jacques said. "The more pain and suffering the better. And I will admit I gave him a taste of his own medicine once when I had him in custody." He smiled ruefully. "It cost me my job with the DST, but it was worth it after what that bastard did."

"What did he do, Jacques?" John asked. "I never got the straight of it."

"Killed half a dozen young schoolgirls. One of them was my daughter."

"How did he kill them?"

"Fire. They burned to death in a locked section of a school dormitory. André locked them in. It was a horrible way to die. My daughter's name was Angelique."

"I am sorry, Jacques."

The Frenchman's eyes were haunted with old memories. He

sighed and shook them away. "A dozen other girls still carry dreadful scars of that night. And they will carry them all their lives. I heard from a former member of the PLF that André used to tell the story and laugh about that awful night. Yes, I do have a personal score to settle with André."

"I would imagine so," John said. His thoughts were suddenly of his own kids; perhaps he'd better call them. Yes, he'd do that.

"You're far away, John," Kemper said. "We lost you for a moment."

"Yes, you did. I was thinking of my two kids. They're here in the city. As are Bob's."

"Did you call them about the, ah, impending crisis?"

"No."

"I would, old boy," Henry said.

"And tell them what?" John asked. "To get out of the city? They'd know immediately that I knew something was up and they'd tell their friends, and on down the line it would go. My son is in advertising; he's sure to have friends in broadcasting. Within hours Manhattan would be in a state of panic. I'm going to call them, probably today, but not about the terrorists. Just to say hello."

"Bob?" Henry called, glancing over at Garrett.

"I'm going to call my kids. But like John, just to say hello."

"I would be sorely tempted to let the cat out of the bag," Henry said.

"It's a big bag, Henry," John reminded him. "And there aren't that many members of the PLF in the city."

"How do you know?" Jacques countered. "How do you know André hasn't picked New York City to be his grand finale? It's certainly possible." He frowned. "Believe me, with André, nothing should be discounted or taken for granted."

"Yes," Henry agreed. "You know of course, John, that André is insane."

"Yes. I know."

"What's the matter?" Jenny questioned, her voice filled with undisguised sarcasm. "Have the shrinks found that his daddy spanked him or his mommy refused to bake him sugar cookies, or he had a hard-on and didn't know what to do with it?"

John sighed at Jenny's remarks and looked heavenward for a few seconds.

The Brit and the Frenchman laughed at both John's expression and Jenny's remarks. Jacques said, "The psychiatrists can find many excuses for criminal behavior, Miss Barnes. It is my opinion that they have to justify their existence, however outlandish their conclusions."

"We all agree on that," Kemper said, holding up a hand. "Wholeheartedly. But it isn't helping to solve the immediate problem."

John looked at his former Agency colleague for a moment before suddenly rising from his chair and walking to the window overlooking the street below. "Maybe it is, Kemp. Or at least giving up a clue."

"What do you mean?" Henry asked.

"What's the one thing André hates more than anything else?"

"He's an anarchist," Henry said. "He hates government. All forms of government."

"Wealth," Kemper said. "He believes in worldwide wealth redistribution."

"Authority," Jacques said. "He hates all forms of authority."

"Yes," John said. "And in this city, where can the epitome of all that be found?"

"Wall Street?" Paul said.

"No," John said, shaking his head. "The United Nations."

Twenty-six

"The others don't buy it," Ballard said. "They are all convinced President Kelley is the target."

"To tell the truth, I am very surprised to see you, Ballard," John told the man. They were meeting in midtown Manhattan, in the middle of a block. The wind had picked up and contained a cold splattering of rain.

"Let's find a café," Ballard suggested. "It's turning colder out here."

In a fast-food place across the street, they took a booth and ordered coffee.

"I've gone over and over the file on André," Ballard said. "He has laid down false trails and leads several times in the past, then done the totally unexpected."

"Yes. I have the same file," John admitted.

Ballard paused in the lifting of coffee cup to mouth and stared at John. "Do you now?"

"Yes."

"How interesting." Ballard took a sip of coffee and set the cup on the table. "Well . . . how you got the file is unimportant at the moment. And I stress 'at the moment.' "

John smiled. "Never going to give up on that, are you, Ballard?"

"Not as long as I'm a working agent."

"You thinking of retiring?"

Ballard laughed softly. "Tell you the truth, the Bureau didn't know what to do with me anymore. So they made me an inspector and thought, hoped, I would just fade away. I'm sort of like that old naval rank between Captain and Admiral: Commodore. I've broken too many important cases and been decorated, so to speak, too many times for them to force me into retirement. As long as I pull my weight, I'll be around until mandatory retirement age."

"No family?"

Ballard shook his head. "Not anymore. Wife and I divorced years ago, the kids are all grown. The Bureau is my family. I've studied your file carefully since you got involved in this case. You know that feeling, Barrone."

"All too well."

"Yes. Well. Enough of this maudlin talk. Back to business. We've got a couple of problems with this United Nations theory of yours."

"Name them."

"One: suppose I could assign people to the UN. At the first sign of heavier-than-usual security, André would back off and strike somewhere else. Maybe a hospital or some children's day care center. Two: I don't have the authority to pull people off the assignment I was handed. There it is. Now what?"

"My people handle it."

"I'll pretend I didn't hear that . . . for the time being. I can't allow some high-priced vigilante group to start a war in the United Nations complex."

"It isn't going to be inside the UN complex, Ballard. Not much of it, anyway. None of it, if we do this right."

"Oh?"

"I thought at first that might be it. But I changed my mind. I think André will be going after the tourists visiting the UN. Many of them will be arriving in tour buses."

"Damn!" Ballard breathed, looking down at his coffee cup. "Yes. You're right about that." He nodded his head. "That would be perfect for André. He's pulled this type of barbaric action in the past."

"Yes."

"All right. I agree with you. I'll see what I can do. But I can't promise anything."

"I know."

Ballard sipped his coffee in silence for a moment. He lifted his eyes to meet John's gaze. "What do your kids know about this . . . mess?"

"Only what they read in the papers and hear on television."

Ballard blinked a couple of times at that. "You didn't advise them to leave the city?"

"I haven't talked with them. I tried to call them today, about an hour ago, just to say hello. I got an answering machine at both numbers. Where are your kids?"

"The girl's here in the city."

"You haven't told her to get out?"

"No. We, ah, haven't talked in several years."

"Bob Garrett's kids are here."

"I know."

The men sat for several minutes without speaking. John finally said, "Now what, Ballard?"

"I wish you good luck, Barrone. But I can't help you. I really wish I could."

"You could detain me. You have the power to do that after all I've told you."

"I know."

"But you're not going to?"

"How? This conversation never took place. Right now I'm resting for a few hours, and my people have orders not to disturb me unless it's an emergency."

"I hope you enjoyed your rest. I know you've been working long hours."

"Yes. One more thing . . ."

"Of course."

"Will you please try to do something about Miss Barnes's vulgar mouth? She's really a good person, but her language is very offensive."

John smiled. "I'll try, but I certainly can't guarantee anything."

"I realize that. I tried for several years."

"Anything else?"

"No. Good-bye, Barrone. Good luck." Ballard rose and walked out the door without looking back.

Strange man, John thought.

He looked at the patrons in the crowded fast-food place, knowing that any one of them could be a member of André's terrorist group, just waiting for the right moment to toss a grenade.

John walked out into the cold night and stood for a moment. Ballard had hailed a cab and was gone. Jenny appeared at his side, stepping out of a store entrance.

"Did anyone buy our theory?" she asked.

"Ballard did. But he couldn't convince anyone else."

"So he can't help us?"

"No."

"That leaves LaBlanc, Thompkins, and Kemper."

"Yes. Kemper might be under orders to stand clear. I don't know for sure."

"The others?"

"LaBlanc has two people with him. Thompkins has one: a Miss Camilla Farnsworth."

"She sounds positively delightful."

"I'm sure."

"Did Ballard say anything else?"

"He asked me to try to do something about your vulgar mouth."

"Screw him."

John sighed in the cold night air. "Ballard is really not a bad person, Jenny."

"I know. He's just an asshole." Before John could respond to that, Jenny asked, "Is President Kelley planning to address the UN?"

"No. This is a fund-raising trip."

"Now what?"

"We check out the UN complex and pick our spots."

"I did some reading on the place. It covers eighteen acres. It has a lovely rose garden. First tour starts about nine in the morning."

"Something tells me the roses won't be in bloom in this weather."

"But if we don't do something, and do it right the first time, there'll be plenty of red on the ground."

"Yes, of the innocent kind."

Jenny looked at her watch. "We've got about forty hours, John."

"We'll spend it looking the place over and picking our spots. There's no point trying to locate André and his pack of loonies. Let's get back to the house."

John had just hung up his topcoat when Paul handed him a sheet of paper. "I just printed this out, John. It's grim from start to finish. Looks like the PLF is pulling out all the stops on this one."

"I'll get you a cup of coffee, John," Bob said. "Or perhaps something stronger."

"A vodka martini, please. On the rocks."

John sat down and read: LATEST REPORTS INDICATE LARGE NUMBERS OF ENGLISH-SPEAKING PLF MEMBERS LEFT TRAINING BASES IN MIDDLE EAST SEVERAL WEEKS AGO. DESTINATION: NEW YORK CITY.

"It's going to be a bad one, folks," John said, handing the message to Jenny.

She read it quickly and said, just as John was tasting his martini, "Well, fuck me hard!"

John choked on his drink and went into a spasm of coughing. "Good Lord, Jenny!" he managed to gasp.

After the laughter from the others quieted down, John cleared his throat, wiped his eyes, and blew his nose. He pointed a finger at Jenny. "If you ever blow off like that again, I'll turn you over my knee and spank you!"

She grinned at him. "Oohh, wow! Kinky, kinky. Is that a promise?"

That got everybody going again. John leaned back on the couch and sipped his martini and let the team have another good laugh at his expense. He struggled unsuccessfully to keep a smile from creasing his own lips.

"Sorry, John," Jenny said. "I'll try to do better from now on."

"Please do." He held up the paper. "Has everybody read this?"

They all had. Suddenly the mood changed and the team got serious.

"Al, get in touch with Jacques and Henry. Bring them up to speed and tell them to bring their people and meet us here early tomorrow. We've got to make some plans."

"Ballard?" Paul asked.

"No help. Although he agrees with us about the UN. Everything is going to be concentrated on the president."

"He's not going to blow our cover?" Bob asked.

"No. I don't know, really, what brought on his change in attitude. But he's going to let us slide."

"The NYPD?" Linda asked.

"As far as I know, we're on our own. All we're operating on is a hunch on my part. The others have seized memos from various PLF cells indicating that the president is the target."

"But those memos might well have been planted to throw off the real target," Al said. "I personally think they were."

"So do I," John said. "But it's still a hunch."

"Historians might end up calling this Bloody Friday," Jenny said.

"Yes," John agreed. "No matter what we do."

"That old saying about a mule sure fits us in this situation," Paul said.

"What's that?" Linda asked.

"All we can do is try."

Twenty-seven

The three young women, all in their early to mid-twenties, were walking home. They had gone out for dinner after work, then decided to see a movie when they noticed that the line at the box office was not very long. The movie had gotten good reviews, but the three friends had been very disappointed in it.

"I'm tired of all the blatant sex in movies nowadays," one of the young women said as they walked along the cold, windy, and nearly deserted street. "I know how it's done. I just don't get it done to *me* very often."

The others laughed. "You're awful, Carol," one said.

"But truthful," the other said.

"Denise," Carol said. "Didn't you tell us one time your father is with the FBI?"

"Yes. He's been with them thirty years."

"Is he here in the city?"

"I really don't know. We don't talk very often. As a matter of fact, it's been a couple of years since we've spoken. He probably is here. He's some sort of big shot with them. Inspector."

A cold blast of wind mixed with tiny frozen pellets of ice sent the young women scurrying into the shelter of a storefront for a moment. They still had several blocks to go before they reached their subway station, and the temperature was hovering right at the freezing mark.

"Does your mother ever hear from him?" Nancy asked. "She's so nice."

"No," Denise said. "Never. They split up when my brother and I were in grade school. They don't get along at all." She smiled in the dim light. "I guess they never did. It must have been a mismatch right from the beginning."

"I don't mean to pry—"

"I don't mind, Nancy. Really. Gosh, I haven't seen my father in . . . oh, I guess it's been six years or so. He was on some assignment when I graduated from high school, and on assignment when I graduated from college."

"That's tough," Carol said.

Denise shrugged her shoulders. "I don't remember him being around much when I was a child."

The three stepped out of the protection of the storefront and once more braved nature's elements on the way to their subway station. The wind had picked up, and conversation was practically impossible, the icy wind sucking the words out of their mouths.

They did not see the car turn the corner and pull up almost silently behind them.

Ballard was jarred out of a deep sleep by the incessant ringing of the phone. He opened his eyes and shook his head, trying to shake the grogginess out of his brain.

He fumbled for the phone and stuck the right end to his ear. "Yes? What is it?"

"It's urgent, Inspector," the voice on the other end told him. "The SAC wants to see you immediately."*

"On my way."

Ballard dressed hurriedly and stepped out into the hall. Libby Carson was waiting for him, a concerned expression on her face.

*Special Agent in Charge

"What's the matter, Libby?" Ballard asked.

"Better let the SAC inform you, Inspector," she replied.

Ballard took her arm. "No. You tell me, Libby. I'm asking you."

"Let's grab the elevator. I'll tell you what I know. Which isn't much."

On the ride down to the lobby, Libby said, "It's your daughter, Inspector. Denise."

"What about her?"

"We think she's been kidnapped."

"What?"

"Please, Inspector. Let the SAC explain it. I've told you all I know."

"Somebody'd better tell me something," Ballard's reply was very terse.

The Special Agent in Charge of the New York City office was waiting in the lobby. The expression on his face was not a happy one.

"What in the hell is going on?" Ballard demanded of the man. "What's this about my daughter? How in hell did anyone find out I even *have* a daughter?"

"I won't candy-coat it, sir," the SAC said. "The PLF has grabbed your daughter." He held up a small cassette recorder. "The message."

"Let's hear it."

"Here, sir?"

Ballard pointed to a spot in the lobby away from the front desk. "Over there."

The message on the tape was profanely blunt: BALLARD, THIS IS ANDRÉ. WE HAVE YOUR DAUGHTER. SHE'S A FINE LOOKING BITCH, I MUST SAY. WE'VE ALREADY DETERMINED SHE'S NO BLUSHING VIRGIN. JUST THOUGHT YOU'D LIKE TO KNOW. YOU'LL BE HEARING FROM US AGAIN. AS THEY SAY IN AMERICA: STAY TUNED.

"I'm sorry, Inspector," the SAC said. "So very sorry."

Ballard clicked off the cassette recorder and stared at it in silence for a few seconds. Then his years on the job took over.

"Thank you. What do we have?"

"A description of the car, and a fair description of the people who took your daughter and her friend."

"Her friend?"

"Carol Wilson. Three young women had been to a movie and were walking to their subway stop. A car pulled in beside them and grabbed your daughter and Miss Wilson. The third girl, Nancy Adams, broke free and ran screaming for the police. When they got there, it was all over."

Ballard looked at his watch. He had been asleep for about three hours. That was enough. "Let's get to work," he said. "I want to interview Miss Adams."

Thursday 0530

John was rudely shaken awake by Jenny. She cut on the light and shoved a newspaper under his bleary eyes.

"André grabbed Ballard's daughter last night, John. Took her right off the street."

That opened his eyes. "What?"

She held out a mug of steaming coffee. "Drink this before you shower away the sleep. I made it. It's good and strong. Then we'll talk."

The coffee was strong all right. It bore a startling resemblance to boiled blacktop road surfacing. The first gulp almost took John's head off.

John's gagging in the bathroom brought a laugh from Jenny. "I forgot to tell you, John. I can't cook, either."

"I never would have guessed it," he called. "Where'd you get this stuff, the La Brea Tar Pits?"

"Oh, be quiet and drink it. At least it'll wake you up."

"Yes. For about a week."

Dressed, John walked out into the den. The rest of the team

was up, some were dressed and alert, others looking bleary-eyed. Linda was missing.

"She's making some decent coffee," Paul said. "Did you try to drink that crap Jenny made?"

Jenny gave him the finger.

"No comment," John said. He looked at Jenny. "And you behave yourself." John sat down and picked up a bagel some-one had gone out and bought. "I just scanned the paper. Who leaked it to the press?"

"No one knows," Linda said, coming out of the kitchen with a pot of coffee and mugs. "But you can bet the Bureau is grilling the reporter who wrote that story."

"I hope they beat the shit out of him," Jenny said. "What a dumb-ass thing to print."

"Well, it's printed," John said. "Too late now. But it sure puts the lives of those young women at risk."

"Anybody got any ideas on what we can do to help Ballard?" Paul asked.

"Nothing," John replied. "We don't want to be caught up in this. You can believe the Bureau will be working with blood in their eyes on this one."

"What do you suppose André was thinking when he grabbed Ballard's daughter?" Bob pondered aloud.

"Arrogance," Linda said. "Daring Ballard to come after him. Among other things."

"What other things?" Paul asked.

"To throw the Bureau off the real target," Al said. "To create as much confusion as possible."

"They've done a good job of that," Jenny said. "Ballard will be concentrating on finding his daughter now. And who could blame him?"

"Ballard will do what he was sent here to do," John said. "And that is finding the PLF cells. This just gives him more incentive. It's all one and the same now. But we stay clear of the kidnapping."

"What's on the agenda for today?" Paul asked.

"We check out the UN complex. That's all we can do."

"LaBlanc and Thompkins?" Linda asked.

"They'll meet us there at nine o'clock."

"I can hardly wait to meet Ms. Farnsworth," Jenny said.

"Will you try to behave?" John asked.

Jenny held up a hand. "Scout's honor."

"I didn't know you were in the Girl Scouts," Linda said.

Jenny smiled and winked. "I wasn't."

André nudged Denise with the toe of his shoe. "Get up, bitch. We're leaving."

Denise crawled to her knees, holding a blanket to cover her nakedness. She was bruised from the beating she'd received and the numerous rapes she'd endured. She looked around for Carol. "What have you done with Carol?"

"She's alive. Don't worry about her. Now get up."

"Where are my clothes?"

André reached down and slapped her. The blow knocked Denise off her knees and sent her sprawling back on the bed. "Do what I tell you to do, bitch," André told her. *"When* I tell you to do it. If you want to stay alive."

When Denise hesitated, André reached down and ripped the blanket from her. "Nice tits," he said.

"You bastard!" Denise hissed at him.

André laughed at her. "That's it, bitch. Show some spirit. Now get up."

A woman walked into the room, threw Denise's clothes on the bed, and walked out without saying a word. She was an older woman, Denise noted, maybe in her late forties, and grim looking. Everyone around her looked grim and determined.

"Now get dressed," André told her.

"I need a bath," Denise said.

"Get dressed or we'll dress you. How do you want it?"

"I can dress myself."

"I would certainly hope so. Do it!"

"You're the ones who killed those people at Grand Central, aren't you?" Denise asked.

"They were sacrificed," André corrected.

"Sacrificed? For what?"

"You wouldn't understand. You've been brainwashed for years by your pig father."

"I haven't even seen my father in years," Denise told him. "And if you think he's able to pay ransom you're wrong. He isn't a rich man."

"I know all about your father. He's a pig. And you're his little piglet." André kicked her on the leg and Denise gasped in pain. "Now get up and get dressed."

André left the room and walked to another part of the old house they were using. The group, now more than fifty strong, were using many different locations in the tri-state area. André was changing safe houses every day now. Tonight would be the last night his group would spend in New Jersey. They would drive into New York City before dawn, using many routes and driving different vehicles.

From the basement of the old house, André could hear the faint sounds of Carol's painful protests as Hurran mounted her again, taking the young woman as dogs do. The man certainly was twisted in his sexual appetites. There was nothing Hurran would not do to humiliate women. André knew that deep down, Hurran hated all women.

André shook his head. Hurran had just about outlived his usefulness. André had thought about sending him to the hospital where Wini was being held under guard with orders to kill the woman, or die trying. But he rejected that. Hurran just might succeed in killing her and getting out alive.

"Damn," André muttered just as a member of his team appeared in the doorway. He looked up. "Yes, what is it?"

"The FBI bitch is dressed. She's whining about a bath."

"If she continues to whine, give her a beating. That will shut her up."

"With pleasure."

"But don't kill her. Not yet."

"As you wish, André. Are we taking her with us into the city?"

"Yes. Insurance."

"The other girl?"

"We'll dispose of her before we leave. Leave the body in the basement. It will be days before anyone discovers it. Perhaps even weeks."

"Hurran is certainly enjoying her."

"Hurran would mount a mongoose if it would hold still."

The woman laughed and walked away.

André suddenly experienced a moment of tension and nervousness. He did not attempt to fight it. He allowed the sensations to wash over him, allowing the feelings to intensify, to take control in order to bring them clearer in his mind. It happened often when on an assignment, and André always knew what to do when the moment had passed.

"Yes," he whispered to the empty room. "Yes. You're right. That is what we must do."

To say that André was about three bricks shy of a load would be an understatement.

He rose from his chair and called for his team. "Get ready to move out. We're leaving this place. Heading into the city. This location has been compromised."

"Now?" Akal questioned.

"Immediately."

"The woman with Hurran?"

"Kill her." André was thoughtful for a moment. "Everyone dress appropriately. We don't want to be stopped because we fit some profile. Max, distribute weapons now. We're attacking this morning."

"What?"

"You heard me. Brigitte, notify all members to converge on the target immediately." He glanced at his watch. "We have plenty of time. The tour buses won't start arriving for nearly three hours. We will hit the first groups to arrive."

André went to his quarters and began packing. The feeling of urgency was strong within him and growing stronger. "It must be today," he muttered. "The authorities will not be expecting a strike today. They will all be gearing up for an attack tomorrow."

André laughed aloud at that as he looked around the room, checking to see if he'd missed anything.

He smiled as he touched a briefcase filled with grenades. With any kind of luck he might be able to make his way inside some part of the UN. And wouldn't that be a coup for all the oppressed peoples of the world?

His packing finished, André pulled on a T-shirt and then secured his body armor—the finest and lightest body armor in the world.

Alain walked into the room. He was dressed in a business suit and looked as if he were ready to go to work on Wall Street. "André?"

"Yes."

"I have assigned Norma to finish the woman."

"Good. Wise choice. Tell her to go home and forget she ever saw us when she has completed her task. It will be her job to begin forming new cells in the city."

"Very well. Brigitte and I will be leaving shortly. We'll be taking the FBI's daughter with us."

"I will see you at the site. Be certain that the FBI's piglet is highly visible when we begin our work."

Alain smiled. "America will never forget this day, André."

"That is our goal, Alain. I want blood to flow this day."

Twenty-eight

Carol ached all over. Hurran had beaten her several times and taken her sexually in the most painful, humiliating, and unnatural ways. The man was a savage.

"Foul-smelling, no-good son of a bitch!" Carol whispered.

She lay on a filthy and stinking old mattress in the moldy smelling basement. She was naked, her clothes in rags, tossed in a corner when they had been ripped from her. And Carol was becoming very, very angry.

She heard that perverted lard-ass bitch Norma clumping down the stairs and made up her mind right then that Norma would not again beat her and laugh while doing so.

I might get killed for fighting her, Carol thought. *But at least I'll go out fighting.*

The clumping on the stairs stopped and Norma called, "Good luck, guys. I wish I was going with you."

André's voice reached Carol. "You have your work cut out for you here, Norma. Good luck to you."

The sounds of doors opening and closing, both in front and back of the old house, reached Carol.

They're all leaving, she thought. *Leaving Norma behind to deal with me and . . .*

No! she thought. *They didn't leave Denise behind. They took her with them.*

Leaving Norma with me means?

"She's going to kill me," Carol whispered. *I'm nothing to*

them, she thought. *But Denise is the daughter of a very important FBI man.*

Carol grew even angrier. While fat-butt Norma was still standing on the steps, talking with someone, Carol forced herself to stand up, gritting her teeth against the pain in her bruised body. She swayed unsteadily for a few seconds, the room seeming to tilt sickeningly. She closed her eyes, and when she reopened them the room had stopped its tilting.

Norma was still talking.

Carol staggered over to the pile of rags that was her clothing and looked at her panty hose. Useless. Hell with it. She pulled on her pants. The zipper was ruined but she managed to get the waist button buttoned. *Pants cost me fifty dollars,* she thought ruefully. *Well, at least I'm alive.*

She could not find her shoes, and could not remember what had happened to them. She did find what was left of her shirt and slipped it on.

She heard Norma say, "Oh! Are you staying, Edward? Really? Yes, we'll have some cleaning up to do. OK. That'll be fine. Bring some beer back. Fine." There was a pause, then: "Oh, Edward! Why? Well, I suppose so. What difference does it make now? All right, all right. I'll wait. Yes, she'll be alive when you get back."

Carol grimaced. She had a pretty good idea what Edward wanted to do. Big ugly son of a bitch. He was stupid, too, Carol recalled. She could understand why André did not want him along when they . . .

My God! Carol thought, suddenly remembering bits and pieces of overheard conversation. *They're going now to attack tourists as they arrive at the UN complex.*

"I'll go check on the bitch, Edward," Norma said. "See you in a few minutes."

Carol heard heavy footsteps on the floor above her and a door slam shut. Norma again began her clumping down the steps to the basement.

Carol limped to the stairs and hid under them. She had already looked around the dimly lit basement for some sort of weapon and could find nothing . . . which she thought was odd. The basement had been carefully cleaned out. Carol huddled under the steps.

Norma made her way slowly and carefully down. When her feet came into view, Carol reached up, quickly grabbed both of the woman's ankles, and jerked.

Norma either didn't have time to scream or was so shocked that she forgot to. She tumbled headfirst onto the concrete floor and did not move.

Carol slipped from the darkness under the steps and prodded the woman with a bare foot. She did not move nor make a sound. "Goddamn you," Carol said as she bent down and pulled off the woman's tennis shoes, sitting down on the steps to slip them on. They were about a size too large, but at least Carol now had something on her feet.

She turned and felt a hand close around one ankle and jerk. She went sprawling to the floor. She kicked out with her free foot and connected with Norma's face. The older woman grunted in pain but doggedly held on to Carol's ankle.

"Turn loose, you bitch!" Carol said.

Norma cussed her and held on.

Carol kicked again and again, connecting each time. Finally, Norma's hold loosened and Carol was able to wriggle away and get to her feet just as Norma struggled to her feet.

"I'll kill you," Norma said.

"No, you won't," Carol panted, balling her fists. She stepped closer and swung a hard right at the older woman.

The fist connected with Norma's jaw and the woman yelped in pain. Carol's right hand throbbed from the impact.

Norma's face was bloody from the kicks she'd received from Carol's foot. Her nose was bleeding, and her lips were beginning to swell. Carol rushed at the woman, succeeding in knocking her down, but Norma grabbed Carol's arm and brought her down with her. The two women wrestled on the dirty floor, Carol finally managing to get on top.

Norma was yelling and cussing as Carol pummeled her with hard fists. The older woman smacked Carol with a fist that knocked Carol from her, sending Carol sprawling to one side. Norma showed some surprising agility getting to her feet. She kicked Carol on the side with the heel of her foot and the younger woman yelped in pain.

Carol grabbed Norma's leg and twisted, bringing the heavier woman down again. She crawled over to her and began hitting the woman in the face with her fists, lefts and rights, as hard and as fast as she could. Norma's face was now red with blood and swollen.

Norma kicked out and a bare foot caught Carol in the belly, knocking the wind from her. She fell back, and for a moment both women lay on the floor, trying to catch their breath and recover some strength.

The pistol Norma had shoved down in her waistband had fallen out when she tumbled down the steps and was nowhere to be seen in the dimly lit basement.

"You damned lousy bitch!" Norma hissed, struggling to get to her feet. She got as far as her knees and crouched there, glaring at Carol, blood dripping from her busted nose and mouth. "You capitalist bitch!"

Carol didn't waste any precious breath replying to that, even though she was weary of everybody in this nutty group, male and female, calling her a bitch. She crawled to her knees and popped Norma on the jaw with a right fist. The blow knocked the woman back to the floor. Carol climbed painfully to her feet and stood there, swaying from near exhaustion.

Norma rolled to one side, came up on her knees, still wildly cussing, and bit Carol on the upper thigh, hanging on like a bulldog.

"Oh, damn!" Carol yelled, trying to shake Norma loose. Norma held on, clamping down harder, as she held onto Carol's leg with both hands. Carol hammered at Norma's neck with both fists, hitting her as hard as she could. Still the heavier older woman hung on. Only Carol's winter slacks prevented Norma from tearing a chunk of meat from her leg.

Carol's flailing around with both arms caused her to lose her balance, and she went tumbling to the floor. That broke Norma's hold, and Carol kicked out, the toe of one shoe catching Norma savagely on the side of the head.

Norma suddenly straightened up, a strange look in her eyes. Her mouth dropped open.

Carol rolled several yards away from her and climbed to her knees, staring at the woman. She was so tired and sore she wondered if she could possibly continue the fight. She really didn't think she could. She was so thirsty she felt as though her throat was on fire.

Blood began pouring from Norma's ears and mouth and the woman let out an awful shriek. She balled both hands into fists and began pounding at the air, screaming. Her eyes were wild looking. Then she began trembling.

Carol stared at her in fascination. It was like something from a bad horror movie.

Norma abruptly stopped screaming and crouched there on her knees for a moment, swaying back and forth, the blood dripping. The silence in the room was broken only by the heavy breathing from both women. Norma collapsed in a heap on the floor and did not move.

Carol crawled over to her and gingerly touched the woman's throat, trying to detect some sign of life. She finally found a faint throbbing, very faint. The pulse was thin and erratic.

Carol realized then that her wild kick to Norma's head must have caused something to rupture in the woman's brain. She backed away and crouched there, in mild shock.

Edward! the thought jumped into Carol's mind. How long had he been gone? How long had she and Norma been fighting? She had no idea. Surely not for very long. She automatically looked at her watch. Or where her watch had been. It had been taken from her, she remembered.

Norma started jerking and making awful noises. Carol carefully skirted her and began looking for the gun that had fallen from the woman's waistband. She found it in the corner and stood for a moment looking at it. Carol had never held a pistol, much less fired one, but it looked really easy in the movies.

She picked it up. It was heavy. She knew this type was called a revolver. She hoped it was loaded.

Carol looked back at Norma. The woman had stopped her moaning and thrashing and was lying still on the floor. Carol wondered if she was dead. She wouldn't go over there to check.

When Carol started up the stairs an almost overpowering feeling of weariness enveloped her. The stairs looked to be a mile high. She managed to make it halfway to the top before she was forced to sit down and rest. She could not ever remember being so exhausted.

She rested for a few minutes and then started up the stairs, finally reaching the landing.

The damn door was locked!

"Crap!" Carol blurted, looking down the stairs into the dim basement.

She headed back down the stairs and went over to Norma. The woman was still breathing, but it didn't sound right. It was labored and raspy. Carol squatted down and began going through the woman's pockets, finding a ring of keys and several wadded up twenty dollar bills. She stuck the money in her back pocket and headed back up the stairs.

"I might need to grab a cab," she muttered, fumbling with the keys. She did not have the faintest idea what this bunch of goofballs had done with her purse.

She unlocked the door and stepped out into the kitchen. Light was streaming through the windows. Carol could see that the morning was cloudy and the skies threatening rain. She walked over to the sink and found a glass on the counter. She drank three glasses of water before her thirst was slaked.

Then she felt a sudden and immediate urge to go to the bathroom.

She hurriedly found a bathroom and emerged a few minutes later feeling much better.

Carol stood in the hall for a moment gathering her thoughts. She did not have any idea where she was. She went to a window and looked out. Definitely a semi-rural area. She walked the house, looking for her purse and for a phone. She found her purse on a beat-up old table in the living room, but no phone anywhere.

She then went looking for her coat and found it in a hall closet.

Carol returned to the kitchen and began looking for something to eat. She was suddenly, incredibly, hungry. She found a can of mixed fruit and a can opener. She ate all the contents, drank the juice, and felt better.

Carol returned to the door leading to the basement and locked it.

"Now what?" she questioned.

She looked around for a newspaper . . . anything to tell her where she might be. No newspaper in the house and no television or radio. Not even an old phone book.

"Damn!" Carol muttered. She knew she wasn't thinking clearly, but she was trying to shake the cobwebs from her head. She wondered if her kidnappers had drugged her. She shook her head. She didn't think so. She felt she must be in some sort of mild shock. She continued to look around. She could find nothing that would help her.

But she knew she had heard a radio or TV, and concluded the terrorists must have removed them before leaving.

She looked in a bedroom and found a pair of socks on a dresser. She slipped them on. They were too big, but would do. The socks made her feet warmer and snugged up the too-large tennis shoes.

"Well," Carol said, looking out the kitchen window at the empty road in front of the house. "I've got to get out of here and get help."

So start walking, she thought as she paced the kitchen, walking around and around the kitchen table.

But what if I run into big stupid Ed while I'm walking down the road?

I've got a gun.

But don't know how to use it.

The sound of a vehicle pulling into the drive brought her back to the window.

Edward stepped out.

"Oh, hell," Carol muttered.

Twenty-nine

Thompkins and LaBlanc and their people met John and his team several blocks from the UN complex. It was cold and blustery with the skies occasionally spitting cold rain.

"You should feel right at home in this weather, Henry," John kidded the Englishman.

"Actually," the very attractive young lady with the MI6 agent said, "London is not this bitter. It's quite comfortable for those of us who are not accustomed to racing inside every time a cloud pops up."

"Well, kiss my ass," Jenny muttered, but not loud enough for John to hear. "I was making a joke, Miss . . . ah?"

"It's Ms., if you don't mind. Camilla Farnsworth."

"La-tee-da," Jenny muttered.

John cut his eyes to Jenny and she smiled sweetly at him and curtsied very properly.

John had to turn his head to keep from laughing out loud at her antics.

"Jacques," John said, turning to the Frenchman. "You all alone?"

"For the time being, yes. My people will join us at the complex at about nine-thirty or so."

"All right," John said. "That'll give us time to get some breakfast." He looked around. "Somewhere. Let's all get out of this lousy weather. How about it?"

"Smashingly good idea," Henry said. "I could do with a spot of tea. Camilla?"

"Whatever you say, sir."

They found a place open for the breakfast crowd and took tables. On the way over Jenny had positioned herself several yards behind Camilla and prissed and minced along, despite the several warning glances John gave her, none of which had absolutely any effect on Jenny.

"I have heard, of course, about the kidnapping of Ballard's daughter," Thompkins said. "Despicable bastards, the PLF. The lot of them. Have you spoken with Ballard?"

"No. But I imagine he's pretty well racked up about it. I know I would be."

"Married to the Bureau," Jacques said. "I understand he always has been."

"He's dedicated, for a fact," John agreed.

Thompkins and Camilla ordered tea, John and his bunch ordered coffee, and Jacques ordered coffee with a snifter of brandy.

"At eight o'clock in the morning!" Thompkins said. "Good Lord, man!"

Jacques smiled. "Takes the chill away."

"I imagine so," John said.

The very aloof Ms. Farnsworth frowned and sniffed with displeasure at liquor being ordered that early in the day.

John cut his eyes to Jenny, but she was maintaining a straight face . . . for the time being.

"The weather prognosticators are all predicting this weather will continue for several days," Thompkins said. "If that is the case, we can eliminate any type of outside gas attack."

"Guns and grenades," Paul said.

"Unfortunately, that is correct," Jacques replied. "But this weather might keep tourists away."

"I wouldn't count on that," Bob said.

"I'm not," Jacques answered. "But I can hope."

Their refreshments came, and for a moment no one said

anything. After the waitress had left, Thompkins said, "Jacques and I have discussed this, and we both are of the opinion that this operation may well be André's swan song."

"Why?" Linda asked.

Thompkins took a sip of tea and said, "André is mad, and his condition is worsening. That report comes from people who were once a part of his group. He's becoming irrational. He receives strange mystic messages. . . . Of course no one else can hear them. He may not realize that he is planning his own demise."

"If given even the slightest of opportunities, I will certainly oblige him," Jacques said.

Conversation waned after that. Finally, John said, "Let's finish up and get to work, people. We can't all go trooping through the grounds in a bunch. That would draw attention. We'll wander through in groups of two or three. Pay particular attention to placement of statues and shrubbery. Ready? Let's do it."

Denise had been trussed up and tossed in the back of a van like a side of beef, her mouth taped shut. But Denise's hearing was not impaired, and she listened in horror as her captives talked lightly, almost jokingly, about killing tourists, including children.

"Grenades first," one of her captors said. "If we get lucky the bus will blow up, and that will create even more confusion."

"Yes," another said. "If we all get into position correctly, we should be able to kill several hundred."

Incredible, Denise thought. *They're all crazy!*

"André said he wanted blood to flow," the driver said. "Let's grant him his wish."

"Including our own blood," another added with a laugh.

They're not even thinking about getting away, Denise thought. *It's a suicide mission and they're joking about it.*

"It's all for the greater good," the driver said.

All agreed.

My God! Denise thought.

Carol quickly backed away from the window and stepped into the living room. She took the pistol from her pocket and looked at it. *Point it and pull the trigger,* she thought. *You've seen it a thousand times in movies and on TV. Simple. But does this gun have one of those safety things on it?*

She didn't know.

And there wasn't time to give it a lot of thought.

Edward was fumbling at the side door leading to the kitchen.

She crouched down behind the couch. It was the only place she could find. She wasn't thinking clearly, and knew it. She took several very deep breaths and tried to calm down. She thought it helped.

"Norma?" the big man called just as the door closed behind him. "Where are you, Norma? Is the bitch naked? I'm gettin' a hard-on just thinkin' about it."

There was, of course, no reply from Norma.

"You ain't messin' around with her, are you?"

God! Carol thought.

"Norma!" Ed shouted. After a few seconds of silence, he said, "Shit. I bet she's downstairs with the damn door closed. What the hell is she doin'?"

Carol listened as Ed walked over to the door leading to the basement and tried it. "Norma?" he shouted. "You down there? Answer me."

Carol silently cursed herself for lingering in the house so long.

"You better come up here and unlock this damn door, Norma!" Ed hollered.

Carol waited, trying to conceal her ragged breathing. She was sure the big oaf would hear her.

"OK, Norma. I hear you. You movin' kinda slow. What's the matter, you sick?"

Moving! Carol thought, as panic filled her, threatening to explode from her mouth. *Norma is moving?*

"What's that, Norma? I can't understand you. Can't you make it up the stairs? What the hell's goin' on?"

Ed began smashing at the door with his shoulder.

The door gave way, and Ed almost fell through the shattered door. "Norma!" he yelled, and began clumping hurriedly down the steps.

Carol jumped up and ran to the front door. It was locked. She went as quietly as she could through the house to the back door. It, too, was locked. "Shit!" she whispered. "It's through the kitchen, or nothing."

She made it to the archway and stopped, horror filling her eyes.

Norma stood there, blood leaking from her nose and mouth and running down one side of her face, out of her ear. She grunted at Carol, trying to speak words, but managing only to grunt and snort unintelligibly.

This is not happening to me! Carol thought. *I'm going to wake up from this nightmare very soon and laugh about it. I just know I will. I have to. Dear God, please let it be only a very bad dream.*

Norma lurched toward her, dragging one leg. Carol screamed, "No!" and shoved the woman back.

Carol fell back into the arms of Big Ed, who had just then stepped behind the woman.

"You bitch!" he shouted at Carol. "What have you done to Norma?"

Something snapped in Carol. She was suddenly filled with an uncontrollable rage. "Me? Done to her? Why, you big stupid son of a bitch! Go to hell, you dimwitted bastard!"

Ed sat Norma down in a kitchen chair and grinned at Carol. "You in trouble now, bitch."

"Stop calling me bitch! I'm sick of it!"

"Bitch bitch bitch bitch!" Ed chanted as he took a step in Carol's direction.

Carol lifted the pistol and pointed it at him. "Don't come near me, damn you. I'll shoot. Get out of the way. I mean it. Move!"

Ed eyeballed the pistol for a moment. "I don't think you'll shoot, bitch."

"You're wrong."

"We'll see." He took another step.

"Stop, damn you!" She aimed the pistol directly at Ed's big belly. "I mean it, Ed."

Ed grinned at her. "Then pull the damn trigger."

Carol stared at him.

"Just like I thought. You won't shoot. You ain't got it in you. I'm gonna beat the shit outta you and then fuck you like you ain't never been humped. And I got the equipment to make you holler, bitch."

He stepped toward her and Carol pulled the trigger.

"You have the unloaded weapon for the FBI's bitch?" the driver asked.

"Ready to go."

"This is going to be funny. She'll be standing ankle deep in blood with an unloaded weapon. Anybody want to make a bet how long she'll stay alive?"

No one did.

"Forty-five minutes to go," he was reminded.

Denise lay on the floor and listened. She wanted to remember all the names and faces. In this big van there were Dave and Rufino and Claire and Taylor. The driver was called Red. She would remember their faces for as long as she lived.

"I'll let everyone off a few minutes before the complex opens for visitors," Red said. "Leave this damn bus somewhere. We won't be needing it anymore."

Denise wondered about that. How did they plan to get

away . . . or did they even have such a plan? If they thought she was going to stand around with a gun in her hand while this bunch of screwballs killed innocent people they had another thought coming.

Denise didn't know just how she was going to get away, but as soon as the ropes were taken off her she would think of something.

"There're some of our people over there," Claire said. "Pulling into that garage."

"That's Carl's bunch," Taylor said. "I haven't seen him in months."

How many people are going to take part in this insanity? Denise wondered.

"We'll outnumber the security guards," Rufino said.

"That's Alfred's job," Dave said. "His people will take care of security."

"The world will know of us after this morning," Claire stated proudly. "And the poor people will build monuments in praise of our work."

Idiots, Denise thought. *Many of the people you'll be trying to kill will be part of the working class you claim to care so much about.*

"It won't be long now," Red said. "Get all your equipment ready."

The bullet from Carol's gun struck Ed in the left shoulder and turned him sideways. He yelled in shock and pain, but didn't go down. Norma opened her mouth and tried to speak. It was a useless effort. Whatever she was trying to say came out as a jumble of grunts.

Ed charged Carol, yelling and cussing. He slammed into her, knocking her down, going to the floor with her, pinning her down, but she doggedly held on to the pistol. Her ears were ringing from the weapon's discharge, and her wrist ached from the recoil.

"Bitch!" Ed shouted.

Carol stuck the muzzle of the pistol against Ed's belly and pulled the trigger. The slug tore into him and blew right through his body, exiting out his back. He rolled away, screaming in agony.

Carol managed to stand up just as Ed was struggling to get to his feet. There was blood all over him and a part of the floor. Ed slipped in his own blood and fell back heavily to the hardwood floor. He lay there and groaned.

Carol stepped around him and walked slowly into the kitchen. Everything seemed to be happening in slow motion. It was like a bad dream.

Norma still sat in the chair, mumbling and looking at Carol. Blood was leaking from her nose and mouth.

"You rotten bitch!" Ed yelled.

Carol ignored him. Still holding the pistol, she walked out of the kitchen into the cold, late fall air. It was drizzling rain. The air tasted wonderful. She walked over to the car Ed had used and looked inside. The keys were not in the ignition. Carol walked on to the road. There was no way she would go back into that house to try to get the keys from Ed.

She walked up the road. There were houses up ahead. She would go up there and use a phone to call the police.

Then she saw a car coming toward her. She stepped into the middle of the road and began waving her arms. She still held the pistol. The car drew closer, slowed, and then stopped.

"Help me!" Carol shouted. "Please help me!"

The car backed up, turned around, and drove off.

"Damn you!" Carol shouted. "Stop."

The car disappeared around a curve. Carol stood in the middle of the road. She was so confused. She just wasn't thinking straight.

And she was very nearly at the limit of her endurance. She just could not go on. She'd been kidnapped, beaten, raped repeatedly, fought a madwoman, shot a man, and she was just about all done in.

"Hell with it," Carol muttered. She sat down in the middle of the road and laid the pistol on the cold wet surface. "Somebody will surely come along and help me."

A car came up behind her and stopped. She didn't look around. She was sure it was Ed, and he was going to kill her.

"Miss?" a woman said from behind her. "Miss? My God, that's a gun."

Carol turned around and looked up into the face of the woman. "My name is Carol Wilson. I've been kidnapped, beaten, and raped. Some of the people who did it are back in that house right back there." She pointed with a shaking hand. "That one. Will you please help me?"

"Don't move," the woman said. "I have a phone in my car. I'll call the police."

"Thank you," Carol said. "They're going to attack the UN this morning."

"What? What are you saying?"

"They're terrorists. The same ones who killed those people in the city the other day."

"Don't move," the woman said. "Stay right there."

"Watch out for Ed," Carol said as her world began to spin into darkness. "I didn't kill him."

"What are you saying?" the woman asked. "Ed who?"

Carol shook her head and passed out on the cold wet road.

Thirty

Thursday 0830

"The buses should start arriving in thirty-five or forty minutes," John said, glancing at his watch. "There is no need for us to hurry."

The gray skies were full of clouds, and had begun dripping a steady drizzle of cold rain. It was downright miserable for the people scurrying along, most huddled under umbrellas. John and his group were spread out along the block just north of the eighteen-acre UN complex. They stood in doorways for protection against the cold wind and rain. Jenny and the so-far unflappable Ms. Farnsworth were with him.

"You believe André planned all that's happened well in advance, John Barrone?" Camilla asked.

"I have very mixed feelings on that, Camilla. Part of me thinks he's playing it all by ear, so to speak. He had no way of knowing that Inspector Ballard would be assigned to this case. So the kidnapping of Ballard's daughter was certainly spur of the moment. I do believe that after the attack on Grand Central didn't produce hundreds of dead, André shifted gears, again, so to speak. But this attack? I don't know. He may have been holding back from his own people all the while. We may never know unless we take him alive and he confesses the truth. And both of those are big maybes."

"André does not have the truth in him," the Englishwoman

said. "He has hate. That's all. If you get a chance to kill him, do the world a favor and pull the trigger."

"Ever killed anyone, Camilla?"

"No," she replied quickly. "Not yet. But when it comes to André or any of his group, I would not hesitate. Be assured of that."

"Rain's easing up," Jenny said, fixing a scarf over her head. "I think I'll head on down to the complex and just wander around a bit."

"We'll be a few minutes behind you," John told her.

"Y'all behave," Jenny said with a grin, then stepped out of the storefront.

"We'll certainly try," Camilla replied, giving Jenny a very strange look.

John and Camilla chatted for a few more minutes, then began walking toward the UN complex. A large van passed them, driving as slowly as traffic would permit. John had his topcoat collar turned up and was wearing a hat. He was unrecognizable in the cold gray drizzle—just another New Yorker walking to work.

"No additional security," André said from the center seat of the van. "The American pigs suspect nothing." He laughed. "What a morning this is going to be." He looked at his watch. "Find a place to park. The buses will be arriving in a few minutes."

"The others are in place," Alain said, after acknowledging the very brief transmission from a small two-way radio.

After circling a few blocks until finally finding a place to park, André asked, "Everybody ready?"

They were.

The first bus was rounding a corner, approaching the UN complex.

"Let's do it," André said. "We'll strike another powerful blow for the oppressed peoples of the world." He put his hand on the large briefcase containing grenades and slid the door open, stepping out into the cold morning. He smiled as yet another tour bus was rounding the corner.

André's group were wearing topcoats, their weapons hidden under the long coats. After the assault, the PLF members would shed the long coats, put on caps and hats, and try to blend in with what would surely be a panicked crowd.

André's people began walking toward the UN buildings in small groups. Denise Ballard was in the center of a group, a pistol pressed into her back.

"If you yell or try to run, you die," she was told. "Do you understand that?"

"I understand," Denise said.

"Very good."

"I want to kill a cop for Wini," Jan told André. "I want to kill many police this day."

André smiled. "We shall. I promise you that. There will be much blood on the ground this morning. Take the group and walk past the first bus. That one is mine. I will strike the first blow. Lay down a field of fire in all directions when the first grenade blows. I want as much confusion as possible. I will try to get inside the General Assembly building."

"If all goes well, I will see you at the rendezvous point."

"If all goes well," André said.

"Here comes another bus." Akal spoke in low tones. "There will be many targets this day."

André was carrying a grenade in each topcoat pocket. The briefcase was in his left hand. He had already pulled the pin on one grenade, holding the spoon down. He felt powerful, invincible, as adrenalin surged through him.

"For the oppressed peoples of the world," André said, and he pulled out the grenade, tossing it under the first bus.

John was crossing the street when the grenade blew. He was frozen for just a few seconds, not understanding what caused the explosion. Then he knew, knew with a cold certainly: André had out-foxed them all and jumped the gun.

The bus shuddered under the explosion and black smoke

began pouring out of the rear. But it did not catch fire . . . yet. The windows along the street side were popped out, and John could see a dozen or more tourists sprawled on the wet concrete. Some were screaming and crying and bleeding, others were lying very still on the driveway.

John made it across the street to the Colors of the World site, where the flags of member nations flew. Then he had to hit the cold wet concrete as automatic weapons fire erupted from the front of the complex and from both sides.

Tourists were going down like pins in a bowling alley as the automatic fire raked everything standing. The other two buses were trying to get away but the PLF members quickly put a stop to that by tossing more grenades under them. One bus blew up, sending shrapnel-pocked men and women sprawling to the concrete, severely wounded and screaming for help.

John and his people were armed only with pistols, not much of a match for the Uzis and the grenades.

John lined up one wild-eyed, Uzi-wielding woman and shot her in the belly just as she was pulling the trigger. She fell backward, her finger still on the trigger, and blew the entire magazine into the drizzling air.

But there was nothing John and his people could do for the tourists who had reached the visitors' entrance. There, they had run straight into half a dozen PLF members, all armed with automatic weapons and grenades. It was carnage—that was all it could be called. Blood was running in tiny red rivers from the broken and bullet-shattered bodies.

"Dear God!" John heard Camilla Farnsworth exclaim from her belly-down position on the concrete just a few feet from him. "Some of those down are children!"

Over the rattle of gunfire and the screaming, weeping, and moaning of the wounded and the utterly terrified tourists, John heard the unmistakable whoosh of a rocket, probably fired from an RPG.

The sound appeared to be coming from behind him.

"Rocket!" he yelled.

The rocket struck one of the already crippled buses and it blew apart in a shower of hot twisted metal and thick shards of glass. Thick black smoke swirled into the cold air, the smoke staying close to the ground due to the heaviness of the air.

Then some of the terrorists turned their weapons on the buildings across the street, where a number of windows were lined with people staring out at the attack.

Dozens of windows blew out under the hail of bullets and the curious were suddenly dead or wounded.

The entire attack had used up no more than ninety seconds so far and the wet concrete was littered with dead and wounded: men, women, teenagers, and small children. But the terrorists had only begun.

Security began pouring out of the buildings and ran straight into death. The terrorists chopped down the guards, and André made it to the front door of the General Assembly building. He laughed as he ran down the hall. His laughter faded when he discovered there was no session scheduled.

André began cursing as he looked around for another target. There was none. The building was nearly deserted.

"Goddamn it!" André screamed in frustration.

A woman ran out into the hall and André shot her, leaving her seriously wounded and bleeding on the floor.

He ignored her screaming for help and moved on.

Behind him, two more members of the PLF had made their way into the building.

"Where the hell is everybody?" one yelled.

"It's deserted," André tossed the words over his shoulder. "Follow me. There's a way over to another meeting hall."

He was talking about the building that housed the Economic and Social Council of the UN.

No one was meeting in there, either.

"Don't these overpaid bastards and bitches ever work?" André screamed out his rage.

Outside, the shooting raged on, but targets were becoming fewer as tourists found cover.

As NYPD patrol cars began converging on the scene, John managed to wave most of his people back, across the street, guns put away. Thick white smoke began pouring out of smoke grenades thrown by the terrorists to cover their actions and retreat.

Out of the corner of his eye, John watched as Jenny ran toward three gun-toting terrorists.

"No, Jenny!" he shouted.

She dived at the middle person and brought the woman down just as several members of the NYPD opened fire and the two PLF members were no longer standing. They were on the concrete, riddled with bullet holes.

Jenny pulled the woman she'd knocked down into a cloud of swirling smoke and disappeared.

"What the hell?" John muttered.

"Ballard's kid," Jenny panted, suddenly appearing out of the thickening smoke a few feet from where John had stationed himself behind a parked van.

"I didn't do anything," Denise said. "They kidnapped me. Oh, God! This is terrible. Who are you people?" Denise asked.

"Friends," John told her. He turned to Jenny. "Find the others. Tell them to get the hell away from here. It's over for us."

"Ten-four, Boss."

John put a hand on Denise's arm. "It's all right, Miss Ballard. You're safe now. Relatively so," he added. The gunfire had lessened somewhat, but bullets were still flying all over the place, most of the gunfire now between the police and members of the PLF.

"Who are you people?" Denise persisted.

"Friends of your father. Let's get the hell away from here. Come on."

John led the woman up the street, away from the scene of violence and death.

They hurried out of the thick smoke and into the gray morning, filled with cold drizzle.

Camilla stepped up beside John. "The Inspector's kid?" she asked.

"Yes. Where is Henry?"

"Waiting at the corner. Just up ahead. Your people are coming up behind us."

"All of them?"

"Yes. I don't believe anyone was hit. We got lucky."

"Nothing short of a miracle," John replied.

"Who are you?" Denise asked. "My God, I'm shaking so much I can hardly walk. Are you FBI?"

"No," John told her. "Get her out of here," he told Ms. Farnsworth. "Get with some of my people. They'll take you both to a safe house. Then we'll call Ballard."

"But—"

"No buts, Camilla. Just do it. Move out."

At the end of the block, they mingled with a knot of people who had foolishly gathered to view the attack.

"Get out of here!" a cop told them. "Move!"

John lagged behind to make certain Camilla and Denise got clear, then turned the corner and walked away, heading up the street toward midtown.

"Goddamn it!" John muttered, summing up the feelings of a lot of people on that cold rainy morning.

Thirty-one

An hour after the attack was presumed over, police were still counting the dead. They were finding dead and wounded all over the eighteen-acre complex, including twenty of the terrorists, all dead—four with self-inflicted wounds.

And John finally got through to Ballard.

"Your daughter's all right, Ballard," John said. "She's with me.

"What?" The FBI man nearly screamed the one-word question.

"I said Denise is all right. She's at our safe house. I thought you might want to question her before your interrogation team does."

"I . . . all right. You gave me one address the other night. Is that still good?"

"Yes."

"I'll be there as quickly as I can. But I might not be alone. This UN thing . . ."

"I know. She'll be safe until you get here. And she's all right, Ballard."

"Was she . . . raped?" He stumbled over that last word.

"Yes. And beaten."

Ballard sighed. "All right, Barrone. I'm on my way."

"Going to be interesting to see how he handles this one," John said.

"I really would like a bath," Denise said. "I know I must smell awful."

"That will be up to your father," John told her. "I don't know how he wants to handle this."

"I haven't seen my father in years."

"Well, you're going to see him today. As you are. He'll take you straight to the hospital from here."

"Are you with the New York Police?"

"No, Denise."

"You're not FBI, are you? Did I already ask that?"

"No, we're not with the Bureau."

"Are you CIA?"

"No, we're not."

"But you have guns."

"How about another cup of coffee, Denise?" Paul asked. "It's really good. I made it."

Jenny rolled her eyes. "You'll make someone a fine mate, for sure."

"I'd love another cup, and another sandwich, if you don't mind."

"Coming right up." Paul left the room, Jenny right behind him.

"I'll fix the sandwich," Jenny said.

"We want to feed the lady, not poison her," Paul responded as they both disappeared into the kitchen.

"Then who are you people?" Denise asked. "You've got to be from some police agency. I mean, you act so . . . professional. That other woman who left with those two men, she was English. I could tell from her accent. I know! What's that international agency? Inter-something or another. INTERPOL. That's it. That's why you won't tell me. Right?"

When John did not reply, Denise sighed and said, "I quit smoking two years ago. But I want a cigarette so much right now I can't stand it. Somebody give me a cigarette, please."

"Are you sure?" John asked. "After two years you want to start back?"

"I'm sure. Just give me the whole pack."

Denise fired up, and after coughing for a few seconds she settled back and sipped the coffee that Paul had brought in. "That is good coffee."

John clicked on the television.

Regular network programming had been suspended. Television crews were as close to the UN grounds as police would permit. Many of the bodies had not yet been removed. The lifeless forms had been covered up and left in place where they had fallen. It was a horrible sight, being witnessed all over the nation and the world. John glanced over at Denise. She was watching the screen, her face impassive.

The scene occasionally shifted to some official, local, state, or federal, for comments. Their statements might as well have been canned; they all said basically the same thing. Then the cameras would cut to someone who had witnessed the carnage, or who had been near and heard the shooting, or who had a friend or relative among the victims.

"That is going to go on all day," Jenny said, bringing out a sandwich and setting it down on the coffee table in front of Denise. She stared at the TV for a few seconds, then added, "As awful as it is, the press is going to milk it for everything it's worth and then some."

"The nature of the beast," John said. "Called ratings. Does this bother you, Denise?"

She slowly shook her head. "No. Not really. I was there and saw it, lived it. I heard them planning it. This is just a replay." She puffed on her cigarette, then grimaced and snubbed it out. "It didn't taste as good as I thought it would. I think I'll stay quit."

Bob walked into the room and motioned for John to join him, away from the group. "The information lid has been screwed down tight," he announced. "We're not getting anything."

"Understandable. I'm just curious as to how many of the terrorists got away."

"On a brighter note, all our team members who were injured back in Louisville are out of the hospital and doing well."

"Tell them to stay put and low. As soon as we get a lead on what's left of the PLF, we're out of here."

"Any clue as to how Ballard is going to handle the recovery of his daughter?"

"No. That's up to him. But I'm betting he won't blow our cover."

"You hope. But there's always Denise. How do you know she won't start talking?"

"I don't. I think after she talks with her father, they'll arrive at a simple story that will stand up." John smiled. "But I think we'd better quietly pack our gear and get ready to pull out just as soon as Ballard picks up his kid."

"I'll advise the others, one at a time."

"Good enough. We're probably going to be followed when we leave. If that's the case, we're going to have to shake a tail. We might have to split up. You take Paul and Linda and maintain contact."

"Will do."

John packed his gear and rejoined the group in the living room. The TV was still on. The scene had not changed, and probably would not for the rest of the day.

"If this had happened on a weekend," Jenny said, "all the dimwitted sports geeks would be screaming about missing their goddamn football games."

"I gather you're not a sports fan," Denise said.

"I was a gymnast in college," Jenny said. "I was pretty good, competed all over the United States. I enjoy a sporting event. But I'm not a sports freak."

"I'm not a sports anything," Denise said. Then she closed her eyes and passed out, hitting the floor before anyone could grab her.

* * *

André and his team made it out of the bloody carnage of the UN complex unscathed, dropping their automatic weapons and shedding their fake glasses and overcoats and hats and blending in with the people running through the swirling smoke from the smoke grenades, looking for the most part like office workers in a panic. But they were still armed with pistols in shoulder holsters and purses . . . in case they ran into trouble getting away.

They had no trouble at all.

Two of the drivers, including Red, chatted briefly and in a friendly manner with pedestrians and one police officer as they made their way back to their vehicles, telling them how awful and terrible the scene at the UN Headquarters had been.

Then they were on their way, smiling at how easy it had all been.

They had left twenty of their own faithful dead or dying back at the attack site, but none of the survivors could be sad about that. They all had died for the cause, and they would be remembered and martyred within the PLF.

Now there were more important matters at hand: new plans to be made. New targets to be selected. More blood of rich Americans to be spilled.

Only one person knew where they would strike next, and that person, of course, was André. So far he wasn't talking. But he would, in time. And his followers would be ready.

Jenny and Linda had quickly taken over the caring for Denise. In just a few moments she was awake and wondering aloud what in the world had happened to her.

"You fainted. From the strain, I'm sure," Linda said. "After all you've been through I'm surprised it didn't happen sooner."

"I feel sort of light-headed."

"Don't try to get up," Jenny told her. "Just lie back and keep that cool damp cloth on your head. Take it easy until your dad gets here."

"He was always so stern," Denise said, closing her eyes again for a moment.

"He's a pussycat," Jenny said.

That opened Denise's eyes. "You've got to be kidding!"

"She is," John quickly stepped in.

"Look at the screen," Bob said, his eyes on the TV.

One of the terrorists had been killed at the bronze statue titled "Let Us Beat Swords Into Plowshares," given to the UN by the Russian sculptor Vuchetich, symbolizing the main goal of the United Nations. The terrorist was sprawled in bloody death at the base of the statue.

"What a shot," Paul said. "The networks will be showing that shot for weeks to come."

"How did the press learn about André being the leader?" Al asked.

"Maybe it was a bad leak somewhere down the line," Linda speculated.

"Had to have been Carol," Denise spoke. "That means she's all right. Thank God."

"I understand."

"Maybe we'll know when your dad gets here," Paul said.

"He's here," Bob said, speaking from the foyer of the brownstone.

Denise sat up on the couch and then stood up, with a little help from Linda.

Ballard went immediately to his daughter and embraced her. There were tears in his eyes that he made no attempt to hide. Jenny had to turn away from the scene for a moment. It was a side of Ballard that she had never seen, and did not know existed, and it visibly affected her.

"Coffee?" John asked when Ballard had released his daughter from a long embrace.

"Yes, that would be nice, Barrone. Thank you."

"I'll get it," Jenny said.

"I don't know how you're going to handle this, Ballard," John said. "But we're out of it."

Ballard nodded. "I'll keep you clear. Somehow. It's time for me to retire, anyway."

"I don't think it has to be that dramatic," John told the man. "We can work something out."

"We'll see," Ballard said. He looked back at his daughter. "Have you called anybody, honey?"

"No. And I haven't had a bath, either."

"You have to be checked out by doctors. It's . . . well, not pleasant. But it's necessary."

"I understand."

"You came over here alone?" John asked.

"No," Ballard said. "There are two senior agents outside. But they'll keep their mouths shut. And they don't know any of you."

"I appreciate that."

"I've viewed a video tape of part of the attack. Shot by a civilian from the other side of the street. I saw Miss Barnes risk her life to save my daughter. It was a very brave act."

Jenny returned with a mug of coffee and set it down on an end table. "Just the way you like it, Inspector."

Ballard looked at her. "Did you make it?"

That broke everyone up, and laughter echoed around the living room.

"He knows you well, Jenny," John said.

"I have to say this," Ballard said. "Miss Barnes and I did not get along, but she was a fine agent. And she couldn't make a decent cup of coffee if her life depended on it."

Thirty-two

Ballard stayed just long enough to drink his coffee and make a phone call. He and Denise left moments after he hung up the phone.

"Let's pack up what's left and get out of here," John said.

The team was out the door and gone ten minutes later, heading for a furnished house in a nice neighborhood in Queens.

John called in as soon as they arrived.

"You think the terrorists are still in the New York City area?" he was asked.

"I don't know for sure where they are," he told the voice. "I don't know whether André is playing this by ear or whether it was all planned out well in advance."

"Well, hold onto your hat for this: our people think he will try for the president tomorrow."

John thought about that for a moment. "The Bureau?"

"Our sources tell us they feel the same."

"If that's the case, there'll be five hundred federal agents in and around that hotel."

"At least that many."

John was silent for a few heartbeats.

"Are you still there, Barrone?"

"Yes, I'm here. Just doing some thinking. Let me voice my opinion now, and you're probably not going to like it: I think what you're telling me, in a roundabout way, is that neither your experts or anyone's else's experts have a clue as to what in the hell André is going to do next."

There was an even longer pause at Control's end. "That, ah, is bluntly put but basically correct."

"And all the rest you said about the president is pure speculation, right?"

"Unfortunately that, too, is correct. But we prefer to call it an educated guess."

"Call it anything you like. Can you tell me the death count at the UN?"

"Sixty-five dead, so far. Seventy wounded. Some of those are not expected to live."

"Then let me add another opinion—"

"I think I already know what you're going to say, but go ahead."

"There will be federal agents crawling over each other. Probably, certainly, doing so as we speak. In short, there is no place for us here, and nothing for us to do."

"Not necessarily, Barrone. I think on the very fringe of the action is a good place for your people."

"Why?"

"You know the answer to that."

"Yes, I'm sure I do. But I want you to say it. I don't want any doubts about this."

"You will follow any PLF members who survive the attack and kill them."

"I thought so. Very well. Understood."

"Are your new accommodations satisfactory?"

"Just lovely."

"I want to apologize to you and your team."

"Apologize? For what?"

"For this operation. No one here thought it would turn out to be so, well, bizarre."

"Well, I thank you, Control. Apologies are not needed, but they are accepted."

"You will pass them on to your team."

"As soon as we hang up."

"Which is right now."

The connection was broken.

John turned to face his team and almost bumped into Jenny, who was standing at his elbow.

"Control sends his, their, apologies for this operation being such a screwup."

"How nice of him, them," Jenny said. "Whatever."

"We have new orders?" Al asked.

John laughed. "Well, sort of. Control admits their experts don't have a clue as to what André and his people will do next. So we're to prowl around the hotel where the president will be staying."

"Smack in the middle of several hundred federal agents?" Paul asked.

"We're to stay on the fringes of any action that might develop."

"And do what?" Linda asked.

"We are to follow and neutralize any PLF members who might get away."

"Is that all?" Jenny questioned. "No prisoners?"

"I haven't made up my mind about that."

"Well, good luck to us," Bob said sarcastically. "If the feds don't pick us up for questioning after spotting us loitering around for hours, and the PLF actually strikes at the hotel, and if we don't get shot by some of the president's own security people if something does happen, we might actually get out of this mess alive. John, who in the hell thought up this one?"

"I think Control realizes they threw us into this assignment without adequate preparation. It was a shakedown assignment that ballooned into something much bigger than they ever imagined. But we're in it, and we're going to see it through. So . . . there it is."

"John," Al said. "Does Control have any evidence that André's group is still in the area?"

"He didn't say. But I very much doubt it."

"So far there hasn't been anything on the news about Ballard's daughter," Bob said. "And it's been two hours since he took her to the hospital."

"He managed to sit on it," John replied. "For the time being. It'll break before long. But that isn't our worry. Ballard can't implicate us without admitting he knew all along of our existence and involvement."

"So what do we do now?" Paul asked.

"Send out for some food, have a good meal, and relax."

"I can fix something," Jenny said. "What would you all like?"

"I'll go get a sack of hamburgers," Bob quickly volunteered.

The president was staying at New York City's most prestigious hotel. He would speak in the same hotel. The political love-fest would cost the party faithful a thousand dollars a plate, and the banquet hall was booked to capacity.

Security was tighter than it had ever been, both inside and out. Standard security procedures had been tightened even further. The hotel had been "swept"—visually, electronically, and with dogs—and would be again just before the president was due to arrive.

The Secret Service had done all that was humanly possible to insure the president's safety.

All that was left was prayer.

Friday 0700

John and his team were up and dressed, sitting in the living room drinking coffee. The day had turned bitterly cold, the skies occasionally spitting bits of sleet and snow.

"I've lost track of time," Linda said. "Has Thanksgiving come and gone and we didn't notice?"

"Next week," John told her. "It's unusually bitter here for this time of the year."

"I wonder where we'll all be on Christmas day." Jenny said.

"You can bet Control has that all worked out," Al said. "Right, John?"

"I'm sure they do. But they haven't informed me as yet."

"I hope it takes us somewhere warm," Linda said. "I'm a California girl."

"Does anybody have any idea what the hell we're supposed to do once we get to the vicinity of the hotel?" Jenny asked. "I mean, come on, folks, we're going to stand out like Bob Jones at a Jim Smith convention."

John smiled at her analogy. "We'll get to the area about thirty minutes before the president arrives. We'll walk around and window shop. Teams of two. Jenny, you're with me. Linda, you and Bob. Al, you and Paul. Once the president is inside the hotel, he's out of our hair and I'm not going to worry about it. We can go back to the house and get drunk."

John's cell phone rang and he picked it up and listened for a moment. "Son of a bitch!" he blurted. "No, not you. Yes. The changing situation. I agree. That might create some problems, for a fact. All right, duly noted. We'll adjust our plans. Yes. I know it's going to be a big mess. And that's just what André was hoping for. If he's in New York, and if he was planning to strike at the president. Yes. Thank you very much. We'll do our best. I assure you of that."

John clicked off the phone and placed it on an end table. He felt like hurling it against a wall. He paced the room in silence for a few seconds. His face registered his anger, and Jenny picked up on it immediately.

"You want to give us the bad news?" she said. "Before you blow up all over the room."

"The president's plane will be arriving a couple of hours late due to bad weather. That will put him in town right in the middle of rush hour traffic."

"André will love that," Linda said.

"If he's in town," Bob said.

"We'll know in about ten hours," John said. "One way or another," he added grimly. "But if André does attack the president at the hotel, we do nothing. Understood? Nothing. We show guns in that crowd, we're arrested at best, dead at the worst. We lay back until it's over, pick our PLF person, and follow. Keep in touch with the other team members."

"When do we neutralize our subjects?" Paul asked.

John hesitated a few heartbeats before replying. "We try to take them alive for questioning, if possible."

"And if it's André?" Bob asked.

"Kill him."

André smiled when he heard the news about the president's plane being delayed. *Perfect,* he thought. *Streets bumper-to-bumper with traffic, many of them trying to get out of the city for the weekend, the drivers already filled with some degree of road rage, the sidewalks packed with people heading home. A great many of those people will never get home, and more than a few will leave the city in body bags, providing the pig police can find all the body parts.*

André laughed aloud, insanely, as he sat alone in his room in a rundown hotel in a very bad section of the city. The other residents in the fleabag hotel—besides a few members of his own team—were whores, drunks, dopers, and all-around losers.

Yes, everything was working out perfectly. He could not have planned it better. This just proved that sometimes it was better to let matters take their natural course and let the chips fall. He still had his Uzi and a number of full magazines. Yes, this would be his greatest coup. He was ready. He had his pistol, and he had a rucksack filled with grenades.

He and his PLF would spread bloody violence and mangled death all over midtown Manhattan. He had picked his people to attack the president, and assigned others to attack various civilian targets. Literature had been printed denouncing the grossly unequal capitalist system and explaining in detail why America was now under siege and would be until the bloated, greedy, fat cats in power were destroyed.

André picked up one of the flyers and scanned it.

OPPRESSED PEOPLES OF AMERICA—UNITE! read the header.

André thought it was beautifully worded.

Actually, it was a ridiculous mish-mash of militant socialist/anarchist/communist crap, but to André's poisonous mind it was the Bible, the Koran, and the Talmud all wrapped up into several paragraphs.

There was a tap at his door. André rose and unlocked the flimsy door. Brigitte stepped in and André waved her to the room's only chair.

"The others are resting," she said.

"Good. This evening will be trying for us all. But if we succeed it will be the greatest blow against this nation since the glorious assassination of Kennedy." He took a sip of water and sighed. "However, it will do little to solve the gross imbalance of power, since the vice president is just as rich and evil and corrupt as the president. But it will shake this government to its very roots."

"It will show the American people that no one is immune from the wrath of the oppressed," Brigitte said, mouthing a segment of the mantra of the PLF.

"Precisely. The PLF will grow into a mountain of resistance after the events of this evening. The oppressed will be clamoring to join our ranks. We might not live to see it, but our spirit will forever be alive."

"Power to the people!" Brigitte said softly, dredging up a weary slogan from America's Sad Sick Sixties.

"Yes. Now go get some rest. You will need all your strength for this evening."

André took the chair and sat for a time looking out at the street below, the concrete slick with rain. He imagined the slickness to be blood, and that filled him with a lust for the mission only hours away. In his mind he could hear the screams of the wounded and the rattle of gunfire.

When those sounds had subsided, André stretched out on the sagging bed and slept very peacefully, a smile on his lips.

Thirty-three

John's team whiled away the morning napping, reading, and just taking it easy. At one o'clock they packed up and got ready to head into the city.

Linda stood in the living room and said, "I wonder how many houses and apartments the organization owns around the country."

"Dozens, I would guess," John said. "It wouldn't surprise me to learn they own some nationwide real estate agency. Maybe several of them."

"That's an interesting thought," Jenny said. "Oh . . . the next time you talk to them, John, ask if they own some nice hotels, with room service and exercise rooms and Jacuzzis. It would be a nice change."

"I'll be sure to inquire. Just for you."

"Thanks. You're a real pal."

John was sure all the neighbors wondered what in the world was going on when six people moved in one day and then moved out the next, but he didn't wonder about it for very long. He knew it was a dead bang certainty this place would never be used as a safe house again. At least not by this team.

John wondered, and not for the first time, if his was the only team or if the organization had other teams working somewhere in the world. Others in his group had also wondered about that. The only answer John could give them was that he didn't know.

The weather was really lousy and traffic was heavy and running slow. By the time the team got into the city and found a place to park their vehicles it was mid-afternoon, and the temperature had dropped a few more degrees.

"Delightful weather," Linda said.

"It'll probably get worse," Bob told her.

"Thanks, I really needed that," she replied. "I should have bought some long underwear."

"Reminds me of winters back home in Missouri," Jenny said. "I miss them."

Linda looked at her and shook her head in disbelief.

"A couple of hours to go," John told the group. "Split up and wander around, window shop."

"And if we spot some of André's group?" Paul asked.

"Keep them in visual and bump me. I'll get word to Control and they can take it from there."

"But we don't take them?" Bob asked.

"No. Not until they've made their move. I've talked with Control three times today. Those orders stand."

"The president might well be dead before we get around to doing that," Al said.

"And so could we if we show weapons around dozens of federal agents," John pointed out again. We'd be shot down in a single heartbeat. Sorry, but that's the way it's got to be, gang. We'll follow orders and do our best. And we'll protect our own asses."

Jenny grinned and patted her butt. "Absolutely right. Very valuable to me."

"Let's go, folks. And don't buy anything you can't slip into your pocket. The agents protecting the president will be looking hard at people carrying shopping bags." John paused and smiled at his team. "Good luck, people."

André and his people had split up into five groups of six each. They all wore loose-fitting overcoats. Under the coats were automatic weapons, a dozen or more full magazines each, pistols and spare magazines, and some of the most powerful grenades ever manufactured.

They had left their various locations and were making their way toward the hotel, where the president was due to arrive in the late afternoon. Some were taking the bus, others the subway. André and his personal group took taxis.

None of the PLF taking part in this upcoming action believed they would make it out alive, even though all would try to do so. They had said their good-byes and were ready to die for the cause.

They arrived a few blocks from the hotel about forty minutes before President Kelley was due to arrive. By listening to small portable radios they knew his plane was about to touch down. Using a cell phone, André issued his instructions to the other five teams.

The streets were lined with New York's finest, braving the unseasonable weather stoically, waiting for the president's motorcade to pass by.

John and Jenny were two blocks from the hotel, strolling along, window-shopping. The two other teams were doing the same. So far, they had spotted no known members of the PLF.

"I am freezing my butt off," Jenny told John. "Let's step into this joint and get a cup of coffee."

"It's a bar, Jenny."

"So we'll have a beer."

"They've got a TV going," John said, peering into the place. "We'll know when the president is getting close. OK. Let's see if they can serve us some coffee."

Jenny touched his arm. "We've got company heading our way."

Without turning his head, John asked, "Who is it?"

"The British have arrived. Camilla and Henry."

"Have they seen us?"

"Not yet. Oops. I spoke too soon. Here they come."

"Good afternoon," Henry said. "What a coincidence, meeting you both in this large city."

"Stranger things have happened, I suppose," John replied. "You and Camilla out for a pleasant little stroll in this lovely weather?"

"Oh, quite, John. Are you and Miss Barnes in the habit of loitering outside pubs in the rain?"

"Actually, we were thinking about getting a cup of coffee. Care to join us?"

"I believe a gin would be more in order," Henry replied.

"I'll take a vodka martini," John said. "Come on."

"Vodka will eventually drive a man insane, old boy."

"Aren't we already?"

Thompkins chuckled. "Point well taken, John. Quite right. Come, ladies. We'll imbibe."

Seated at a back booth in the warm establishment, drinks in front of them, John said, "So you think André will strike when the man arrives today, Henry?"

"It's only logical."

"André isn't logical," Jenny said. "He's nuts."

"Oh, quite right, Miss Barnes," Henry agreed. "But brilliantly so."

"Isolate your target, create a diversion, and strike," Camilla said.

John looked up from stirring his martini with the olive-laden toothpick. "What will be the diversion?"

"I wish we knew," Henry replied.

"Level with me, Henry?" John asked.

"If at all possible."

"What are your orders concerning André?"

"Kill him," the MI6 man said bluntly. "What are yours?"

"Follow any survivors of the attack."

"To the core of the cell and then kill them?"

"Yes."

"All right."

"Have you seen Jacques?"

"He's at the hotel."

"What does he hope to accomplish by staying there?"

"I can only presume he's under orders. The Canadians have backed off, as have the Germans."

"All at the hotel?"

"Yes."

"I find that odd."

"Orders, old boy. The talk is that directive came from your president."

"Really? Now, that is odd."

"Yes. That's the way I view it."

Henry took a drink of his gin and tonic. "Interesting group you have, John."

"Thank you. We work well together."

"But who do you work for? That's the question."

John smiled. "I run a security service primarily. I thought I gave you one of our cards."

"Stuff and nonsense. I don't believe that for an instant. And neither does anyone else."

"Oh, but it all checks out, Henry. Don't you think Ballard ran us?"

"I'm sure he did, and I'm sure it does. On the surface. But. . . ." He paused and cocked his head to one side. "I thought I heard sirens. Thought it might be your president's party motoring through traffic."

"Not yet. If the TV doesn't announce it, we'll know anyway."

"How?"

"Through the magic of electronics, Henry."

"I beg your pardon?"

"Cell phones."

"After that tiny bit of information, I shall quickly finish my drink and be on my way. Are you going to dawdle over that hideous drink of yours all day, John?"

"A while longer, Henry."

"Very well. Be sure to eat your olives. They'll help you

keep up your strength." Henry downed his gin and tonic, and he and Ms. Farnsworth left.

"That man is a character," Jenny remarked.

"One of the best in the business, Jenny. He's been around as long as I have."

She frowned. "You make it sound as though you're over the hill."

"I'm not very many years away from that point. And that's the truth."

"I don't believe that. I went through training with you, re-member?"

"And believe me, several times I thought I wasn't going to make it."

She patted his hand. "Well, for an old goat you do pretty well."

John smiled at her. "Thank you so much, you young whip-persnapper."

They both looked up as a special bulletin flashed on the television; President Kelley's plane was on the ground.

John sighed, picked up his martini, and made a mock salute toward the television. Then he drained his glass. "Time to go to work, kid."

"Well, it was nice and warm for a while."

"I distinctly remember you saying that you liked this type of weather. Twice, as a matter of fact."

"Oh, the first time I said that for Ms. Iron Pants' benefit."

"Ms. Iron Pants? You're not referring, I hope, to that dear sweet Camilla?"

"John?"

"Yes, Jenny?"

John's ears were blistering as they walked out into the cold air.

Thirty-four

The president's car was three blocks from the hotel when the PLF struck. A grenade was furtively rolled under a parked police car. The woman who pulled the pin on the minibomb walked on unnoticed in the crowd. Fortunately for the police, the vehicle was unoccupied. When the grenade blew, the patrol car bowed up in the middle, the light bar was blown off, the windshield was blown out, and the crowd panicked. The patrol car did not blow up or catch on fire.

The president's motorcade barreled on toward the safety of the fortress-like hotel, being waved on through the lights by the police.

"It's started!" John said, as the muffled crumping sounds of the explosion reached him. "That crazy son of a bitch is really going to try for the president."

"Look around us," Jenny said. "There are plainclothes agents everywhere."

John stood with Jenny on the sidewalk, in the gathering crowd, and looked around him. A dozen men and women, on both sides of the street, had brushed back their coats and were ready to pull sidearms. A couple were talking into their shirtcuffs, using tiny, miniaturized transmitters. Others had opened and dropped briefcases, pulling out automatic weapons.

"Stand easy and quiet," John said softly. "We're just on-lookers here."

"You bet," Jenny replied. "My hands are in my pockets."

A half a block away, across the street and up from where they stood, another explosion ripped the cold, rainy late afternoon. The show windows of a store blew out, filling the air with sharp and deadly shards of glass and bits and pieces of mannequins and ripped articles of clothing. Half a dozen passersby were knocked to the sidewalk, cut and bleeding.

A young man ran from the crowd, an Uzi in his hands. He opened fire indiscriminately and began slowly swinging the weapon toward where John and Jenny were standing. The pair made a dive for the safety of a doorway a few yards behind them just as the PLF terrorist began spraying the area where they had been standing with 9mm fire.

The wet sidewalk was suddenly littered with wounded men and women, lifeblood leaking from their torn and shattered bodies.

Those men and women still standing on both sides of the street panicked and began screaming and running in all directions, preventing the plainclothes agents from opening fire on the terrorist.

The PLF member laughed as he slipped in a fresh magazine and resumed firing, triggering off short bursts, sending more wounded men and women to the sidewalk and street. He shouted unintelligible words above the screaming and moaning and crying of the wounded.

"What the hell did he say?" John said.

"Shit!" Jenny muttered, lying close to John. "Who knows? Who cares? I just wish somebody would hurry up and shoot that crazy bastard."

Somebody did. Two federal agents suddenly got a clear field of fire and put several rounds into the man's chest, knocking him down. As the terrorist lay severely wounded on the cold concrete, he released his Uzi and pulled the pins on two grenades. Using the last of his strength, he tossed them. Then he lapsed into unconsciousness.

The grenades exploded, one on the sidewalk, the other in the street. The one that landed in the street killed or injured no one, but the grenade that landed on the sidewalk blew a woman and her child into eternity, splattering them all over a parked police car.

Several hundred yards away, closer to the target hotel, another explosion cut the fading light of late afternoon, just as the president's car began to pull into the hotel's parking garage. But it could not pull all the way into the garage, for the entrance was blocked by the smoking ruin of a car.

Another heavy explosion rocked the late afternoon air. Smoke and flames could be seen for blocks.

"They've blocked the president's party!" a uniformed cop yelled. "Front and back. He can't go anywhere."

"Now it gets real interesting," John said, getting to his feet. Jenny had already bounced up.

"Do we notify the others?"

"No. They have their orders. We wait. Let's see if we can help these wounded."

Only two of André's five groups had attacked. The other three had held back, waiting. Now they struck simultaneously, and struck hard.

Two more NYPD patrol cars blew up from live grenades being rolled under them. No police officers were in the units, but that was about to change.

A PLF member sprayed a patrol car with automatic weapons fire while standing on a street corner, across from John and Jenny. An unarmed man with more guts than sense tried to wrest the Uzi away from the terrorist and got a belly full of 9mm rounds for his efforts.

The two officers in the unit were wounded but not out of the game. They rolled out of their crippled unit, sidearms drawn, but could not get a clear shot at the terrorist. The PLF member had grabbed a young woman and was using her as a shield as he laughed and fired his weapon into the crowd standing at the intersection.

John could hear the wild laughter, and wondered if the terrorists were popped up, high on something.

The terrorist slowly backed away from the two officers, still holding the terrified woman in front of him. The cops crouched behind their bullet-riddled unit, pistols ready, but could not risk a shot for fear of hitting the woman.

The PLF terrorist suddenly pushed the woman away from him and ran into a store. The released woman staggered for a second, then tried to run toward the officers. The terrorist gave her a short burst from his Uzi, the 9mm rounds slamming into her back and knocking her to the sidewalk. She was dead before she impacted with the concrete.

The police officers fired, their rounds hitting the PLF member in the chest and belly. He screamed and dropped the Uzi, then fell to the sidewalk.

The entire terrible scenario, from the instant the woman was released until she was shot dead and the police fired, killing the terrorist, had taken no more than a few seconds.

Up the street, the Secret Service was in a panic trying to get the president to safety.

The sidewalk and the street in front of the hotel and the entrance to the hotel's parking garage were all a jumble of smoking, explosion-shattered vehicles and broken and bleeding bodies. Cars and Secret Service SUVs had pulled up on either side of the president's limo, to protect him from bullets and grenades. Agents were all around the president's limo, forming several defensive lines.

A block away from the hotel, on a street that had not been blocked off for the president's arrival, a PLF terrorist tossed a couple of grenades under a bus. The crippled bus stopped in the street and the explosion blew out the windows. The terrorist was shot and killed by NYPD officers seconds after the blast, but that did not help those riding the bus. Several passengers were killed immediately, a dozen others wounded, and the bus caught on fire. Police and EMTs worked frantically in the smoke and flames to get the remaining passengers off the bus.

A terrorist, screaming hate for America and shouting idiotic

PLF slogans, jumped out of a crowd of people huddled in a doorway and charged the line of agents protecting the president, firing his weapon. He did not even get close before Secret Service agents shot him dead.

André and Max, both dressed in nice suits and expensive topcoats, clean-shaven and with their hair freshly cut and combed, made it inside the hotel with several dozen other pedestrians, as if trying to escape the terror raging outside.

"Shove that goddamn vehicle out of the way!" a Secret Service agent shouted to the driver of the president's limo. "Ram it!"

The driver of the custom-built, bulletproof limo told the president, "Hang on, sir!" And he rammed the crippled vehicle.

It moved only a couple of feet.

The street in front of the hotel had turned into a traffic nightmare.

"It's in park, with the emergency brake on," an attendant shouted.

"Shit!" an agent said. He waved at the limo driver. "Ram it again."

This time the crippled vehicle was moved enough to allow the limo to maneuver past. Once inside the garage, the limo pulled quickly to safety. A net of security people was immediately around it.

"Stay in the car," the driver told the president. "We're pulling other vehicles around, creating a shield."

André and Max had slipped away from the crowd and walked to the men's room. There, they stuffed their hats and topcoats into the trash and changed the type of fake eyeglasses they were wearing. Their Uzis, spare magazines, and grenades were in oversized briefcases. They carried pistols in shoulder holsters.

"We may get a chance to kill the son of a bitch, after all," André said.

"If not him, at least many others." André really had no illusions concerning his chances of killing President Kelley. If the opportunity presented itself, fine. If not, that was all right. He just wanted to kill Americans.

Max moved toward the door. "Now?"

"Let's do it."

They stepped out of the men's room, looking just like dozens of other men in suits, carrying briefcases and milling around in the lobby of the hotel.

No one gave them a second glance.

"Split up," André said. "And good hunting."

John used his cell phone to contact the other members of his team. They all reported basically the same thing: death and panic in the streets.

"It appears there are at least five teams of the PLF working," Linda said. "Maybe more."

"We've had a report that federal agents have exchanged fire with agents from a different department," Paul said. "We can't confirm that."

"Where is the president?" John asked.

"In the hotel parking garage. Surrounded by dozens of Secret Service agents."

"Any sign of André?"

"Negative."

"Orders?" Linda asked.

"Stay put. Stay clear of the hotel. Remain on the perimeter."

Inside the hotel, André had walked past an agent guarding the exit stairs, paused, turned around and asked, "When do you think it will be safe outside, sir?"

"I don't know, buddy," the agent said. "But it's going to be a while."

"My wife is going to kill me," André said. "I've missed my train, and we were supposed to go out to dinner tonight."

"I know that feeling."

"Oh, well," André replied. "Time to head for the bar."

The agent smiled understandingly and nodded.

André returned the smile and walked over to the bar, now crowded with men and women who had ducked into the hotel when the shooting started, looking for safety. He pushed his way to the bar.

After a moment, André caught the busy bartender's eye and called, "Beefeater martini, please. Straight up."

"What a fucked-up mess," the man standing next to him said bluntly.

"It is that, for sure," André replied. "Are you staying here?"

"Yeah. I picked a hell of a time for a weekend in New York, didn't I?"

"I just ducked in here when the shooting started. I missed my train, and my wife is going to be some kind of pissed at me. Say, where's the men's room?"

"Ah, it's . . . well, hell, I got to go myself. Come on. I'll show you."

When André stepped out of the men's room a few minutes later, he had the stranger's electronic room card, still in its registration envelope, the room number on the envelope. The stranger was sitting on the commode, the stall door closed. He was quite dead. André had taken all the man's identification. He might not have to use the room card, but it was added insurance in case he was questioned by the president's bodyguards.

André did not return to the hotel bar. He walked confidently through the lobby to the elevators and was stopped by a plainclothes guard. He showed the man his room card and was admitted onto the elevator.

André went straight to his floor and walked down the deserted hallway to the correct room, very much aware that he was probably being monitored by the hotel's video cameras, placed in every corridor.

He entered the room without trouble and fixed a drink from the minibar. He walked to the window and looked out. The street several stories below was still blocked off. The rain had stopped. The day had slowly melted into deceptive dusk.

André sat down on the bed and pondered his next move. He didn't have a clue what that might be. Killing the stranger at the bar and taking his room seemed like a good idea at the time. Now he wasn't so sure.

But at least he was now inside the hotel, and that much closer to the president of the United States. That was something.

The presidential suite was above his floor, André thought. To get to it the president had to use the elevator. André smiled as he opened his oversize briefcase and touched one of his grenades.

Now he had a plan.

Thirty-five

"I saw that bastard at the UN," Jenny said, cutting her eyes to a man with blond hair standing on the corner across the street from them.

"I see him and recognize him," John replied. "He was using an Uzi there."

"It's in his briefcase. Bet you."

"No bet. OK, he's walking across toward us. Get ready to tail him. I'll be half a block behind you."

"When do we grab him, and what the hell do we do with him?"

"Both are very good questions."

"In other words, you don't know."

"You catch on fast."

"Wonderful. OK. I'm off."

"Stay cool, kiddo."

"That's me."

The terrorist did not even glance at Jenny when she stepped in behind him, about two dozen yards back. It was now full night in the city and the cold rain had resumed—rain mixed with tiny pellets of ice. His name was Vani, and he had become separated from his team and was lost in the strange city. He had been in the States only a few weeks, and most of that time he had spent in hiding. He did not realize he was only a few blocks from the hotel.

A huge fire truck turned the corner, coming straight up the

street at him, sirens wailing and lights flashing. Jenny saw a bum come staggering out of an alley in the middle of the block, and decided that was as good a spot as any to take the PLF member.

Just as the truck passed, Vani felt something slam into his back. It felt as though he'd been hit with a block of concrete. He was thrown into the alley and pinned there on the filthy alley floor. *I've been mugged!* he thought. *I've survived all that has happened this day in this city, only to be mugged.*

Vani felt the cold muzzle of a pistol pressing against his neck. He had lost his grip on his briefcase.

"Don't move, sucker," Jenny told him.

A woman? Vani thought. *I've been mugged by a woman!*

"Good work," a man's voice said. "You sure you've got him?"

"If he moves he'll never use this shoulder again," Jenny replied, moving the muzzle of her pistol to Vani's right shoulder. "You understand me, asshole?"

"I understand," Vani said. "But I will never talk. I will never tell you anything. I promise you that."

"Yeah, right. I've heard that a few times. What the hell are you doing, John?"

"Calling Kemper."

"Not Ballard?"

"Kemper is Agency. He knows how to keep his mouth shut."

The CIA man answered his cell phone and John gave him their location and told him what they had waiting for him.

"He's alive?"

"Very much so. Get over here pronto."

"In less than five minutes, partner."

"Sit on him," John told Jenny. "If he starts anything, rap him on the noggin."

"I will remain quiet," Vani said. "Now that our mission is concluded, I have no death wish. I assure you, I am not a fanatic."

"Just a killer," Jenny said.

"I kill to draw attention to the world's oppressed. Not because I enjoy it."

"How wonderful for you," Jenny said sarcastically. "I'm sure the dead really appreciate what you're doing."

"You don't understand," Vani said.

"I sure don't."

"Forget it," John told her. "Trying to plumb the depths of a terrorist's mind is reminiscent of some of Kipling's words."

"You'll have to explain that to me sometime, John."

"You never read Kipling?"

" 'Fraid not."

"I have," Vani muttered, his face pressed against the cold, wet alley floor. "The man was a racist pig and a terrible poet."

John shook his head and walked toward the mouth of the alley. Before he reached the street a car slowed, pulled in, and stopped. Four men got out, one of them Kemper.

John jerked a thumb at the darkness behind him. "He's all yours, Kemp. And you're welcome to him."

"This will be the only one of the bunch taken alive so far," Kemp said. "You've been a busy boy this evening, John."

"Lucky is the word. We were just passing by when we spotted this one."

"Oh, I'm sure you were. Just out for a quiet stroll in this pleasant weather, were you?"

"That's right."

"I don't know just how I'm going to explain this, but I'll come up with something."

"I'm sure you will. That's exactly why I called you and not Ballard."

Vani was hauled to his feet and stuffed into the backseat of the car.

"The president?" John asked.

"Safe."

"The death count so far?"

"Not too bad. Maybe a dozen dead. Twice that number wounded."

"That's bad enough."

"You and I have seen much worse around the world, ole buddy."

"But this is America."

"And it's going to get worse," Kemp responded. "You know it, and I know it."

"Yes. Unfortunately, I have to agree with you."

The wind and rain suddenly picked up, blowing cold and wet up and through the alley.

"Lousy fucking weather," Kemp said. "What now, John? For you and your people, I mean."

"Oh, we'll get a new security assignment. We have quite a waiting list of people requiring our services."

Kemp laughed at that. "I'm sure you will. By all means, stay with that story. It's amusing."

"Glad you like it."

"I didn't see you tonight, ole buddy."

"You got that right, Kemp."

Kemp turned away without another word and walked back to the car. The car backed out of the alley and was gone.

"What happens to that PLF member now?" Jenny asked.

"Don't ask."

Jenny got the message.

André took a chance and used his new cell phone to call Max. Max answered on the second ring.

"You're all right!" Max said in a low voice. "I was worried."

"You?"

"So far, so good. I haven't even drawn a suspicious glance so far."

"Where is the president?"

"In the parking garage. I heard some people talking."

"All right. I have a plan. I will outline it to the others. You listen carefully. . . ."

* * *

"Let's make our way toward the hotel," John said. "I have a bad feeling about all this."

"What do you mean?" Jenny asked.

"I can't explain it, kiddo."

Jenny looked at him in the dim light that made its way to the center of the block where they were standing, near the mouth of the alley. "Indigestion, maybe?"

"I wish." John called the other team members and told them to get close to the hotel.

"And do what?" Paul asked.

"I don't know," John admitted. "Maybe nothing. Just get close and play it by ear." He tried Kemper's number. Busy. He tried to call Ballard and was told the FBI man was not available for personal calls. He turned to Jenny. "Let's go."

"You think André made the hotel, don't you?"

"I think there's a chance he did, yes."

The two began walking up the street. They turned the corner and again faced the blast of cold wind and drizzle. John tried Kemper's number again. It was busy. "Damn," he muttered.

Jenny glanced at him as he stuck the cell phone back into his pocket. "Ballard?"

"He's out of pocket—not receiving calls."

"And now we're going to do what?"

"Stay as close to the hotel as we can and hope for the best, I suppose."

"Maybe Kemper can get something out of that goober we gave him."

"Goober?" John smiled in the cold darkness.

"Old Missouri expression."

"It certainly fits him. But as far as that . . . goober goes, anything Kemp can get out of him will be too late. If André made the hotel, whatever is going to happen will happen in the next few minutes. All we can do is try to sweep up the pieces."

They rounded a corner and stopped. "My God, look at that up ahead," Jenny said.

For several blocks around the hotel, there was a nearly blinding array of red and blue flashing lights.

Using his cell phone, John called the other teams. "Can anybody get close to the hotel?"

Negative, from both teams.

"We're facing wooden barriers less than a block away," Paul said. "Any closer and we'll draw attention to ourselves."

"Not a chance," Linda said. "We're blocked from getting any closer to the hotel."

"All right," John told them. "Get as close as you can and maintain that position. It's all we can do. Everything is out of our hands now."

Inside the hotel, standing in the lobby, Max called André on his cell phone and whispered, "The president is approaching the elevators."

"As soon as you hear the explosions, open fire," André ordered calmly. "Kill as many as possible. This will be our last chance."

"I understand. The president is now in the elevator. Doors are closing."

"I will see you in eternity," André said, then broke the connection.

Max slipped his phone into his topcoat pocket.

André took a small flat crowbar from his briefcase and pried open the elevator door. Holding the door open with his foot, he pulled the pin on the grenade.

"Freeze!" a Secret Service agent shouted from the other end of the hall.

André dropped the grenade down the elevator shaft and opened fire with his Uzi.

Thirty-six

The grenade bounced to one side and became wedged between the wall of the shaft and the elevator before it blew. One side of the elevator was blown inward, seriously injuring several of the president's invited guests. The cables were not damaged, but the elevator was stuck and filled with hysterical passengers.

President Kelley was not in that elevator; he was in the one just to the right.

The Secret Service immediately hit the stop button on the president's elevator and headed back to the lobby. There, they hustled the president into a nearby office and sealed it off with a human wall of armed agents.

"Jesus Christ!" were the first words President Kelley said after being seated.

"How in the hell did they get inside the hotel?" a senior agent questioned.

"I'd like to know that myself," President Kelley said.

"Probably came in with the rush of people when the shooting started," another agent answered.

"We can worry about that later," another agent said. "Heads up, and stay that way."

Max's mini-Uzi had caught on the inside of his suitcoat and then in the shoulder holster. He had missed his chance to kill a lobby full of Americans, and he felt like a fool.

"To hell with it," he muttered, and laid his briefcase on a

table and opened it. He took out two grenades and, in front of a dozen horrified onlookers, pulled the pins and laughed aloud. "The PLF forever!" he shouted. He released the spoon, tossed one grenade into a knot of men and women standing close by, and then threw the second grenade into the bar.

Before either grenade blew, Max had grabbed half a dozen full magazines from his briefcase and was off and running. He jumped behind the registration counter just as the grenades blew.

It was absolute chaos in the hotel lobby. Men and women were sprawled on the floor, dead, dying, and severely wounded. The bar was a broken shambles, bleeding and broken bodies piled on top of each other.

Max stood up and opened fire on the panicked crowd. He burned a full magazine that knocked half a dozen people to the floor before one of President Kelley's guards got lead into him. Max was thrown back by the shot, badly injured and bleeding, but managed to crawl to his feet and slip a full mag into his Uzi. He gave the agent who shot him a short burst that knocked the woman down, then turned his weapon toward any target he could find. He killed two of the reservation counter staff before half a dozen federal agents put him down with a dozen rounds in his body. Max hit the floor, dead.

André tore the body armor off the dead federal agent, slipped the agent's weapon and spare mags into a jacket pocket, and ran to the door to his room. He dumped the contents of his briefcase into a cloth sack and exited the room, walking calmly to the door leading to the emergency stairs. He took the steps two at a time, pausing at the door to each floor. They were all locked.

"I believe this is against the law," André said with a strange smile. "I should write a letter to the fire marshal protesting this irresponsible action."

André paused long enough to slip into the body armor and check all his weapons. They were loaded up full and ready to bang. He still had several grenades.

But he had no idea where the American president was.

"No matter," André muttered, catching his breath. "One rich American is as good as another. As long as they're dead."

He heard footsteps racing up the stairs. André grinned and leveled his Uzi, waiting for his targets to appear.

With any kind of luck, he thought, *I can kill or at least stop all of them with ricochets.* He angled the muzzle toward the concrete wall and laughed as he pulled the trigger.

"Another terrorist down in the hotel," Jenny said, walking back to John. She had been standing near a line of New York cops, listening. "But he killed a dozen people and wounded two dozen more before they nailed him."

"The president?"

"Safe and unhurt. So far," she added. "You talk to the other teams again?"

"Yes. They're as close as they can get. All we can do is wait. André?"

"They're sure he's in the hotel."

John thought about that for a few seconds. "Jenny, that slippery bastard just might make it out of the hotel. But I don't believe it will be out the front entrance. Bump the others and tell them to watch the alleys closely. Just watch them, don't go in them."

"Got it." She looked suspiciously at him. "What are you going to do, John?"

"Wander around."

"Alone?"

"Yes."

"What do you want me to do?"

"Wander and stay ready for anything. There are a lot of alleys and not enough of us."

"Well, with all the cops around at least the danger of getting mugged is just about nil," she said with a smile.

John glanced at her, thinking that any mugger who tried to take Jenny would be a fool. "You be careful, Jenny."

"Ten-four, boss man. And you do the same."

André stepped over the bodies sprawled on the landing. The wicked, flattened-out ricochets had done exactly what he had hoped. He spat into the face of a Secret Service man who was bleeding profusely and just barely clinging to life, staring up at him through pain-filled eyes.

"American pig," André said. "If I had the time I would finish you."

"Fuck you," the agent said. "You'll never get out of this hotel."

André laughed. "I might not. But then, maybe I will. Justice is on my side."

"Justice is on your side? You're crazy!"

André kicked the man in the face, laughed, and walked on down the steps.

John had entered a store and walked past groups of people who had taken refuge there when the shooting started. No one questioned him. He walked to the rear of the store, hit the safety bar on the door, and stepped out into the alley. He smiled at how easy it had been.

He was facing one side of the hotel.

He stood in the dark alley, pressed up against the wall of the building he had just exited. There was activity at both ends of the alley, left and right, but he could detect no one in the alley. The rain had stopped, and the temperature had dropped. John thought it was probably at or below freezing. With the wind blowing at a brisk clip, it seemed much colder than it actually was.

John slowly unbuttoned his topcoat and reached inside his jacket, closing his hand around the butt of his .45. He eased it out and slipped the weapon into his right hand pocket for easier access. He waited in the dark cold, listening to the sighing of the night wind. A tin can, pushed along by the wind, rattled along the littered alley. John cut his eyes at the sound, but did not move his head. He was only a dim shadow in the night as he waited.

Inside the hotel, André used his small crowbar to jimmy the door open and stepped out onto the second floor. A Secret Service agent walked around the corner of the hall, and André shot him. The baffles in his sound suppressor were just about all blown out, but would do for what André had in mind for the time left.

André fanned the dead agent's body and took his pistol and spare magazines, dropping them into the sack he carried. He thought about taking the man's tiny transceiver, then said to hell with it and walked on around the corner of the hall.

Just as he was approaching the elevators, one donged its signal and the doors opened. André paused. The elevator was empty. André looked at it for a couple of seconds, astonishment in his eyes. Then he shrugged his shoulders and stepped inside.

"How convenient," he said as he punched the lobby button. He smiled and hummed an old song as the elevator descended. He slung his Uzi and pulled the pins on two grenades.

The doors slid open and André stepped out, a very strange smile curving his lips. He popped the spoons and tossed the powerful grenades before anyone could make a move to stop him, then quickly moved behind a group of women who had sought safety in the hotel. He jerked the Uzi into firing position just as the grenades exploded.

The crowded lobby of the beautiful hotel was filled with panic-driven chaos as a dozen people were hit by shrapnel and went down to the floor, lifeblood leaking from their broken and torn bodies. Dozens of people were trying to run in all directions, yelling and screaming in fear. All most managed to do was slam into each other, creating more terror and confusion. Some were slipping on the blood-splattered floor and falling, others tripping over them and hurtling to the floor.

Using a terrified woman as a human shield, André opened fire into the mass of confused and horror-stricken people in the lobby, sending more wounded and newly dead to the floor.

As he reached a door leading into the dining room, he shoved the woman aside and jumped into the room, racing for the kitchen.

He slammed into a waiter, knocking the man spinning to one side, and ran into the kitchen.

"Somebody kill that son of a bitch!" a woman screamed from the lobby.

"Not quite yet," André panted, that very odd smile still on his lips. He paused and lobbed another grenade toward the swinging doors he'd just entered through, then turned and ran out into the alley.

John was waiting for him. He had called Jenny at the first faint sounds of gunfire from within the hotel and told her to come on the run.

John stepped out of the cold darkness and tripped the terrorist, sending André sprawling face first to the alley floor. Then John coolly and deliberately kicked the man on the side of the head.

Jenny came running up and slapped handcuffs on André. John jerked the man to his feet and propelled him into the store he had used to exit into the alley.

"Jesus," Jenny said. "This is the main gun, John."

"André in person, kiddo. Hold up here. Call our people and tell them to get a car and come over here for us. We'll meet them in front of the store."

"How are they going to get a car?"

"Hell, steal one!"

Thirty-seven

Linda rolled up in a stretch limo with diplomatic plates. John and Jenny, with a still addled André, hurriedly piled in. Linda was in the front seat, a pistol stuck into the ribs of a very frightened driver. Bob, Paul, and Al were in the spacious double backseat.

"Good move," John complimented her. "Now let's get the hell out of here."

"Drive," Linda told the man behind the wheel.

He said something in what appeared to be Russian and shook his head.

Linda prodded him with the muzzle of the pistol and he got the message.

"Move this goddamn boat!" a New York cop yelled, running up. "Get this thing outta here! How the hell did you get into this area, anyway?"

John lowered his window just a bit and said something in German to the man.

"What?" the cop yelled.

John repeated it.

"Get outta here!" the cop yelled. "Goddamn it, learn to speak American!"

The limo driver backed up, made a U-turn in the street, and drove off.

"What did you say to him?" Jenny asked.

"I asked him where the rest rooms were."

John had the driver drop them off a few blocks from where they had parked their vehicles. André had not spoken a word since being taken prisoner. Just before exiting the limo, John handed the man two one hundred dollar bills and said, "Thanks for the ride. Buy yourself a nice dinner."

The driver smiled and slipped the money into his pocket. "I don't know who you are," he said with a heavy accent. "But I sense you are not terrorists. I will give you fifteen minutes before I call the police."

"Good enough." John stepped out of the limo. "Thanks for the ride."

John and Jenny hustled André into a vehicle and pulled out, the others right behind them.

André finally broke his long silence. "Where are you taking me? And who are you?"

"Mr. and Mrs. Santa Claus," Jenny told him. "And the elves."

"Very amusing," André said. "Well, no matter. I can make an accurate guess."

"Oh?" John asked.

"Of course. You're CIA. That's obvious."

"Glad to hear it," John said. "Now that we've got that settled, we can move right along."

Jenny was handling the wheel, John in the backseat looking after André. The other team members, in two vehicles, were tagging along behind.

Doubt suddenly appeared in André's eyes. "Where are you taking me?"

"To a safe place, André. Then we'll hand you over to another group of people."

André stared at John for a silent moment in the dimness of the interior of the vehicle. "Yes, you're CIA, all right."

John smiled. "Good guess."

André leaned back against the cushions. "I am finished, then. There will be no trial for me. I know how you people operate. Very well. I am ready to meet my fate."

John had watched Jenny speaking low into the cell phone. After she had closed the phone, he asked, "Did you make contact?"

"Yes. We'll meet your friend in a few minutes."

"Good."

"But he wants you there for the initial interrogation."

"We'll all be present. I'll insist on it."

Jenny did not have to say that John was going against orders by not killing André immediately. She had never thought he would unless the terrorist pushed him into it. But she wondered how John was going to explain this to Control. Then she wondered if perhaps John had received new orders and had not told the others about it. No matter, she concluded. This assignment, as screwed up as it had been, was almost over.

Ten of the PLF terrorists were dead; two, including André, had been captured alive. The rest had managed to escape by mingling with the panicked crowds. Eighteen dedicated PLF members were still on the loose in New York City.

But dozens of people with pocket cameras and the presence of mind and the opportunity to do it, had taken pictures. Store video cameras had hundreds of feet of the various PLF members on their vicious rampage. The TV networks had done their filming as well, with sophisticated equipment. Every member of the PLF who had taken part in the attack in New York City was now captured on film . . . which would be used in an effort to track them down.

The FBI and Secret Service now had that film and many of those cameras. The film was being processed and developed, and would soon be transmitted to every police organization in the world . . . with the exception of those countries who harbored terrorists and supported their actions.

And President Richard Kelley was alive and well and planning to make his speech. But not just to the party faithful. It would be carried live to the nation.

* * *

"The bad boy himself," Kemper said, looking at André. "Good work, John. Very good work."

"I got lucky."

"I demand a public trial!" André said. "With judge and jury. That is my right."

Kemp cut his eyes to the terrorist. "You demand? You have rights?"

John and his team had driven to one of the Agency's safe houses just a few miles north of the Bronx. Kemper and a team of his people were waiting for them.

"I certainly do have rights," André said. "Especially here in America. And a public trial is one of them."

Kemp surprised the terrorist by saying, "You'll get a trial, André. I guarantee it. You'll be tried with Vani and the others we captured."

"Vani?" André blurted. "I don't believe it."

"He is still alive and unhurt," Kemp told him. "Not a mark on him."

John's face remained expressionless. He did not believe Vani was still alive.

Jenny arched an eyebrow in surprise at the news.

"Very well," André said. "I shall say no more until the trial. Then I will make my statement."

One of Kemp's agents walked into the room. "Three more of the group captured," he announced. "Alive and not seriously hurt."

"I don't believe it," André said.

"What don't you believe?" John asked. "That we captured them, or that they're not hurt?"

André smiled and shook his head. "No matter. This is only the beginning for America. You are all unprepared for the waves of violent discontent that will soon sweep into this nation."

"Brought to us by more nutty groups such as yours?" Kemp needled the man, prodding him to talk.

"Nutty?" André said. His eyes touched on the mug of coffee John was sipping. "May I have some coffee?"

"Sure," Kemp said, signaling a man. "Coming right up. How do you like it?"

"Black."

"You got it."

A moment later a mug of coffee was placed before the terrorist.

"Thank you," André said, holding up his cuffed wrists. "I suppose it would be too much to ask to have these handcuffs removed?"

"Not a chance," Kemp told him.

"I thought not. Well, it was considerate of you to handcuff me in the front." He cut his eyes to Jenny. "That sadistic bitch insisted on cuffing my hands behind me. It was very uncomfortable."

"You have my totally insincere apologies," Jenny told him.

"Fuck you," André replied. "You capitalist cunt."

"Drink your coffee," John told him. "Before your ass overloads your mouth."

"I don't like you at all," André said, looking at John.

"I can live with it," John replied.

André took a sip of coffee. "Very good." He glanced at Kemp. "My compliments to your people." He nodded at John. "His people can go to hell."

"I'm beginning to feel like a redheaded stepchild," Jenny said.

"What?" André asked. "What does that mean?"

"Old midwestern expression," Jenny said.

"What a horrible thing to say," André told her.

"Good God," Linda said. "Now I've heard it all: a politically correct terrorist."

"Yeah, André," Jenny said. "You missed your calling. You should have been part of the Speech Police here in America.

"I am proud to be a spokesperson for the millions of oppressed people in the world," André informed the group.

"Two more PLF people just picked up," Bob said, walking into the room.

"How many people did you have, André?" Kemp asked.

André laughed. "We have hundreds around the world."

"I don't doubt that," Kemp said. "How many did you have here in New York?"

"Enough."

John stood up and walked into the next room, motioning for Jenny to follow him. "Linda, see if you can find out if any of the PLF people have talked."

"Will do."

John sat down on a couch. He would leave Kemp alone with André for a time. Kemp was very good at quiet interrogation. But John would bet a year's pay that André would never talk. He would take whatever he knew of the PLF to the grave. André was a one hundred percent, hardcase terrorist. John had dealt with many just like him.

"You think Kemper was serious when he told André he was going to trial?" Jenny whispered.

John looked at her and slowly shook his head. "No. André will never talk. He won't tell Kemp anything of any substance, anyway. And Vani is no longer with us, either. We don't make a habit of bringing terrorists back alive."

"By we, you mean the Agency."

John smiled.

Kemp walked into the room and motioned for John to join him. "You'd better hear this, John."

"He's not really talking, is he?"

"Nothing of any value. But this is interesting. It confirms what we've suspected all along."

John and Kemp sat down at the table with André. "Go ahead, André," Kemp said.

"I will tell you both this, and then I will say no more. For I know that I will never come to public trial. You, Mr. CIA man," he said, looking at Kemper, "are a liar. And you," he cut his eyes to John, "whatever you are, and whomever you work for, are five times worse."

Neither John nor Kemp said a word.

"I don't remember who wrote the novel, or even the name of it," André said after draining the last of his coffee and setting the cup down on the table. "But I do remember this line: 'Fear is the only weapon of the weak.' America is filled with fear. In every state, every city, every town. You all saw it tonight. A stampede of fear-induced panic. And tonight was only a small taste of what is coming to America. We have an arsenal of biological weapons. And we're going to use them. Not just us, but every group around this globe who advocate rights for the oppressed peoples of the world and who are willing to lay down their lives for that belief. Everything from anthrax to powdered cholera. I know you are recording this." He shrugged. "That's all right. I'm just verifying what most of you in the intelligence community already knew." The terrorist paused and looked down into his coffee cup. "May I have another cup, please?"

"Of course," Kemp said, and took his cup. He left the room and was back a moment later with a full cup of coffee.

"Thank you," André said softly, adding a smile.

John didn't trust the bastard, not for one second. André was going to pull something, John was certain of it.

"You want to tell us the rest of it, André?" Kemp gently urged.

"Yes. Of course. But there isn't that much more to tell." He took a sip of coffee. "You know, of course, there were thousands of Russian scientists suddenly unemployed when their country shifted politics and the economy collapsed? Of course you do. Many of them are no longer unemployed. They work for us, for China, for other countries who, shall we say, are very weary of being bullied by the mighty America. Those men and women whose life's work is in biological weapons are being paid rather large salaries for their knowledge." André again smiled, but this time it was a hard, cruel smile. "You in America will soon taste their handiwork, and you will die by the hundreds of thousands. I wish I could be here to see it." He took a sip of coffee. "Now you can turn off the recorder. I am finished." He suddenly laughed aloud. "But then, so are you."

John lunged to his feet, startling Kemper. "The son of a bitch has a hound dog on him, Kemp."

"Impossible! He was searched."

"Search his shoes, his belt buckle. Look in the crack of his ass, dammit."

Before Kemp could respond, the front door of the old brownstone was smashed in and the foyer was filled with men and women, all carrying machine pistols.

Thirty-eight

André, still laughing, dived under the table just as the old home erupted in gunfire. Two of Kemp's people went down, bloody and dying, riddled with 9mm rounds from sound-suppressed weapons. Jenny dropped to one knee behind a chair and opened fire, killing one of the PLF members with a head shot.

Paul took a round in the leg which knocked him down. Bob was hit in the side. One of Kemp's men took a burst in the stomach that was meant for Al. Al got two rounds of automatic weapons fire, in the shoulder and arm, that slammed him back against the fake fireplace. Another of Kemp's personnel took a burst in the face that splattered Linda with bits of bone and brain and knocked her down. She slammed her head against a coffee table and was out.

André crawled from under the table and ran into the living room, diving into the foyer and crab-crawling toward what remained of the front door.

He didn't make it.

While John and Kemp were laying down a hail of lead at those PLF members in the foyer and living room, Jenny snapped off a round and shot André in the ass.

André screamed and pitched face forward in the foyer. The bullet had entered his left buttocks and exited out the right cheek. André rolled around on the floor in his own blood, yelling in pain and frustration.

John took aim with his .45 and put a slug into the chest of a terrorist. The hot and heavy lead doubled the man over. He pitched forward, landing on top of André.

"Get off me, you bastard!" André screamed.

But the terrorist was beyond hearing anything. The .45 round had shattered his heart, killing him instantly. His body had pinned André to the floor. The leader of the terrorist group could not move. He lay on the floor and cussed in several languages. And did a lot of moaning.

Kemper fired just as a terrorist was trying to jerk the pin from a grenade. The slug struck the woman in the throat and she staggered back against the foyer wall and slowly sank to the floor, leaving a trail of bright crimson on the wall. The grenade slipped harmlessly from her suddenly limp fingers and rolled away.

The two terrorists who were still on their feet ran out what was left of the front door. The house became quiet—except for André's moaning and the gurgling of the woman who was missing a throat . . . who finally had the good grace to shut up and die.

"Shit!" Kemp said, slowly rising to his feet and looking around him at the blood and bodies. "I've lost all my team."

"So have we," Jenny said, after inspecting the bloody human mess in the foyer and making sure André could not reach a weapon. "Asshole," she told the leader of the PLF.

André cussed her.

"You hear any sirens or see any flashing lights?" Kemp asked her.

"Nothing. And those two we didn't get are gone. I watched their van pull out and turn the corner."

"Let's get the hell out of here," John said. "Get our vehicle, Jenny. Kemp, you'd better call in for a cleanup crew."

"I know my business," the CIA man said testily.

"Then tend to it," John popped right back.

Paul was on his feet, hobbling around, helping Bob get to his feet. Linda was sitting up, blood pouring from a gash on her forehead. She had a dazed look on her face. Al was struggling to get up. John walked over and helped him up.

"Sorry, John," Kemp apologized. "This has not been a real good evening."

"It's OK."

"I can walk," Paul said. "It's just a flesh wound. I'll help Jenny with the cars."

"You sure about that?" John asked.

"Yeah," the ex-Border Patrol officer said. "Bleeding has almost stopped. The bullet didn't hit anything vital."

"I'll get André," Kemp said, pocketing his cell phone. "People are on their way. Let's be gone when they get here."

"Any of your team alive?" John asked.

"No. I'll help you get your people out." He looked around him. "Christ, what a mess."

"The night isn't over yet," John reminded him.

Thirty-nine

"Our clinic still open and in the same spot, Kemp?" John asked.

"Yes. I'll call and tell them you're on the way with some patients."

"Thanks. You're going to handle André?"

"I wouldn't miss it for the world."

"You'll take good care of him?" Jenny asked.

"Rest assured of that, Miss Barnes," Kemper said with a smile. "He will be taken care of."

"Let's get out of here," John said. He stuck out his hand and Kemper took it. "Luck to you."

"Same to you. Stay loose."

"Will do."

"You rotten son of a bitch!" André yelled from his position on the floor.

"Which one of us?" John asked.

"Both of you! And that lousy cunt with you."

"I'm so offended." Jenny spoke from the shattered doorway. "I might never recover. And I hope you don't. By the way, André, how's your ass?"

André cussed her again.

"Here's Paul. I'll get our car," Jenny said. "What about the other one?"

"Leave it," Kemp said. "My people will take care of it. Get your people together and take off, John."

"Yes. See you."

Jenny took the wheel, John in the front seat with her, Bob and Al in the backseat. Linda, the least hurt of them all, was riding with Paul. Only John and Jenny had come out of the wild shoot-out unscathed.

"That was weird back there," Bob said. "Not a single neighbor showed up."

"There are no neighbors, Bob," John told him. "Not a single house on either side of that block is occupied. They're all being renovated."

"That's odd," Al said, gritting his teeth against the pain in his shoulder and arm.

"Not really," John replied. "The Agency owns them all. The renovation has taken a long time. But after the events of tonight it will speed up dramatically, and the houses will all be sold. At a nice profit, too, I might add."

After dropping off the wounded at the clinic and being assured by the doctors that they would be all right, John and Jenny headed back into midtown, John at the wheel.

"What are we going to do back there?" Jenny asked. "You think the remaining members of the PLF will attempt another strike at the president?"

"I rather doubt that," John said. "But the group is leaderless now; their hero is in custody. According to the information we have, this Brigitte woman is now running the show—if she isn't among the dead or captured, and we don't know that for sure. She's as warped in her beliefs as André. Anything could happen, and probably will."

"Midtown?"

"Your guess is as good as mine, kiddo. They might try the airports, the bus stations, the subways. There is just no way of knowing."

"Or they might just give it up and hunt a way out of the city."

"Possibly. But terrorists being what they are, I rather doubt that."

"John? Did André have an electronic tracker on him?"

"I don't know. But it's either that or the PLF has a mole reporting back to them."

"Not in our bunch!"

"No, I don't think so, either. Perhaps one of Kemp's team, or someone in the Agency's New York office. I'll opt for the latter. Kemp will find out, you can be sure of that."

"Who in the hell is financing the PLF to give them so much power?"

"Nations, private individuals, companies, corporations. Many people right here in America. A lot of them unknowingly doing so. The money is being siphoned off a few pennies or a few dollars at a time. It can add up to hundreds of thousands of dollars, even millions worldwide."

"Almost impossible to find out for sure."

"Yes. Unfortunately, that's correct. Look at that, Jenny." John pointed. "We're still blocks away from the hotel, and the flashing emergency lights are visible."

"What now?"

"We find a place to park, if we can, and hoof it."

"Wonderful. A nice pleasant stroll in the Big Apple."

"I'll make you a wager we run into someone we know."

"Please don't let it be that insufferable Ms. Iron Pants."

For the first time in several hours, John enjoyed a good laugh. "It probably will be."

"Oh, God! I hope not."

It was.

"Crap!" Jenny muttered. "About ten million people in this part of the country and we run into Ms. Ramrod Ass. Henry seems like a real nice guy. I know I've asked this before, but how in the hell does he put up with Ms. Refrigerator?"

Before John could reply, Henry Thompkins and Camilla Farnsworth had spotted them. Henry and Camilla were standing on the other side of an alley, in the middle of the block.

John and Jenny had just crossed the street to the far corner of the block.

"Hi ho, John!" Henry called, waving a gloved hand. "Camilla and I got two of those miserable buggers! They'll throw no more bombs."

"I think Henry is a bit excited," Jenny said.

"It certainly appears so," John replied.

Henry and Camilla stepped off the curb and into the dark mouth of the alley. A car engine roared and bright lights highlighted the MI6 people. The pair jumped back, but Henry was a split second too late. The car slammed into him, the front bumper catching him on the right leg and knocking him several yards back onto the sidewalk.

A pistol appeared in Camilla's hand and she pumped several fast rounds into the driver's side of the vehicle, hitting the driver in the head. The fast moving car slewed to one side, slowly did a half spin on the wet, slick road, and slammed into another vehicle parked across the street.

John and Jenny were running toward the unmoving form of Henry when four people, two men and two women, jumped from the wrecked vehicle and opened fire with automatic weapons.

Camilla gamely stood her ground, standing over Henry's body and returning the fire before she was hit and slumped to the street.

"Dammit!" John yelled, dropping to one knee and putting three very fast rounds into the chest and belly of a terrorist. The man stumbled back and fell facedown onto the sidewalk.

A woman began screaming PLF slogans and charged John and Jenny, firing and shouting as she ran.

Jenny calmly and carefully shot her twice, both rounds striking the woman in the center of the chest. She stopped as if hit with a giant fist and flipped backward, dying in the middle of the street.

Another of the terrorists leveled his Uzi at Jenny. John shot him twice, the .45 rounds hitting the man in the chest and throat. His feet slid out from under him and he dropped to the concrete, clutching the mini-Uzi, his finger still holding the trigger back. The weapon hit the sidewalk and blew a full magazine on full auto. The rounds struck the remaining terrorist, starting at her legs and working upward, the last few rounds striking her in the head and blowing her brains out.

"Move!" John ordered. "Holster your weapon and get into the alley. Go!"

"Henry and Camilla?"

"They'd do the same. Move, goddamn it!"

John and Jenny disappeared into the darkness of the alley just as several NYPD units screamed around the corner. The pair exited the alley and turned the corner, stepping onto the sidewalk just as officers cautiously shone flashlight beams into the now empty alley.

"Keep walking," John said just as several reporters, complete with camera crews, came running toward them.

"Here we go," Jenny muttered. "You can bet they'll ask us something."

"Be careful," John told them. "There was some sort of shoot-out at the other end of that alley." He pointed. "My wife and I are getting the hell out of here. Like right now. Damn place has gone crazy!"

"Did you see anything?" a reporter asked, lingering as the others ran toward the alley.

"No," Jenny said. "But we heard shooting."

"Neither of you saw anything?"

"No," John said.

"We're going back to Toledo in the morning if we can change our tickets," Jenny said. "To hell with the Big Apple."

The reporter ran off to catch up with the others without asking another question.

"Toledo?" John asked, as they resumed walking.

"It was all I could think of at the time."

"Toledo sure beats Washington, DC."

They reached the corner and paused. "Which way?" Jenny asked. "Toward the hotel?"

"No. We're finished, and the PLF is finished. At least this New York bunch is. It's all mop-up now. To hell with it. Somebody else can do it. Let's walk up the other way and find us a bar and relax."

"That's a wonderful idea. My nerves are just a little bit jangly."

"Join the club, kiddo."

They walked on for several blocks, seeing bars and passing them by, none of them appealing. At a corner, John spotted a bar in the center of a dimly lit block.

"Want to check out that one?"

"Sure."

They looked in the window. The bar was almost deserted.

"Just right," John said.

"Let's do it. It looks nice and quiet in there."

The lounge was about to get very lively.

Forty

Jenny and John sensed something was wrong the instant they entered the lounge. Tension hung in the air. The bartender stood with his forearms on the bar and did not greet them. He did not smile, just stared at them. There were half a dozen others in the room—four men, two women. They stared at the newcomers. John and Jenny took a table and waited.

After a very long moment with no service, John asked, "Is this place open for business?"

"What do you want?" the man behind the bar finally asked.

"Vodka martini on the rocks for me, a draft for the lady."

"Coming right up." But the bartender did not move, just continued to stare at them.

"What the hell?" Jenny muttered.

John had caught a glimpse of someone standing in the darkness at the end of the long room. "Get ready for trouble," he whispered to Jenny. "I think we walked into a holdup."

"Wonderful," Jenny replied in low tones. "What else is going to happen tonight?" She slipped her hand inside her coat.

John had already stuck his hand inside his jacket and gripped the butt of his .45.

"Goddamn terrorists are here," a man suddenly blurted. "They're holding us prisoners."

Jenny sighed and John shook his head minutely, whispering, "Get ready, kiddo."

"Sittin' on go, boss," Jenny murmured.

"I've seen them both!" a woman shouted. "They're federal agents. Kill them."

Jenny and John threw themselves out of their chairs and rolled on the floor, John overturning the table where they'd been sitting and then kicking over another table. It wouldn't be much protection from bullets, but certainly better than nothing. Reaching out, Jenny turned over another table.

The lead started flying then, all the PLF opening up with automatic weapons. Most of the lead that didn't hit a nail or screw tore through the first two overturned tables, but lost a lot of punch in doing so. The third table stopped most of the rest of it. The sound of gunfire in the lounge was deafening, and when John added his big .45 autoloader the noise level peaked to high.

Those few customers who had been trapped in the bar hit the floor, scrambling for safety. The bartender had dropped down behind the bar.

"No, no, Karl," someone shouted. "Don't use grenades. Oh, shit!"

The bartender came up fighting mad, a double-barreled, sawed-off shotgun in his hands. "You sons of bitches and whores!" he shouted. He gave the terrorist called Karl both barrels at a distance of no more than ten or twelve feet and literally blew the terrorist in two, the buckshot catching the PLF member in the belly. The upper half of Karl fell on top of the grenade. The bartender dropped back behind the bar to reload just a split second before the grenade went off.

Bits and pieces of Karl got splattered all over the room, and the terrorist lost his head. It bounced on the floor and rolled to a wide-eyed staring stop.

Jenny opened up and laid down a full magazine of lead, two of her rounds poking holes in a terrorist's belly. The man went down screaming, both hands on his perforated stomach.

"Hurran!" a woman shouted. "Grab a couple of civilians and let's get out of here. Use them for hostages."

Hurran stood up from behind cover, and before he could

take a step both John and Jenny drilled him in the belly and chest. Hurran fell back against a woman. Before she could recover her balance, John and Jenny nailed her, their rounds taking her in the chest, throat, and face.

"You bastards!" another women screamed, jumping up from behind cover.

"Get down, Brigitte!" a man yelled just as the bartender opened up with his sawed-off shotgun. Brigitte took the full blast in her face and went down holding back the trigger on her mini-Uzi. The automatic weapon spat out a full 32 round magazine in a couple of seconds, the 9mm rounds taking the bartender in the stomach, chest, and face.

Several of those who had been trapped in the bar made a run for the front door. A PLF member opened up with her Uzi and brought them all down in a heap before they could make the door and get out.

John and Jenny fired at the terrorist and both hit their target.

"Claire!" a man yelled.

"No use, Jan," another man yelled. "She's dead. Took one in the forehead. Let's get out of here."

They didn't make it.

John and Jenny emptied their weapons and brought them both down with killing head shots just as the pair of PLF members turned to run for the back.

"Let's go," John said. "Out the back."

NYPD units were howling up to the front of the bar as John and Jenny exited out the rear of the lounge and into the alley.

They ran to the end of the alley, then as calmly as possible stepped out onto the sidewalk and began walking until they reached the next block. There they mingled with pedestrians and walked with the flow.

"John?" Jenny said.

"Yes."

"I hate to tell you this, but I really, really have to pee!"

* * *

"I guess that about wraps it up," John told the voice. "I guess you might say that once again luck has overcome skill and training."

"It was a difficult assignment, Barrone," the voice replied. "Berating yourself is not necessary."

"Any word on our next assignment?"

"Nothing that I can discuss at the moment. You will be notified."

"I'm sure."

The line went dead.

John clicked off his cell phone and slipped it into his jacket pocket. "What a jerk!" he muttered.

Jenny laughed at the expression on his face. "Control doesn't go in for much chitchat, right?"

The two of them were sitting in a motel room just outside Philadelphia. They had driven through the night and had grabbed a few hours sleep before calling in.

"Not much. But he did clear up a few missing items on what happened in New York City."

"Oh?"

"Several of the captured PLF people broke. There were thirty of them in the attack in and around the hotel. All but one has been accounted for. Ten were taken alive. Two of them died in the hospital. Vani, Winifried, and André didn't make it."

"André died from getting shot in the ass?"

"Apparently so."

"How tragic."

"Yes. Wini, as she was called, died from wounds sustained during her capture."

"Sure she did."

"Vani tried to escape and was killed."

"Poor fellow."

"Yes. I'll light a candle for him."

"I didn't know you were Catholic."

"I'm not."

Jenny laughed. "How about I make a fresh pot of coffee?"

"I'll do it!" John quickly volunteered.

"John, everything is pre-mixed and packaged, except the water. I can't screw it up."

Reluctantly, John agreed, and Jenny headed for the small coffeepot in the bathroom.

"What else did Control have to say?" Jenny called as she filled up the small canister.

"The president's speech was well received by the American people and his approval rating shot up . . . no play on words intended, I assure you."

Jenny stuck her head out of the bathroom and grinned at him. "You're a regular Johnny Carson, boss."

"I always liked him. I was sorry to see him leave *The Tonight Show.*"

"Our guys we left at the clinic in New York?"

"Everybody's doing well. Linda's all right, except for a bump on the head, and will be released sometime today. The others will be out for a few weeks. Henry and Camilla will live."

"So this screwed-up assignment is over?"

"Yes, thank the gods of war. And I hope the next one is a little bit better planned out."

"Or we have something to say in the planning."

"Yes. That's something I touched on with Control last night while we were driving in. You were sleeping."

"I thought I heard you talking with someone. Did they agree with your suggestion?"

"To some degree."

Jenny disappeared back into the bathroom to check on the coffee. She came back out with a very sheepish look on her face.

"What is it?" John asked.

"Well . . . it'll be a little while longer, I guess."

"Why?"

"I forgot to pour in the water."

Epilogue

The day the team reunited in a hotel in Chicago, John received new orders, hand-delivered by courier.

"Where are we heading?" Lana asked.

"The northwest," John said. "Washington, Oregon area . . . for starters."

"Starters?" Don inquired. "Are we all over the United States again?"

John held up the single sheet of paper for all to see. "It doesn't say. We'll know when we get to Portland."

"When do we leave?" Jenny asked.

"Right now."

William W. Johnstone
The *Mountain Man* Series